THE LIGHTNING TREE

THE LIGHTNING TREE

PJ Curtis

BRANDON

A Brandon Paperback

This edition published in 2008 by Brandon
an imprint of Mount Eagle Publications
Dingle, Co. Kerry, Ireland, and
Unit 3, Olympia Trading Estate, Coburg Road, London N22 6TZ, England

First published in 2006 by Brandon

ISBN 9780863223877

2 4 6 8 10 9 7 5 3 1

Mount Eagle Publications/Sliabh an Fhiolair Teoranta receives support from
the Arts Council/An Chomhairle Ealaíon.

Cover design: Anú Design
Cover photographs: upper: © Getty Images; lower: Bord Fáilte
Typesetting by Red Barn Publishing, Skeagh, Skibbereen
Printed in the UK

Go and open the door
even if there's only
the darkness ticking
even if there is only
the hollow wind
even if nothing is there
go and open the door
at least there'll be a draught.
(From "The Door" by Miroslav Holub.)

FOREWORD: REMEMBERING MARIAH

"I shall remember while the light lives yet
And in the night time I shall not forget."
"Erotion" by A.C. Swinburne

OLD MARIAH LOOKED as if she had been hewn out of the stone which surrounded the cottage in which she had lived for all of her ninety-six years: slate-gray, weather-lined, ancient. Sometimes, when, as a mischievous lad of five or six, I peeked in through her doorway and caught her snoozing in her whitethorn armchair, it seemed as if some life-sized carving had replaced her in the chair. Until, that is, she awoke and her bright, sloe-black eyes transformed her features utterly.

Mariah lived close by our house in a sheltered, compact, white-washed house at the southern edge of the Burren region of north County Clare. This cottage, built by her own people in the late 1700s, was without electricity, running water or any modern convenience. She was a namesake and a first cousin to my paternal grandfather, and she was, as my mother never tired of telling us, the oldest, wisest and most feared woman in the whole of the Burren.

She was an extraordinary woman in both looks and spirit and she possessed a razor-sharp mind right up to the day she died, shortly after my tenth birthday in 1954. Tall, straight-backed, gaunt, white hair piled high in a plait under a lace-rimmed black bonnet and usually dressed, whatever the season, in long, black, flowing clothes over high-laced boots.

For several generations, people had flocked from far and wide to her family's cottage, where she lived with her bachelor brothers Brian and Tomás, to avail of their power to cure all manner of physical – and often psychological – complaints. Where regular doctors or apothecary's remedies had often failed, Mariah and her family could bring about extraordinary cures that were deemed almost miraculous.

Though this gift of natural healing brought relief to all who sought it, Mariah's family endured an uneasy relationship with the local clergy, who perceived their extraordinary healing powers as coming directly from Satan himself. And so it was that Mariah and her siblings were demonised to the point of persecution.

Mariah fascinated me as a small boy, and I visited her every chance I got. Initially I was scared to approach her cottage. She was, after all, a "witch" who, if displeased, upset or crossed in any way, might cast the most horrible of spells. Her stark and imposing appearance only seemed to confirm my worst fears, and so my first tentative visits to her house resulted in no more than speedy and furtive glances over her half-door, before scurrying away tingling with fear and delight, her laughter ringing in my ears. When – on her invitation – I finally drummed up enough courage to venture beyond the door into her dark kitchen, I found myself in the company of a severe-looking, though truly gentle, wise old woman.

It was the beginning of many such visits, which before long became almost daily, and soon I grew to love her as I would a favourite aunt. I loved her for the fact that she talked to me as an adult, and I would sit at her feet, entranced and enchanted, and listen to her reminiscing aloud.

She probed and exposed those dark corners in which lurked some unspoken family secrets. Her uncles Tomás and John had soldiered in Europe and fought at the great battles of Waterloo and the Crimea. I marvelled at her rambling yarns populated by ancient, heroic warriors with their fierce battles, great feasting and tragic romances. I thrilled at her descriptions of the long-dead heroes and-wizards, magicians and giants who once walked this land and raised the great stone forts and mysterious dolmens which now dotted the stony landscape all about us.

In the fading light of an early winter evening, Mariah whispered to me of the shadowy inhabitants of the Otherworld, whom she swore she could see and with whom she conversed on a regular basis. Sometimes she would recite, mantra-like and low, the names of the long dead (the famine dead of the locality, so my father said) and the names of local people who had died long before Mariah was born.

For me, as a boy not yet ten years old, each visit to old Mariah was special. Even as she knowingly faced her last few weeks on this earth, she still radiated an undimmed hunger for, and love of, life. I think of her often these days. I remember so much about her; her inner strength of spirit; her indomitable will to accept, experience and treasure each day as it came.

Though half a century has passed, I still hear her voice as a haunting music, still capable of stirring my imagination and touching my soul. And still, in my mind's eye, I see her as she relates her treasure-store of stories, told as if unfolding the book of her long, eventful life to a small boy who, enthralled, sat and listened. Somebody once said that only our memories allow that some people ever existed; that their lives, their thoughts, their actions mattered. That Mariah lived and touched my young life matters to me. This is her story.

PJ Curtis
January 2006

CHAPTER ONE

I WAS UP before dawn this morning. It's the best time to see what the young day is made of. . . when all about has been washed and rinsed fresh and clean by the darkness. I sat by my window and watched the moon set over the hill yonder. This morning, as she prepared to disappear from human eyes, she was wrapped in a halo. A double halo, if you please! The colour of apple skin in September.

There's unsettled weather on the way. I can tell. I can feel it in my bones and I can read the signs just like that heron that sits in the marsh below and points his arse to the east and his beak toward the river. Whatever the season, he stands in that same spot at the river bend every time there's rain on the way. He's never been wrong yet.

My mother would point toward the marsh by the river and say. "Will ye look! There's that old heron. We're in for a flood of rain."

And so the rains would follow soon after. I wonder if that is the same old heron standing there with his rain-face looking to the west? If he is, he must be as old as Methuselah.

The wind has shifted too. It swung to the north-west this morning at dawn. It's a sure sign we're due a spell of bad weather if it shifts with a Hallowe'en moon in the first quarter. The moon and the wind are my weathercocks. The old fishermen and farmers, tinkers and travelling folk know the moon and the wind and should set their lives by them. Those that don't are only half-awake and will never truly come to know this world at all.

Have you ever seen a moonbow? Few have. There's no sight like it. Puts rainbows with all their fine sky painting in the ha'penny place!

Once seen, a moonbow is never forgotten. You have to be up before the lark to see a half-decent moonbow.

As a young girl I loved to dream and to step outside and beyond my waking world. Now, as an old woman, when I dream it's always the same one. I am up in the attic room I slept in as a child and hearing a voice below in the yard. It is the voice of my father Michael, as plain as I hear my own voice now. Michael is dead fifty years or more, yet in the world of my dream he's outside in the yard tackling Paudie – our pony – and talking to my mother Mary Ellen. Then, when I look out the window down on to the yard, there are two black horses, all decked out in silver bridles and buckles and with tall black plumes, harnessed to a black funeral carriage, their great hooves knocking sparks off the cobblestones in their eagerness to be off. My father turns from the carriage, looks towards my window, smiles, and beckons to me to come and join them.

They are preparing for a journey and one of these nights, I know, I will join them on that journey. And it will not be far; for the graveyard sits on a mound not one hundred paces from the back of our house. I know right well where it is they are going, and when I hear my father call – and he always calls the same call: "Come, Mariah! Hurry! We'll be late!" – I always come awake, his voice still ringing clear in my ears.

I used to be greatly troubled by that dream, but not any more. Now when it comes – and more and more it comes to me in broad daylight – it seems less a dream and more like I am wide awake.

One night soon the dream will come again, and I know I will get up and dress and join them and be glad to be off with them on their journey.

The year of Our Lord, 1858. The twenty-seventh day of January. That's when I came into this world and was named Mariah Honoria. I was the third-born of four living children. First was Frank, the eldest, Brian was the second-born. Then came myself, and then Tomás – the youngest and always called "Robin" – born to my dear long-departed mother Mary Ellen and my father, Michael.

There was a great storm the night I came into this world: so my mother would often tell me. About five o'clock of that morning, a bolt of lightning was followed by a crack of thunder so loud and so near that it shook the doors and windows and lit the land with a bright flashing flame.

I wasn't due for several days it seems, but the lightning flash was so bright and the thunder so loud and close and it so frightened my mother that she went into labour, and so it was I arrived into this old world while the forces of nature tumbled, rumbled and flashed all about my crib. She told that story to me so many times, I sometimes think I remember hearing that thunder and seeing the flash of lightning.

This cottage where I was born and where I have lived all my days has changed but little since those far-off days. Settled at this crossroads, beneath the south-facing graveyard, my great-grandfather, Patrick, built this house in about 1765. It was always a cosy dwelling, warm and snug in the depths of winter, cool and airy in the heat of high summer. In those days there were few other houses about this crossroads. But now we have for neighbours a school, a shop, a post office, a tailor's shop, a carpenter's shop and not one but two forges, if you don't mind!

Every March, Father – and later, my brothers Frank, Brian or Robin – would whitewash the walls inside and out, except for the north-facing gable wall, which was thick with clinging ivy and home to swifts and swallows who would come in April or May to build their nests and raise their young.

Even as a small child, I loved to ramble and roam and explore the woods and fields all about the house and go to the high stony places to the north.

To the east sat the hill of Mullaghmore, its frozen river of stone coming alive only under the magical light of a Burren moon. In spring, with the song of a skylark keeping us company every step of the way, I would walk the three miles there with my school companions to gaze on the strange stone shapes or sit at the banks of the blue-green *turlough* or pick the blue gentian, the purple orchid and the blood-red cranesbill.

To the west, the big hill of Clifden stood guard like a giant mother hen over the haunted lake of Inchiquin, the village and our house at the crossroads. We youngsters listened as Mother told us that the moon had its bed deep within that hill and it was there it went to lay its weary head after sailing across the night sky.

To the south, the land stretched away towards distant places we could only imagine: to the town of Ennis, Limerick city, the Shannon River and blue hills of east Clare and Tipperary.

Look at me now! I'm ninety-six years of age, having had a foot in each century, and you might think me old enough to remember Queen Elizabeth herself!

Mother used to often say that I was a child of the winter: that I would thrive on the wind and the rain and that I would grow wan and sickly in the summers. My brothers Brian and Robin never liked the black months, but I never minded. Even from a small girl, I was at my happiest in the days of low sky and dark winds and rain. I slept soundly only when western gales caused trees to shiver, shake and bend and the old house to creak and rattle. Nor did I fear the thunder or lightning, because I came into the world to the sound of it.

In the dog days – in August and September – the storms would come, and the rains would flood the low ground, and animals would take shelter in fear. I remember the first time I ever saw lightning was in late autumn. The storm had been brewing all afternoon. First there was a crack of thunder so loud it rattled the delft on the cupboard shelves as it rumbled across the darkening sky. This was followed by a bolt of jagged lightning that lit the sky and fell to earth as brilliant arrows fired off by an angry sky-god.

I wanted to run to it and capture it: to grasp its brilliance and clasp it to me. I remember its fiery dance across the floodwaters that October night, illuminating the land all around. I wanted to run into the open field or stand in the floodwater. I longed for the arrows of the lightning flash to seek me and find me and strike me and flow all through my body and set me alight. Somehow I believed if the lightning bolt did strike me, I would be filled with some great power. With lightning in my blood, I could never be harmed, and perhaps I would live for ever.

From my window that night, everything – the stones, trees and bushes and even the hills themselves – looked to me so *alive*, lit up as they were in those lightning flashes.

In a field between the house and the potato garden, there was an old ash tree that I used to climb and play in and hide among its branches. I fancy, so, too, did my father and his father before him. It was a giant of a tree and had stood there for several generations. Now I looked on in amazement and I saw it all aflame, having being struck by a single bolt. There was a "crack" and a groaning so loud, it was as if the lightning in its fury wanted to tear the tree from the roots. I stood for hours at the bedroom window and gazed on as the stricken tree burned: a torch in the black night, like a huge naked man spitting flames high into the sky.

The following morning the storm had passed over and all was now quiet as the grave. Even the birds were silent and the air all about tasted like wine yet smelled of sulphur. I ran out to the field, only to see what remained of the ash tree standing there, shunned by birds and animals alike, a black-boned skeleton with its arms reaching out to the sky.

"Avoid the ash, it courts the flash." That's what the old people used to say. I looked on this forlorn sight and tears filled my eyes. This old ash had been a secure place of refuge. Now it was reduced to this shapeless, jagged, lifeless stump before my eyes.

While it still lived, tall and strong, I would often nestle among its limbs, safe and secure from the world's prying eyes. It was my secret hiding place when I wanted to find time on my own and to be with my thoughts; and now there it stood – charred, scarred and leafless.

Right away, I ran home and got a pail of water, returned and poured it – along with my own tears – about its roots to ease its suffering. I thought my act might revive the parched tree. But, in truth, I felt the pain of the tree, and I was heartbroken at its dying.

After seeing what the lightning did to that poor ash tree, I lost my longing to have a lightning flame run through my blood and bones.

The "Lightning Tree". From that day on, that's what I called the blackened skeleton that remained after its ordeal that night of the great storm. How many times as a child and as a young girl, and even as I grew to be a woman, did I sit beside – or sometimes inside – my Lightning Tree and whisper to it my private thoughts and deepest secrets?

Sometimes, these days, I feel more and more like that old tree, so perhaps I have been stricken by lightning after all.

I was born when the Great Hunger was still upon us all. It came upon the land in '47 like a black killing mist out of the skies and never left till thousands of men, women and children fell to its hot anger and fierce wrath. Sometimes I can still feel its cold and grasping fingers gnawing at my gut. There are many still in want, but few starve now as they did in the days of the Great Hunger.

My earliest memory is of me in my cot crying out for milk or bread, and nothing for me but to suck on a piece of wood or a stump of turnip. I can still hear the sound of Mary Ellen, my mother, gently singing as she rocked me in the same old brown cradle made from hawthorn that had rocked my own father when he was a *leanbh*. And I can taste that sour turnip to this very day! I could eat anything and everything growing up, eat it with relish, but turnips I could not stomach.

I was hungry every day of my growing, but then so were all the family and many of the neighbours who shared the hardships of the years. Everybody wanted for food and nourishment in those black years, and neither God nor government nor Queen Victoria in all her majesty reached out with a helping hand. Old Uncle Tomás, who had fought with Wellington at Waterloo, and Uncle John, who had soldiered in the Crimea and had fought at the Battle of Balaclava in 1854, never forgave Queen Victoria for her treachery and abandonment of the Irish in their time of need.

If it wasn't for my father Michael and his knowing the herbs and plants the way he did, we might all have vanished into the earth as the others did, though my grandmother Maud and Mary Ellen carried the haunted look and fear of the hunger with them to their graves. The people who came to us to be cured, no matter how much they themselves were in want, always left something by way of thanks. Sometimes a bag of turnips or cabbages, or carrots, and sometimes we would find a piece of salted bacon or fish, whatever those poor people could spare.

So many families and neighbours gave up the fight and left while they still had health and strength, abandoning their little cottages to the briar, the nettle and the nesting crow. The McCarthys, the Nestors, the O'Tooles and indeed a great many of our own blood: all gone, many to the grave, and so many more across the seas to England and the Americas and others to Australia or Van Diemen's Land.

And so the people everywhere went hungry for the want of food, and the land itself went hungry for want of people to tend to it and to till and sow and reap. There were only a few households left after Black '47 with living human beings within their walls, and many of them were no more than walking skeletons.

It was frightful to behold.

The old people said even the birds of the air stopped their singing as the people moved about like grey ghosts in their world of shadow and nightmare.

And birds do not sing in nightmares.

It was the priests who told the people that the great blight and the terrible hunger that followed were punishments sent by God.

"Sent down from God as a testing of the faith of the people," they thundered from the altars, "and as punishment for sin!"

What class of sin this was, the priests could not say and the people could not fathom. If their sin was only that the people starved to death, then they surely were in sin. It was well noted – though rarely ever spoken aloud – that while men, women and children starved, there were few priests who went hungry and unfed to their beds.

The people who survived the Great Hunger lived in mortal fear that the potato blight would return, and they were forever vigilant for signs and portents.

Did you ever walk on a piece of ground and get stricken with the *féar gortach*, the hungry grass?

No? Pray to God that you may never do or go hungry or be in such need or want.

You could be walking through a field, having only stood up from the table, and suddenly be filled with a great cloud of melancholy and a terrible hunger. A hunger so great that it tears your gut and would leave you without the strength to walk away from that place. When that comes on you, so said the old people, you are suffering the pains of one of those poor souls who died of the Great Hunger. You have to carry a crust of dry bread, a potato or a handful of wheat or barley in your pocket to ward off the fearful pangs of that hunger.

When Father died, I threw out into a corner of a field an old worn jacket he loved to wear. I returned the following spring to find shoots of oats growing through the now-rotted mulch of material and rich, warm earth. The kernels of oats which Father always carried in his coat pockets to ward off the hungry grass had sprouted.

These are the black, unholy places where once somebody died or lies buried after dying from the hunger. That land is cursed land, land to be avoided at all costs, and will never bear fruit. Not till the Judgement Day.

So many died then. There was no counting of the poor people who passed over in those terrible days.

Is it any wonder that the deserted houses, stripped fields and sad roads all about were filled with troubled, hungry ghosts? The wise woman from east Clare, Biddy Early herself, once said that the stretch of road that runs past this crossroads and house is the most haunted road in the country.

I believe her. I saw those grey ghosts: the "pale ones" as I called them. I still see them, though not so many these days, as I prepare to become one of them myself. I still pray for those spirits: that their poor, lost souls will find rest and peace at last. As a girl I saw them walk about, all rags, yellow skin and white bone, with hollow eyes and open mouths, and so many of them walking the roads that a person dare not go out after dark for fear of becoming one of them.

"Maybe they're the lucky ones," my father said. "Now they hunger only for the life they might have lived."

This old land never forgets. History forgets, people forget, but the land does not.

But I'm not going to fill your head with spectres, ghosts and spirits. You want to hear about life and about the living. That is how it is in the world of the young, where there is no death and no ghosts and no past, only the ever present.

You can have a past only by earning it yourself . . . or maybe by me giving you mine.

CHAPTER TWO

THERE'S A DROP in the eye of the wind today. You are young and your blood runs warm, but I am old and there's only one thing that will warm old blood: a drop from a bottle in the parlour, which I will fetch by-and-by. I never used to feel the cold. As a girl, I ran without leather on my feet from dawn till dusk. Off came the brogues on Easter Monday, and my feet did not feel leather again till ice crusted rivers and pools and the water in the horse troughs and barrels in the yard outside. I ran like a young deer in the grassy fields, through carpets of daisy and clover. I raced across heathery bog and over flagstone, and there was no feeling like it. It was as if I had wings on my heels, and I was never bothered by sharp stone, nettle or briar.

And then, to sit and plunge my bare, dusty feet into a clear and sparkling river or pool of pure cold water and waggle my toes! Aahh. . . but that was a lovely feeling. Through the water my toes looked like little brown fish attached to the end of my feet, struggling to swim free.

After the great blight, people often went barefoot for much of the year. This was to save their boots for important outings

21

such as fair days and for mass and for weddings and funerals. On Sundays, people would carry their boots with them on their long walk to mass. They would then put them on to go inside the church and immediately take them off when they came out and carry them home under their oxters.

I hated having to put my boots on when the first frosts came in November. I remember my leaden feet choking for air and freedom inside my boots . . . and how light and free they would feel when I cast them off at night-time.

One of my earliest memories is from when I was two, maybe three years old: I am hand in hand with my mother and my brother Brian, walking through high rushes and wild iris to the spring well for water. We arrive at the rushy well side, and my mother lays down her bucket. She takes me in both hands, lifts me high and holds me over the well and whispers, "Look down, Mariah. Look deep in the well. Do you see her? Do you see the old Woman of the Well?"

Safe in her arms, I looked down and could but see my own face and the water sparkling and dancing in the bright sunlight. I must have been dazzled by its glistening surface, for I saw no old woman.

But I saw her face later on when I was old enough to go to that well on my own to daily draw water for the house. I looked deep and long in the well till I finally saw her smile up at me through the bubbling spring water and strands of watercress and weed. Even when I would cup the cool water in the palms of my hands to drink, her face looked up at me and did not dissolve or disappear.

I never feared her! Even then, I felt I knew her. I felt, though invisible to human eye, she was always close-by, and I came to believe her to be the sister I never had. As I grew, I fancied I heard her voice, low and whispered, from deep within the well.

Later still – from deep inside myself – I sometimes heard her whisper to me in the night.

But I was young and I did not understand her words.

I used the water from that same well all my life. Whenever I drank it, I felt she was near at hand. I've given that same water, pure and undiluted, to many a person needing the cure. They would drink of it, thinking it some powerful potion, and feel its benefits. There are times when ordinary water and simple belief can work miracles!

I've never taken or used water from a well where I felt she was not there present. Neither have I touched wood from a tree where her spirit does not live within its timber. Nor a plant or herb or flower from the earth where she is not buried. Mother told us that when she abandoned the land during the blight, the people took sick and died. But she returned to inhabit once again that ancient well.

"If that well ever dries, the people will suffer again as they did in '47," Mother used to whisper, believing that the welfare of the people depended on her spirit being present in that well.

But maybe you have never seen her in the well? There are those who cannot – or ever will. I will tell you where that well is, and so when you go there . . . look deep! Look deep!

My father saw to it that Brian and young Robin learned about the cure. It was the tradition. It was in the family, this gift of healing. Father said he got his gift from his father, who got it from his father and so on, back though the family bloodline to a time beyond memory and knowing. The cure – a mystery to some but natural to our family – also came down to Uncle Patrick's family, and they use it still. Their gift, however, is with animals, especially horses, and they are rightly famous because of it.

Father could see that for Brian the gift of healing and the laying on of hands came as easy as breathing in and breathing out.

But for Robin it was harder. It just didn't come natural for him, if you know what I mean. But in his own time, Robin grew to learn the cure – or the charm, as they called it – though his true gift was the buying and judging of livestock, especially the training of horses. Robin did not have the gift that came so naturally to Brian. None of us did! Not even Father, and he was known all over for having the cure.

Day and night, for as long as I can remember, people from all over came to our house to find relief from all manner of ailments and sicknesses. And Father and Brian – and later myself – were there for all that needed healing.

When Brian died in '22 – God be good to him – those with ailments turned to Robin or me for help. They came to me to cure complaints of the liver, kidneys, blood, the yellow jaundice, fevers and worse. Those whose spirits were unsettled and whose souls were heavy with some unspoken malady also asked for help.

Being a woman I wasn't supposed to have the power. Supposedly it was only the men in our family who had it, but it came to me unbidden. The charm came to possess me, and in the end I could neither hide it nor refuse it to any living soul who asked for my help. God knows, I didn't ask that I have it, but it chose me and I could not refuse it. Looking back, in some ways, having this unasked-for "gift" brought as much pain to my life as it did relief to others.

The land was still bleeding when I was yet growing. So many had perished or gone. There was neither laughter nor story nor music nor song to be heard in any corner of the land. Even the birds seemed to have lost their song. It was as if some cold, dark wind had stripped the land of everything but the promise of death.

CHAPTER THREE

MY POOR OLD memory is not as good as it was. Like my blood, it grows cold and sluggish and, these days, is perfectly content to curl up and doze, as would an old dog by a fire in winter. But I'll try, through the hazy, drifting smoke of the years, and remember the girl I was. In my younger days, I had the gift to recall from any period of my life, but now my memory is as a spider on a damaged web. I have to crawl slowly down the strand of one memory to get to the centre of my thoughts and then crawl out another strand to reach the memory I am searching for. When that memory-spider was young, it made a quick leap across the web, and it landed exactly where it wanted to be. But the weight of the years is cruel indeed.

While the men worked the fields and the gardens, the meadows and the bog, I helped my mother about the house. From dawn till dusk there was much work for us to be doing. Inside the house there were the daily household chores: the baking of loaves of brown bread, sewing, darning, knitting, clothes washing and ironing. Out in the farmyard, the gathering in and milking the cows, churning the milk for butter, feeding of calves, pigs and poultry was woman's work. The men did the heavy farm labour in the meadows and the boglands, but the kitchen garden was our domain. My mother spent every spare minute of her day tending ridges of potatoes, carrots, parsnips, runner beans, onions, cabbages, garlic, rosemary, thyme and other herbs.

To me she looked like a giant dark slug, as I watched her move slowly up and down between the rows of vegetables, occasionally raising her head from between the high stalks to check on me and see if I was safe.

Of all the vegetables grown in our garden, the potatoes were watched and nursed and mollycoddled as you might a sickly child.

"How are the stalks?" Mother would enquire.

"Healthy! Without blemish, praise be," Father, whose responsibility it was to be vigilant of such things, would reply. When it came to the growing of potatoes, we could never rest for fear of a return of the blight.

In spring, while I sat out of harm's way on a hessian bag under an apple tree at the edge of the back garden, my mother spent most of her daylight hours on her knees between the rows of vegetables, tending and weeding and removing slugs.

I became a lesser slug creeping alongside her up and down between those lines of stalks and root vegetables in our daily war with weed, worm and weevil. I remember at night she would light a candle-lantern and go into the garden to creep like a thief among the cabbage heads and runner beans.

"What are you doing, Mother?" I once asked.

"Removing caterpillars – the enemy to the cabbage and most all things green and fresh," she whispered.

Mother was very proud of her little garden. In her hands and in her loving care, it flourished and blossomed. She knew its humours and she knew the smell and feel of its earth, and it rewarded her for that love and attention with abundant crops.

I can still see the flowers – a profusion of lupins, lilac, lark-spur, delphiniums, azalea, hollyhocks, phlox, sweet-pea and old English roses – she grew on the garden borders or in old iron ket-tles, pots or timber pails set on stones placed about the farmyard, She took great delight in caring for them: pruning and pamper-ing them while watching them come to life in full summer blos-som, and mourning their dying in autumn. She had a way with them; everybody said so. Mother had "green fingers", so they said. Sometimes I think that in those hard, flinty days, other than her family, those blossoms offered the only real beauty she found in her life.

In late spring and all through summer, I loved to open my bedroom window at dawn and dusk and breathe in the perfumes that wafted in from the garden. When the wind moved across the apple trees, my room was filled with such a mixture of garden fra-grances it became difficult to breath. I remember my mother when now I catch the scent of wild rose in the air. The peppery scent of wild garlic, too. She taught me the healing power of gar-lic, and I still use it to this day.

There was little time left for either pleasure or pastime other than hard work when I was but still a lass. From early morning till darkness fell, there were so many chores to do. When I wasn't working with my mother in the kitchen garden, I fetched water from the spring well. I milked goats and cows and twisted the churn handle to make butter from the cream till my hands ached. I collected rotten faggots and felled tree branches for fire-wood and stacked turf against the gable wall of the stable.

In high summer, I went with the men to work the bogs and save the turf and, when midsummer neared, into the meadows to save the new-mown hay to the song of the skylark and corncrake. Barefoot and tanned nut-brown from the summer sun, the boys and I followed the men in the cornfields to make sheaves of the golden wheat and oats that fell to their scythes. In October, at the first sign of the days shortening, we followed the potato diggers to pick the crop from the black earth, examining each one for the telltale signs of corruption. At the end of each day picking potatoes, my back ached and my hands and fingers were red raw and sore from the chafing of the earth.

But there were never complaints from my brothers or me! None would be tolerated. Each one of us – man, woman and child – was required to work to earn our daily bread. After all, we were the lucky ones – Father would tell us so often – when thousands of other less fortunate than we had perished.

Father could hardly contain himself with satisfaction and happiness when the potato crop showed no signs of blight rot.

"Let the winter come as hard as it might, we have potatoes. We will not go hungry," he would say as he placed a bucket of new potatoes, still smelling of the rich earth, on the kitchen floor.

Mother would cross herself then and say, "Thanks be to God!"

When my work was done, I picked mushrooms into a chipped, cream-coloured zinc bucket in the dewy fields at dawn, and blackberries into a timber milk bucket in the shortening September evenings. I knew where the wild honey could be found and often braved many bee stings to retrieve it from some hidden tree stump down by the river. In the shallow pools in the river, I stood and waited silent and still under the old stone bridge to entice and snatch a speckled trout from the sparkling waters. I knew where the gooseberries, fat purple plums and wild strawberries grew, and in autumn I gathered in hazelnuts, crab apples, sloe berries and rose-hips with Frank, Brian and Robin.

Mother made sweet black and red jams from blackcurrants and damsons from the kitchen garden, blackberries, wild plums and crab apples from the hedgerows. And from sloes and rose-hips, she made strong wine that she and my father drank on Christmas, New Year's Day and Patrick's Day.

My father was always able to produce from some secret hiding place a small bottle of *poitín* on those days too! Nobody ever asked where he got it, but he always had a bottle or two hidden away in the bedroom.

"Payment in kind," is all he would smile and say, and Mother would nod her head knowingly. Whenever anybody in the house came down with a severe cold, chill or flu, she would always prepare a *poitín* punch with cloves, honey and ginger for us to drink. We hated it, as it burned both tongue and throat and our insides, too. But Mother swore by its merits, and we took our medicine regardless of our complaining.

When I was around ten or so, my mother began to teach me about the herbs and plants to be found in the hidden places in the fields and among the hedges, mosses and rocks – when they grew and how to recognise them. Later, my father taught me of their hidden powers and which plant and herb worked on which illness or disease.

When I found time to play games, I sometimes played children's games with Brian and Robin, but mostly I climbed up to the craggy rocks and wild hazel groves behind the house to roam and dream or simply to chase yellow butterflies or seek out robins' nests to count their hatching eggs.

It was up there on the high crag that I first met Nora. She was a girl of about ten or eleven, the same age as myself at that time. I met her one late spring evening and she sitting under a whitethorn bush weaving a garland of daisies and buttercups. The whitethorn was in full blossom, and you could scent it all over the hillside. She sat by herself on the hillside some distance from me, her daisy chain passing through her hands like a rosary beads. I could hear her singing quietly to herself. I stood apart and listened for a while. I was amazed and fascinated at seeing her there. As far as I knew, I was the only girl of my age in the locality at that time, and apart from my brothers I had no friend my age. How could this girl be here on the hill with me? Where did she come from and what was her name?

Her song floated in the wind over the hillside. I had never before heard any girl singing as she did. I drew near, and looking up, she saw me and spoke.

"*Cad is ainm duit?* What's your name?" she said.

"*Is mise Mariah.* My name is Mariah," I told her shyly.

"My name is Nora." She sprang to her feet and smiled. "Will you play with me, Mariah? We can pick flowers together and make daisy chains."

Nora had the biggest, saddest eyes I had ever seen; she looked so alone, and her clothes were ragged, old and torn. Soon we were laughing and running together towards a nearby marsh where I knew we could find flowers and tall wild iris growing in profusion. When we had picked two bunches of these flowers, Nora said, "Come! I want to take you to see where I live."

She led me to a place not far away and stopped at a spot in the middle of small field by the side of the road. I could see no house or cottage anywhere close. I did not follow her into the field and kept my distance.

I stopped because I was afraid of this place. I knew this place, and I knew it to be a haunted field. This was *Gort na Marbh* (the field of the dead), where Father said were buried the bones of the hundreds who died in the Great Hunger.

"Those that buried them there did not themselves have the strength to dig graves in hallowed ground, and so there they will lie till the final trumpet."

I had often passed here on gloomy winter evenings and had seen the "pale people" near by. Now, as I stood here watching Nora, I did not wish to be there. Nora knelt on the grass beside an old hawthorn bush and laid her bunch of flowers on the ground. She remained on her knees for what seemed like forever, and finally I called to her.

"Come on, Nora! I don't like this place. Come away from here." I had a strange feeling in my bones. "Let's go back and play up in the crag."

She turned towards me and looked at me then with the saddest face I had ever seen on a human being.

"Don't be afraid, Mariah. This is my home."

Then her face brightened and she laughed, and together we ran from that place and were soon back up among the hazel and stone. We played together on that hillside till it was dark, and then she said she had to go. I ran home delighted but never told my mother of my new-found friend. I played with Nora – Nora O'Loughlin, she said her name was – the whole of that long summer. I never asked how it was I had never seen her before that day in spring. I was happy just to have a playmate, a girl my own age and my first real friend – a secret friend – other than my brothers.

The summer passed and the nights were closing in. One evening in late September, as twilight's shadows fell and the swallows were like black clouds in the sky, I was on the hillside playing with Nora when I heard my mother, who happened to be close by gathering rose-hip berries, call my name.

I left my companion and went to her.

"Who are you talking to, Mariah?" she said.

"Nora," I said. "I'm playing with her. I like her. She's my friend."

"Nora?" said my mother, looking all about her. "Nora who? Mariah, there is nobody there but you. You were playing and talking with yourself!"

I looked, but Nora was nowhere to be seen. She seemed to have just melted away.

But I told Mother all about her and that her name was Nora O'Loughlin and she was ten and that she lived in a cottage in the village behind the hill. My mother said nothing but took me by the hand and quickly led me home, telling me that I must never go on that hill alone or play with that girl again.

That night I overheard my mother and father speaking in low voices in the kitchen, and I knew they were discussing Nora and me. I heard my father speak the words "second sight", the first time I had ever heard such words, and they meant nothing to me.

The following morning, I asked my father if I could go to Nora's house and visit her. His face darkened, he looked at me for a long while and said, "Mariah, what I'm going to tell you, you will not fully understand till you're a bit older. Yes, there was a girl, a lovely slip of a girl about your age, called Nora O'Loughlin who lived near here once a long, long time ago. But Nora and all her family died in the Great Hunger a few years before you were born, and they were all buried in Gort na Marbh. If you saw this girl – poor Nora – it was her unearthly spirit you saw and not a living person of flesh and blood. Say a prayer for her soul tonight that her poor restless spirit may find some peace. God rest her soul."

I could not understand what Father was saying at first. How could Nora be dead? She seemed as alive as myself, and had I not seen her with my own eyes and had I not played and run with her on the hillside and hazel groves behind the house? Had I befriended not a living girl but a ghost? One of the pale people who I had seen wander the roads since I was a child?

I was confused and troubled and wondered for a long time afterwards what was real and what was dream. And after all my years, I still do; for I believe the veil that separates both is thin indeed.

That night we all knelt together to say a prayer that Nora would find eternal peace and rest, and I thought I saw her face as if in a dream, and she looked both sad and happy at the same time.

"Goodbye, Mariah," I thought I heard her say. "I'll wait for you on the hillside."

In the years that followed, though I searched for her often on that hillside where I had first seen her, I never spoke to Nora again. But I knew then I could sense and see a world beyond this world.

I knew then that I had the gift of second sight.

CHAPTER FOUR

WHAT DAY IS today? Wednesday? This is a good day to sow crops and till the fields. Fridays are good, too. Never cut your nails on a Monday for it will bring you bad luck. Never move horses or cattle on a Tuesday. Never kill a pig on a Friday or at the waning of the moon: its blood will not flow as freely as it would in the waxing of the moon and its meat will be the sweeter then. It's not lucky to get married on a Saturday, and if you start work on that day, that work will go unfinished.

Piseoga, that's what we called those superstitions, proverbs and old sayings, and that's what the old people believed and would recite for each and every occasion. They were seldom wrong. Sometimes it seemed to me that there was not a single daily activity that did not have a *piseog* to bless or to hinder it. But the world is turning and people turn with it and many, I fear, away from the old ways, the ways of their fathers and forefathers. And *piseoga* no longer seem to have the power or the truth in them as they did for my generation and the ones that went before.

I can recall my grandfather, old and ailing at that time, sitting here where I'm sitting now, reciting the names of herbs (sometimes in English, sometimes in Irish and sometimes in old Latin) that went to make up his own charms. From him, Father learned his healing lore. He learned of the power hidden within the mushroom – *an beacán* we called it – and knew how to turn even the poisoned mushroom into a healing paste. He had great faith, too, in watercress and in St John's wort. From the comfrey plant he would make an ointment for use on ulcers and other wounds. If there was no comfrey paste on hand, there was nothing better – so he said – than a simple spider's web to heal all cuts and wounds and bruises. He would never let us touch, sweep away or damage a spider's web and would say to us children, "They're my little helpers, working while we sleep."

He knew, too, the power of the Scottish mountain yew – or the juniper tree as it's also called. He would tie a sprig of that tree on the tails of cattle or horses to ward off the charms of evil hags who might wish them harm. Or he would place it in the thatch of the house to ward off the danger of fire and recite the words:

I will pluck the gracious yew
Through the nine fair ribs of Jesus
In the name of the Father and Son
And the Spirit of Grace
Against drowning, against danger, against fire.

Garlic. Father put great faith in the curing powers in garlic. As I do myself. To this day I collect it growing wild and use it in all my cooking. So, too, with watercress leaf and dandelion to clear bad skin of pimples, rashes and the like, and the juice of the stinging nettle to purify the blood. Nothing better in spring than to boil fresh, young nettles for tea or broth or to put the stinging leaf into colcannon, stews, gruels and porridge.

"Good for cleansing the blood," Mother would tell us.

She brewed nettle wine and nettle beer for several years, but I admit I never had a taste for it.

"It's all in the earth," Father told us. "Both the poisons and the cures: they are all there in the good earth, growing side by side, if we care to seek them and know them for what they can offer us."

There were some who had no time for the gathering of such knowledge.

The clergy did not believe in these cures and did their best to dissuade us from using them on the poor sick people who came to our door, saying that in doing this we carried out the work of the devil. But we knew from whence came the power. The plants and herbs we used were nature's bounty and came from God's good earth!

The knowledge held by our family was but the result of generations of learning, experimenting and observing the ways of nature. The using of that knowledge was always to bring relief from suffering and illness, never for financial gain.

If these things were put on this earth by the devil – as the priests claimed – then, unknowing, we did the devil's work. Those same priests would eventually drive poor Brian, whose healing gifts they saw as being from Satan himself, away from the Church, and I would claim they drove him into an early grave with their hounding of him. But I will tell you more of that by-and-by.

I don't know where it all started. Neither did my father, nor his father before him. Some believe it was St Patrick himself that came here and our family did him some great service. In return, he bequeathed us the charm, the power to heal humans and the power to heal all animals.

They also used to say that our family got the charm when a monk on the run from Cromwell's soldiers rode into our forge asking for the smithy to shoe his horse. My ancestor gladly shoed the horse, but put the horseshoes on back to front in order to send the monk's enemies in an opposite direction. It is told that, in thanks, the monk gave the clever smithy the power to heal animals, particularly horses.

But I think that these gifts are within us all. If we want to find them, they are there, buried deep inside us all.

So it was that our family became known for healing. The people came from far and near with all manner of ailments. For kidney and liver diseases, we would give them dropworth boiled in milk. The cure for nosebleeds and sore throats is black knapweed; cat's-foot is good for throats, too; garlic for colds and flu and all stomach ills. Horseradish and olive oil will relieve muscle pain; valerian will cure sleeplessness.

Water from the forge trough is a cure for warts, and to drink a glass or two is recommended for the anaemic and those with poor blood.

And, if I may say, I myself caused the mending of many a broken heart down the years with a special love potion I brewed from the early purple orchid in spring. This is the season when that most virulent of maladies strikes the hearts of young men and women most cruelly – as it surely will your heart one day! For young girls who pined for a certain man, I would make a perfume from the most delicate of Burren herbs and the essence of the petals of rare flowers which, when worn by the young woman, could in a short time win the heart of the man of her fancy. Another sure way for a maid to win the love and attentions of her man was for her to lie on the bed of her reluctant suitor and say his name forty times. But I know of none who tried that particular love spell – none at least who would admit to it.

Ahh, but I could fill your young head with a hundred such cures and remedies for yellow jaundice, warts, fevers, mumps, measles, dropsy, colic, bile, ulcers, poisoned blood, ringworm, rare rashes, smallpox, sore throats and septic wounds. With these ailments – and some unknown to us and a few that they had no name for – they came from far and near, knocking at our door at all times of the day and night.

And we never turned anybody away, no matter what creed or station in life.

It was the custom then for most people with normal ailments to come and seek advice or a cure from the men in our family. But there were ailments, which – as you will understand – were peculiar to women, and it was then that they sometimes came to seek the help of the women in our family. When, for example, a woman could not conceive, and her condition drove her to seek help, there was no doctor to whom she could go. She then would turn to the old ways and come to us – either my mother, when she lived, or me – to ask for our help. My mother would invariably send these desperate women to seek the power of the Sheela-na-gig.

They did not have far to travel, for the Sheela sits over the door of the church, as she has done for a thousand years or more, not one hundred steps from this house.

On moonlit nights, I would sit by my bedroom window and look across the wall into the graveyard and watch the evening shadows sweep across her old stone face. In the moonlight, it seemed as if she looked directly into my eyes and into my heart. Try as I might, I could not stop looking at her, sitting there in her silence, watching over us all and all our comings and goings. If only her old stone lips could speak, what a tale she could tell.

There were nights when she put the fear of God in me, especially at *Oíche Shamhna* – Hallowe'en – when the dead are all about us. It is then she sits a queen holding court to her subjects.

For as many years as anybody could remember, childless women who craved a son or a daughter came to this place and prayed to the Sheela directly for help. They would first kneel in front of the Sheela. Then they must walk around the church seven times and fall on their knees to beseech her to answer their prayers.

That was the usual ritual. Some women would come in the dark of the night. From my bedroom skylight window, I would often see figures move about in there in the dead of night. I would see them hold a lantern high to light her face as they asked her blessing. Some left little offerings, as they would at the holy wells – coins, medals, keepsakes, that sort of thing – at the foot of the doorway where she sits.

I've no doubt but that the Sheela-na-Gig heard and answered many of their prayers, for I know of many a woman from this place who stood in front of the Sheela in the midnight hour and prayed to be blessed with a fruitful womb and who in time bore children. But I also know of many women who after bearing ten or more children came to pray and plead with her that she might grant the opposite and make them barren! There are those who have not, and pray to have, and there are those who have, and pray to have not. It's a strange and funny old world.

I must confess that I have often since pondered on what a strange plan our Creator has for us in this vale of tears. How or when these women first started to come to ask the Sheela to put a good word in for them with the Man Above, I've no idea, but my mother used to say that it had been the practice in this place for several hundred years.

Now that I think of it, I never did hear of a man praying to the Sheela-na-Gig or seeking her aid. I'm inclined to think that a glass of juice extracted from dandelion and burdock – coaxiorium, they sometimes called it – usually gave the men, no matter what age they be, whatever help they might need in that department.

It used to be said that sometimes a man and his wife who remained childless would go and lie together inside a *leaba Dhiarmada agus Ghráinne* and a child would be crying within the house of that couple within the year.

But what cure could we offer by way of relief to the lovelorn maiden?

There were none we could, in honesty, recommend as a panacea for that particular heart condition. For, as I well know, it's true what the proverb says: "Love's a disease that no herb cures."

Father always praised the liquors brewed from nature's store of natural crops: from wheat or the potato. A glass of whiskey or the original *uisce beatha* – *poitín*, that is, from a Doolin still – taken every day. One glass and one glass only . . . no more, mind you! That's the only drop that will warm the blood and fortify the soul. I myself can swear to that panacea. In these latter years, I've developed a taste for such liquor, for it stirs and fires the blood and blows on the embers of memory.

Fresh oysters are good for the body too when we can get them, especially those caught within sight of the Ballyvaughan or Liscannor quayside and washed down by a glass or two of brandy. There is no better mixture for any human ailment.

Many who came were not sick at all, but suffered from the most common affliction known to humankind.

Those poor troubled souls – how do I say it? – carried the mental burdens of dark secrets within their hearts and bosoms. They sickened because they were in need of a special balm that cannot easily be found either in a doctor's chambers or across a pharmacy counter. What they craved most was an understanding, sympathetic ear.

"Look in their eyes, Mariah," my father used to say. "You'll be able to tell by their eyes if they are sick and what it is that truly ails them."

I never forgot that advice. Man, woman, child or the beast in the field: their eyes will mirror all their troubles, all their ills, all their strengths and all their failings.

CHAPTER FIVE

I SEE YOU looking at that old blue bottle on the window. I can't tell you how old that bottle is, but I can tell you that it was there when I was a girl, and its one and only use was to hold the curing water. My father, and my grandfather before him, would add a single drop of the water it held whenever they put together a healing potion or paste. We all grew up regarding that old blue bottle as a very special bottle, and woe betide any one of us if the water within was used for anything other than that single purpose. It was a long-standing tradition that the water in that bottle was replenished once a year and on a special day – at the crack of dawn on May Day morning – from a certain spring-water well three or so miles from this place.

It's many a year since, as a young girl, I first made that journey on my own, and I remember that May Day morning as if it was yesterday.

I was up well before the dawn and was already on my way even as the half-moon was still dropping towards the dark hills to the west.

I was thirteen, maybe fourteen, at that time, and I was to

journey before first light to the well to fill the blue bottle with the curing water. I had walked this old path many times with my father, and now I was grown enough to make the journey alone.

That year, all in the house save my mother and I were weak and housebound with a bad flu. (For the colds, flu and chills and such, there was nothing for a person but to take a garlic crush, a strong hot whiskey or *poitín* punch and take to the bed and let the fever burn itself out.)

I hardly slept a wink all that night with the excitement of embarking on this important journey the following morning. Every May Day morning since he was a boy, my father had made this pre-dawn journey. Father told us how the well took in its magical waters from the magical Seven Streams of Taosca that flowed from out of the Sliabh na Glaise stone fort to spill down a cliff face a few miles to the north. The story is told that, many thousands of years ago, the streams first flowed as milk from Lon Mac Liomhtha's cow called the Glas Ghaibhneach. Lon was Ireland's first ironsmith and the first to make edged spears and swords in his fortress-forge at Sliabh Na Glaise. Lon had stolen a magical cow from the King of Spain, and she became famous the length and breadth of the land, for she could fill any vessel – no matter how big – into which she was milked. One old hag-witch swore there was one vessel she could not fill and milked the cow into a sieve. The cow gave and gave of her milk till she could give no more. The milk ran in a great torrent and flowed as an endless stream, till eventually it turned into the seven separate streams. Those same seven streams still fall like silver milk over the cliff at Toasca. There is a cure to be found there for diabetes if you go to that place for one Monday and two Thursdays.

What happened to the poor cow? It's told that the poor beast died of a broken heart, and the spot where she died can be seen to this very day. From that day to this, not a blade of grass has ever grown there, and no bird will settle on that bleak place.

The well that I was to visit that morning was an ancient well, as old as the hills around it, and known only to my father, my brothers and me. The water had to be taken from this well as the first light of May morning struck the water; otherwise, so my father told us often, it had no power.

"When the light of dawn strikes the surface and you can see the sky reflected, that is the moment when it gains its greatest power. That is the moment it becomes filled with a spirit and becomes a healing water."

This was also the moment, so Father would tell us, the blue bottle had to be filled with this magical water.

Without this special water – *May water*, so he called it – Father could not mix his potions he used to ease the pains and ailments of the suffering who came to him seeking relief.

Without fail, we made that journey each May Day. Long before the cock crowed, we would rise in the dark and, come hail, rain, snow or gale, we set out without drinking or taking any solid food. In fact, not a morsel of food passed our lips till we returned home from the journey, our task complete. On arriving home, Mary Ellen always had a good breakfast of steaming porridge and hot fresh griddle scones or oatcakes covered with butter and home-made plum jam waiting for us on the kitchen table, which we ate with relish, washed down with mugs of hot, sweet tea.

"Mariah!" I heard my bedroom door creak open and Father whisper, "Arise, *alanna*. It's time to make a start if you're to get there before first light."

It had been a long night for my father. Though running a high temperature from his flu, from the coming of nightfall he had stood guard over our own spring-water well till long past midnight. This was to see to it that no living person might come and interfere with the water and bring bad luck to the family.

Oh yes, there were many who would wander abroad that night to bring bad luck on their neighbours. Like Midsummer

43

Eve and Hallowe'en, *Oíche Bhealtaine* – May Day Eve – you see, was a time of great magic, and everybody took some precautions against those who would wish him or her ill luck for the coming year.

Every May Eve, as night fell, Father would cut fresh rowan and place it above the doors and around the windows to ward off evil spirits. Earlier in the day, as was also the custom, he would make a wreath of elder, which he wrapped around the milk churn to protect it during the coming year from bad spirits. He also wove a wreath from a green bough of rowan and marsh marigold with two balls, one covered with silver and one with gold paper, suspended within it.

As a child, I helped make this bough, and I loved wrapping those tiny timber orbs in gold and silver paper I had saved since the previous Christmas. The old people used to say that these balls represented the sun and moon. I liked to think about that as I rolled them into small balls: the sun and the moon held for a moment in the palms of my hands.

On return from his vigil at the well, Father would hang the bough on the door, and there it would hang till it withered.

"May this bough banish all misfortune from our house," he would recite. We indoors knew then that we were safe and secure for the months to come from bad luck, curses, charms and all hexes that might be directed towards us by those who would wish us harm, ill-health or bad fortune.

I was out of my bed and into clothes and lacing up my strong boots before you could say "Jack Robinson". I had miles to go, and the sooner I was on my way, the sooner I would get to the well in good time to catch the dawn that May Day morning. Ready and prepared on the kitchen table was a small lantern, which I lit with a taper lit from the still-glowing embers.

Finally I took the blue bottle from the shelf, and placed it in the canvas carry-sack which I had hung on the back of the chair before I went to bed the night before. Now ready, I strapped the bag over my shoulder and stepped into the sharp, cold night air.

A half moon hanging low in the western sky still gave off a strong pink glow which would help light the dark places I would have to pass through on my journey to the well. Though I had my lantern, I was glad of the moon and the light it would shine on me. I could see it reflected on the thin crust of ice formed on top of the horse trough outside the barn door.

I hurried past the graveyard, my head turned away from the dark shadow it cast on the ground, and made my way past the garden and through the small meadow and climbed up to the first ridge of the hill.

I won't say I wasn't a little nervous or scared. I was, though I could not name my fear. Yet I knew I had to overcome my thumping heart and racing blood. I had, after all, made this same journey since I was six or seven, trailing behind my father as he led the way. And what of it if I saw spirits or ghosts? I did not fear them; so I told myself as I tramped along my way. I saw ghosts sometimes in the clear light of day. Anyhow, if Father had considered me grown enough, I had to face the journey on my own. I had resolved I was not going to let my father down.

It is true what they say: the darkest hour is before dawn. The final mile of my journey was travelled without the light of moon or star, and my feet were placed one after another in pools of lantern light till, at last, I emerged from the hazel growth close to the winding path that would lead me to my destination.

At last I stood looking down at the still waters at my feet. Though I could not yet see the water through the gloom, I could sense it there, deep, still and silent.

I laid my lantern on the ground beside me. From my carry-sack I took the bottle, found a dry stone close by and sat myself down to await the coming of the dawn and the light.

I didn't have long to wait. A single bird sang out his shrill note of dawn song, and the rising sun was a painted halo of light across the sky to the east.

One moment there was absolute silence upon the earth, and then, in the drawing of a single breath, a high-pitched sound – almost beyond human hearing – sounded far up in the still darkened sky.

I thought maybe I was imagining the sound, but the small birds could sense it, for they soon started up such a singsong and flapping that would wake the world from the soundest sleep. A bat flew low close by where I sat, and several crows lifted off from a nearby nesting place to begin their day's scavenging.

I looked down into the well. In the breaking light it remained a dark, still, shadowy pool. I uncorked the bottle and turned my eyes towards the east. The rising dark veil was turning a deep blue, and then the first streak of pale sunlight pierced the morning gloom like a shooting arrow.

I took a deep breath and gently slipped the bottle underneath the surface. The water was cold and stung my hand and wrist as I angled the mouth of the bottle to allow the water to flow inside. I shivered at its sharp sting and felt the power of the moment and the place and the water now safe within the bottle.

Beneath me a shower of golden drops had been sprinkled on a silver net. A small grey spider rushed to the centre of the web to see what all the commotion was about and just as speedily rushed back to the safety of her hidden shelter. A gentle breeze blew up to ruffle the water's surface, which now changed colour from silver to amber and then to dark purple as the light rippled and played on the surface. I corked the bottle and placed it back in the carry-bag. Then I knelt and from the well cupped as much water as I could in both hands and drank deeply.

I swung the carry-bag on my shoulder, and in the increasing glow of morning light, I walked from the well and started back on the pathway I had followed to this place. Retracing my steps as

46

dawn spread across the stones, I now had the opportunity to look all about and to marvel at the land that lay out before me like a huge quilt on a bed of green and grey.

I was about halfway on my journey home when I heard the voices. I had taken shelter from a passing shower in a thick clump of hazel near a place called the Glen of Stone. As I crouched deep in the shade, I thought at first that I was hearing some May Day spirit, or that I was imagining them, but the voices soon grew louder. I peeked out from my hiding place to see who it was out so early and walking in this lonesome place.

Even from a distance I recognised the two shawled figures as they drew near to my sheltered hiding place in the hazel grove. Coming down the rough path towards me were two women, a mother and her daughter, who was a slip of a girl no more than two or three years older than myself. Though the morning was still and calm, the girl was hunched and clutching something to her breast, and she stumbled ahead of her mother as if she was struggling against a stiff gale. The mother – also hunched as if pressing against that same wind – followed behind.

I was about to step out from my shade and hail them both on this fine May Day morning, but something stopped me: probably the tone and hard edginess of the voice I now heard as they drew level with where I hid out of sight. The mother spoke in Irish, and her voice was biting hard and sharp and her tone full of emotion and anger as she pushed her daughter before her. I now could hear the terrible sobbing cries of the daughter as she tried to catch her breath while stumbling ahead of her mother.

"Animals! The both of you! Did you believe that God in His heaven would not see into your souls and see your black sin? Eternity in hell for you and your own father will be the price of this sin!"

I held my breath at the venom of her words and hardly dared look from my hiding shade till they were past and down the pathway from where I had just come. I now saw that the girl, who was barefoot, bareheaded and wild-looking, carried a small bundle hugged tight to her breast.

"This is far enough. We'll do it here."

The woman fell to her knees not fifty steps from me on the pathway and with her bare hands began to scrape the earth and stones away from the ground at her feet.

"We must finish this here and now!"

The woman snatched the small bundle from the arms of the girl, who screamed as if stuck in the heart with a knife. She began to flail at her mother with all her might, but it was to no avail. The woman pushed the girl roughly aside and laid the small bundle in the shallow hole at her feet. Then, as quickly as she had dug, she commenced to fill it with the black wet earth and covered it over with heavy flagstones from a nearby mossy wall.

The desperate wails from the girl at that moment will stay with me till my final hour. With a great howl, she threw herself down on the spot where the bundle had been buried and clawed at the earth and stones and tore her hair and cried as if her very heart was been torn from her breast.

"Come away from this place, girl. It's done. It's in the Lord's hands now. Let's be gone. It's finished!"

With those words, the mother pulled the poor wretch to her feet, and together they stumbled back along the path toward their home, which I knew to be to the north, about three or four miles distant from this place.

I don't know how long I remained in my hiding place in that hazel grove, but I do remember that for a long, long time I sat and shivered. My heart was racing and thumping in my breast and I was sore afraid to draw a breath or peek out as I feared that they would suddenly return to this cursed spot and discover I had witnessed their activities. So, hardly breathing, I sat as still as a mouse while playing in my head the scene I had just witnessed.

What exactly that was I was still not entirely sure, but I knew it was surrounded in a dark, unnatural energy.

When, finally, all about me once again was quiet, I composed and gathered myself and I crept from under the cover of the hazel bush. As silently and as stealthily as I could, I emerged from my hiding place and – with eyes at the back of my head – I made my way homeward. Though that May Day dawn crept across the face of the land, filling the air with the perfume of spring and of birdsong, my heart was troubled and heavy as those voices and words and cries still rang loud in my ears.

My mood had improved when I arrived home to find my father preparing to circle the house with fire.

"Good girl, Mariah." Father smiled and ruffled my hair as I handed over my bag with the blue bottle safe inside. "You're home in good time for the setting of the May fire."

This was a tradition he and those who went before him had carried on for generations. As I entered the house, he moved to the fireplace and, picking three glowing sods of turf from the fire, placed them on a pan.

May Day in our house, and indeed most houses, started with the ritual of carrying fire from the hearth three times around the house to ward off evil and bring good fortune for the coming year. Along with my mother and my brothers, I silently followed Father and the glowing sods in silent procession three times about the house before returning the sods to the fire. What glowing ash remained in the pan was then shaken about the doorway and windows to bring us luck in the coming year and keep away all evil and trouble from our household.

As Mother busied herself filling every vase in the house with all kinds of flowers to celebrate this new May Day and the coming of a new summer, Father was full of praise for me for undertaking and completing the journey on my own. Though I desperately wanted to find a voice or a tongue to tell them of what I had witnessed on the path to the well, I did not. In truth, I still did not fully understand what I had seen that morning.

It was two, maybe three, months later that the same woman I had seen that morning arrived at our door in a distressed state and asked to see my father. Though it was high summer, I remember she was dressed in the same heavy plaid shawl she had worn that morning on the path to the well.

She came into the kitchen and sat where you are sitting now, with her shawl pulled tight over her head, her face lined and haggard, and only her eyes, wild and darting hither and thither, showed her agitation and her troubled soul.

By now I was attending my father whenever he saw visitors – he never called them patients – who might come for the cure. Now I sat quietly behind him in the room as he questioned the women before him on the kitchen floor.

"Michael, I come to your house for help. Not for myself, but for my only daughter who sickens to death before my eyes. She touches not one morsel that is placed before her! She eats neither bread nor meat nor even a vegetable for these several weeks past. Neither does she speak or thrive on any medicine offered her. She is stricken, and if she does not come out of her sickness, I fear she will waste and sicken unto death. I come to your house to ask your help, Michael. I know you have the gift to heal her . . . to help her! God help me, I have nobody else to turn to! I know you will not refuse me your gift."

The poor woman wrung her hands as if she was intent on rubbing from her fingers some invisible dirt or stain that only she could see. Her face was a mirror of a troubled, suffering soul.

Father gently took her trembling hand in his and quietly asked her to describe and relate to him more of the girl's condition, how long she had suffered and how it had progressed.

"I know what will heal the girl," I heard myself quietly say. I

50

had been content to sit quietly and listen to what passed between the woman and my father. Now I heard myself speak and could hardly believe I had uttered the words.

Both the woman and my father turned their eyes towards me.

"What do you see, Mariah?" Father gently whispered.

In that moment I saw clearly for the first time the truth of what had actually happened on that pathway that May morning.

I closed my eyes and spoke.

"I hear the crying of a lost, unbaptised soul who can find no rest. I see your girl and know the cause of her sickness. I see if she is not helped to undo the binding that chokes her heart and soul, she will continue to pine and waste and die of a broken heart. But I see, too, how she will live and heal and be well."

My voice sounded to me as if it came out of another's mouth.

"Tell me how? Tell me how, girl, for pity's sake!"

The woman fell to her knees in front of me and grabbed my hand in hers, her face lined with the weight of her turmoil, her eyes showing her terrible pain.

"Go with all haste to a place you well know by the Glen of Stone and from there remove what has not long since been abandoned by you and the girl and which still cries to be lain to rest in sacred ground. Day and night your daughter hears those cries – as I now do – and she will surely die of her grief unless you do this. Do this without delay. Do this thing this very day!"

A look of sheer grief and terror came over the woman, like an animal caught in a trap. In disbelief she glared first at me, then at my father, and covering her face with her shawl, she began to sob most piteously.

"Listen to Mariah's words." Father laid his hand on her hand and looked directly into her tear-filled eyes.

"Do as Mariah says," he gently said to the woman. "Ask for God's forgiveness for her sins and yours. And give the poor girl this to drink."

He got up, went to the closet and from it he took out a small brown bottle, filled it with a clear liquid from a larger bottle and handed it the woman, who was now quiet, deathly pale and trembling like a leaf.

Inside the bottle was a mixture I knew to contain the juice of the whitethorn blossom, the hawberry and the elderberry. I also knew that it contained a few drops of the curing water I had gathered from the well on the very morning I had last seen the woman and her poor daughter in that lonely valley that now haunted both their dreams and waking hours.

The old woman uttered not another word but grasped both of Father's hands and then mine in silent thanks.

After she had departed, my father never asked me to explain why I had said what I had said to the woman. He just looked at me for a long while and smiled in his knowing way,

"Ah Mariah, *maith a'cailín!* Good girl! I always felt it was in you and now I know. You have the gift . . . you have the sight. You have the cure. Use it wisely and well."

He nodded slowly and, still smiling, went about his day's work.

You are wondering what happened to the poor girl? And the mother? Well, she must have done as I told her to do, for shortly thereafter the daughter got her full physical health back. A few weeks later, I saw her one Sunday at mass with her mother. Neither raised their eyes nor spoke to me, or to a single soul, that day before they scurried away like frightened rabbits.

Some time later, around Hallowe'en of that year, news came that the misfortunate girl had packed her few belongings and departed her home, never to be seen again. We later heard that she had made her way to Australia where she married a wool merchant and raised a family, but she never, ever again returned to her home. It was told to me many years later that one of her sons became a famous outlaw: bushrangers they call them in Australia.

The lad went on to became almost as famous there as Ned Kelly or the Wild Colonial Boy. He had his neck stretched – so it's told – when he was finally cornered and captured by the Peelers following a daring robbery in New South Wales.

As for her poor mother, she fell silent from the day her daughter left and never again spoke to a living soul till the day she died a few years later – of a broken heart, so it was whispered.

And what of the husband? I have not yet spoken of his dark part in this terrible tragedy, and neither will I. All I will say is that he bore the look of a man with a demon within his breast and a sackful of them on his back.

He died a year or so after that awful event. Some said that he died from drinking bad *poitín*. Some whispered that he met his end from eating a deadly root of hemlock, a Devil's cup mushroom or some other deadly poison. I also heard it whispered that the poison that claimed his life was administered by somebody who knew the terrible secret hidden deep in his black heart.

Others whispered that he took his own life: damned and cursed and haunted as he was by a terrible deed known only to himself, his wife and their poor daughter. More than most, I felt I knew the reasons that destroyed this family. But it is God's place to judge, not mine.

In any case, their black secret went with them to the grave.

And so, that was that, the story of my first journey on my own to the well of the curing water on that May Day morning, more than eighty short years ago. I never forgot what I witnessed there that morning. Each May Day morning, for as long as I was fit and able, I went to that spot on the pathway to lay a sprig of cherry or whitethorn blossom on the lonely grave site in memory of that forgotten, innocent soul.

I would kneel on the dew-wet grass to say a silent prayer for those poor troubled souls now reunited in the other world, in the hope they have at last found forgiveness and some lasting peace.

CHAPTER SIX

I REMEMBER MAUDIE, my grandmother, used to play the concertina. It was a tattered, wheezing old contraption, and she
would take it down from over the fireplace, take it gently
from its battered case, cradle it in her lap and draw it out to its
full length and start squeezing the music from it. Sometimes I
think my memory is like that old concertina. There it sits, settled,
solid and dusty, until I take it down from its safe place and start
to draw out the folded years and see what half-forgotten tune of
memory might come spilling out from within the folds and dusty
corners of its heart.

Sometimes those dim tunes of memory are slow to unfold and
play out their songs and music, but at least there is always a tune
there to be had from that old box: the sad and the glad, the good
and the bad.

Today, try as I may, I recall but little of my years 'twixt fourteen
and twenty. They must have been happy ones, for they say if you
can't recall a particular time in your life, then it must have been
happy.

I do recall my last day at the hedge school. This was built of rough limestone, mud and reed thatching, and I and my childhood companions had spent eight or more years of our childhood with Mr Maloney – the Master, we called him. He's long gone to his reward, but I recall him as a fine, learned and gentle teacher, who imparted to us reluctant, and sometimes unappreciative, scholars our reading, writing and arithmetic, and much, much more besides.

In 1884, a fine, sturdy cut-stone, one-room schoolhouse was built as replacement for the old school that has long since disappeared under brier, moss and hedgerow.

Through all those hours, days and weeks and years, I see a young girl, no great beauty, though not plain either, tall for my age, eager for knowledge, thin, barefoot and hardy.

And so I lived out my life in this place, as I still do today, and grew to womanhood here. On lovely spring evenings when my work was done, I would sit by the river, surrounded by fields of wild iris and honeysuckle, my feet in the clear-running water, watching the rainbow trout and perch leap and catch the mayfly.

Or I would climb to the hill behind the house, perch myself on a mossy bank or stone and look out over the valley spread beneath me. From this vantage point, I could see the house I lived in and garden, the ruined castle of Ballyportry, and two ruined church graveyards – the nearest to our house with its old crumbling round tower in the grounds.

They say that tower was destroyed when Cromwell's armies marched through here in the 1600s. Others say it was ruined in 1632 in a great battle between the clans of the O'Briens and the McMahons. Now that I think of it, there is still little love lost between those two families to this very day. Some local tiffs take a very long time to heal indeed!

From that high mound, I could see the entire world I was to inhabit all my life. I learned to know every square inch of that world from the stony ridges to the north to the fields of foxglove, meadowsweet and cow-parsley and on to the hazel groves and hazy woodlands on the distant blue horizon at the edge of my known world. Cutting this world in two was the Fergus River, which meanders through the meadows, fields and woodlands into Lake Inchiquin and then out of the lake through the village and – though I have never seen it – on into the River Shannon.

On those clear spring and summer days, I would climb to the hill behind the house to gaze at the distant hills of Tipperary and Limerick to the east, all the way across the distant Shannon, and Mount Callan to the south-west. The old people said that long ago it was a sacred hill on which druids held their magical rites. This mountain was our weathercock in summer. When it seemed distant and misted over, the outlook was poor and we would surely get rainy, damp weather. When Mount Callan looked blue and near and clear of cloud, we could expect fine, settled weather.

The land that spread as a carpet before me always looked hazy and misted – sometimes even ghostly. It was as if nothing had changed since the making of the world. Often, in my reverie, I would think I was dreaming it all ...or it was dreaming me? It had its own voice, and I would lie there, my cheek pressed to the soft mossy grass, listening to it sing its song of the seasons. I would spend hours sitting up there on that hill on my own and feeling as if only minutes had passed.

I dreamed one night that the door to *Tír na nÓg* was somewhere close to where I was sitting, and though I searched I never did find it. Even when I was grown, I would catch myself searching for it still whenever I walked alone in the groves on the stony hillside.

Sometimes on that hill, from the corner of my eye, as the sun dipped in the west and the valley below me turned purple, I would catch glimpses of my old playmate, Nora O'Loughlin, hiding behind rocks or hazel clumps, and she would laugh and beckon me to join her in play. I remembered then what my mother had told me: that Nora was no longer of this world. I would close my eyes tight, and when I opened them, she would have dissolved as smoke or mist, back to her separate spirit world. But perhaps I only dreamt that I was seeing Nora again.

I would come back to earth from my daydreaming when I would hear our old dog bark, or hear my mother call out to me from the field behind the house. After a while I stopped seeing Nora, though I always felt she was never far away . . . waiting . . . watching . . . keeping an eye out for me as would my guardian angel.

With my three brothers out in the fields working alongside my father, I spent most of my time with Mother or rambling the fields and woodlands all about on my own. I suppose I had become a lonely sort of girl. So many children had died during the Great Hunger that I had few friends of my own age to spend time with, and so I made my own diversions.

In any case, many of the people all around treated the family with a certain caution. What I mean is, they tended to keep a distance between them and us. At the time I didn't know why this should be, but later I came to understand that it had to do with the family possessing the gift of the cures. That frightened some people. Others resented it, as they would a neighbour owning a bigger field, a bigger cattle herd or a better horse. Sometimes it would happen that my father or Brian or myself might be out and about, especially on a Friday, and we would meet a superstitious woman on the road – and God knows there were many. They would cover their face with their shawls and turn their eyes from us and walk quickly away.

"Why do they do it? What do they fear from us?" I asked my father once, as it greatly bothered me to see not only the old women but also my own few friends cower away whenever they might meet me on the road on certain days of the week.

"Pay them no mind, Mariah," Father would answer. "They

believe we have the power to put the evil eye on them if we have a mind to. They have been led to believe that we have the power to do harm, especially on Fridays. God knows, all we do is banish their ills and pains when they come to us for help."

My father blamed the priests for putting these *piseoga* into the minds of the people, even the honest, trusting ones. They were made to believe that our cure did not stem from the power or love of God, but that in some way we were in league with Satan himself and that was where we got our powers to cure and to heal. As if Old Nick would give humans power to do good for the world!

Yet it never stopped the people coming to our door for help when they needed it. They came to *this* house with their illnesses and not to the priest's door. And more than once, the priest himself came to our door in the dark of night, for a cure for some sickness or other. Once, so Father later told us, a certain priest came with a disease that he could not heal with potion or powder or incantation. This clergyman, Father added, had fallen grievously sick with an ailment that no man of the cloth should contract. The same priest might preach from the pulpit the very next Sunday that those who sought out healing from such "charms, spells and incantations" were putting their mortal souls in danger.

My growing years passed by quietly and quickly. Though the years were hard and there were few comforts in those days, I knew no other way of life but the one I lived and I was happy with that.

"We have fields which yield their harvests. We have a roof over our heads to shield us from the wind and rain. We have food to put on our tables. We have our God-given health. We should thank God for what we have."

Father would tolerate no complaints from us young ones about times being hard or not having this or that bauble. There were always those worse off. Even as a young girl I knew that to be true. Many times I saw small boys and girls – ragged and barefoot, even on frosty mornings – root and grub in the earth for old potatoes or other vegetables missed by the diggers.

I saw the poor, white-faced women in their shawls with their babies, some of them near neighbours, walk the roads, their sad eyes empty and hollow and their bony hands stretched out to beg for pennies, bread and milk.

I saw the weary labouring men – those lucky to have work – trudge, like living skeletons, home from the fields or gardens or from relief labour building roads. And all for sixpence a day in winter, eightpence a day in summer. Tom Canny and Peter Foley worked as stonebreakers from first to last light on the Ghost Road on the other side of Mullaghmore Mountain: a public work road to no particular place, where destitute men could earn enough to put stirabout or the gruel made from yellow Indian meal in the bellies of their starving families.

Many a time I watched as the carts carried the old, the sick and starving from the three parishes to the grim old workhouse in the village.

Of course I knew there were worlds other than the one I inhabited: strange, mysterious, far-off lands like the ones I read about in my schoolbooks at the hedge school or the ones my Uncle Tomás had seen and described to me as I sat on his knee. Uncle Tomás was but a lad of sixteen when he left the parish and joined the Munster Fusiliers.

Within the year he was shipped to a bloody war fighting Russians in a land called the Crimea. He came home an old man before his time with a silver medal pinned to his jacket and a hundred stories or war glory and bravery or death waiting to be told.

I had also heard about the great lands of the Americas across the great Atlantical Ocean to the west to where so many fled after the Hunger; but I never longed to see them. Unlike so many others, I had no desire to take that sea journey to live in the great cities of New York or Boston or Philadelphia. Neither did I have a wish to explore mighty rivers or travel into the hills and jungles or the Great Plains or prairies.

What would I do away from these fields, these rocks and these rivers that I knew and loved so dearly?

I remember someone saying how it would take an entire lifetime to know – to *really* know – just one small field not a mile from your own front door.

How could I be separated from the song of the lark, the linnet or the corncrake on a summer evening, or the calling of hungry crows from the low meadows on a winter evening or the curlew or wild duck on the far marshes? Nor could I abandon the soft springtime, the swirling mists of autumn or the crunch of ice under my boots in raw winters, and the ghosts who spoke to me on the dark night-winds.

No, I could not live or survive away from the very ground that held the bones of my people and those who have gone on ahead. I knew deep in my blood that if I did leave I would wither and die from the pain of such a separation from this land that I love. I could not, would not, leave or abandon this old place.

Not for all of Solomon's treasures.

In any case, I've never believed that the other man's grass is always greener. Though, God knows, I could not criticise the many who did decide to abandon the land of their birth and leave all behind to find a better life.

For better or worse, I knew my mind and I knew that it would take me a lifetime to truly know even the smallest field my father owned, and what would it gain me to spend my life searching for a field I did not know? Why would I wander the earth in search of something that I knew, deep in my heart and in my blood and bones, was right here at home?

I remember when my friend and old schoolmate, Mary

Mulqueen, come to me to tell me she had set her heart on taking the boat to America and a better life. She begged and pleaded with me to come with her across the Atlantic to Boston, or New York or Philadelphia, where the both of us would find a new and better life – and maybe even marry and raise a family far from starvation and want on those far-off shores.

But I did not, could not, even for a moment, contemplate the leaving, as so many had done from almost each and every cottage in every parish of every county.

I felt in my heart that this was my place. I knew in my deepest soul that here between the stones and the sky was where I was meant to be. And so it was I knew in my blood and bones that here I would stay and live out my days till they carried me the few short steps to the graveyard up the road.

Now the years and decades have flown, and my time for my final leave-taking cannot now be too far distant. And when my time comes, I will become the very earth I never abandoned.

CHAPTER SEVEN

W HEN THE SKY falls, we'll all catch larks!"
I remember my mother used to say that. I never understood the full meaning of it when I was a young girl, but as I grew older I came to see the wisdom of the words. We should never yearn for more than we can rightly expect and should accept and give thanks for what we do get on our journey through life.

Not that there was that much to hope for in the days when I grew to be a young woman. The hardness of the times and the poverty of the people saw to it that wishes and dreams would only be exactly what they were: wishes and dreams!

I said to my mother, "I wish I could have a lace shawl and a new bonnet for Easter."

"A lace shawl! Ah, Mariah, *a ghrá*, we can only receive what we are due in this world. Marry a wealthy man and you will have your lace shawls and your fancy bonnets and maybe even a coach and four. When the sky falls, we'll all have larks." And then my mother would laugh.

My mother was born in a fishing village on the Clare shores

of Galway Bay with the sound of the sea in her ears. She came from good stock, and though she was frail and pale and work-worn and had lived though the black years of the Hunger, she had the strength of a lioness. Now that I think of it, she was the backbone of our family, and I don't think she ever enjoyed a comforting luxury or an idle moment in her entire life.

While my father Michael and the boys worked outside in the fields, gardens and bogs for all the hours God gave them, Mary Ellen arose before first light to kindle the fire on which she did the baking and cooking for that day. She milked the four cows and ten goats we owned and made cheese and butter from their milk; she sowed and tilled the small garden at the side of the house; she picked, cut, dried and stored apples for winter. In autumn she made jams from great sticks of rhubarb and ginger, from wild red plums and from blackcurrants, redcurrants and gooseberries. After a pig-killing, she cut and salted sides of pork alongside my father and, from the intestines and blood, she made the best black and white puddings you could ever taste. She had hundreds of recipes in her head, although in those lean times she rarely had the ingredients to put many of them to use.

She washed and scrubbed bed sheets, tablecloths and work clothes by hand at the washing stones at the riverside in summer or in an old wooden, hooped tub in winter. She stitched and sewed and darned and knit every garment we wore; she made bolsters and quilts from horsehair, from hen and turkey feathers and from goose down. She cooked and baked soda breads, potato cakes, currant loaves and scones, porter cakes and honey cakes and cleaned and ironed and dusted and polished all hours of the day and night to keep our house spick and span. When we were sick, she was our faithful nurse, night and day, and in all that time she hardly ever made time to visit a neighbour or took time off for herself.

Beyond all that, she never turned a stranger or traveller or begging tinker from our door. Even when we had little to give, she would give bread or milk or meat, if we had it to spare, to a tinker or traveller in need. She never complained or raised her voice to any of us, and she always had a smile and a soft word for us all, even during those bitter years when it seemed as if the land had been drowned in tears. No matter that she was bone tired from her day's endless labours; she gave each one of us time and she gave us stories and she gave us songs. But the hard times took their toll. Her black hair had turned to silver and her gentle face was lined with care by the time she was fifty, but yet she lived on to see out her ninety-fifth year.

She gave up the struggle in the winter of 1909, and I remember her coffin being let down by the graveyard wall not fifty steps from where she had lived most of her adult life.

Though she's at her rest now these forty years or more, I still feel her presence in the house and, in the long blackness of the winter night, I talk to her often, and I know that she hears me and is waiting beyond this thin curtain of life.

In the good years, when the winter skies closed about us, Father would sit by the fire after his hard day's work and smoke his pipe and say, "Thanks be to God, another Christmas is almost upon us, and we have hay and wheat in the barn, turf by the wall and fletches of salt-bacon in the barrel. God willing, we will not go hungry this year."

We did not grow fat in those days, but neither did we go hungry, as did so many of our neighbours. That's not to say that we did not have lean days, months and years, especially when a bad summer yielded bad harvests and in spring when the potatoes and turnips were few or rotting in the pit and the sides of meat in the barrel or the bacon-fletch smoking in the chimney were reduced to the rind.

Many families lived off the land: snaring rabbits, fishing the rivers or killing the occasional wild fowl, and surviving as best they could. I knew of some that trapped and killed pigeons or even swans for the pot when they came in on the February floodings to nest and lay their eggs.

I suppose we were luckier than most of our neighbours as whenever somebody visited my father for the cure – and later, when they came to me or Robin or Brian – they would always leave behind a gift of food, perhaps a sweet cake or a cut of cheese or a cut of ham or mutton. If the family were well-to-do, they might even leave a goat or kid around Easter time. We did not hunger, as did so many in those times, though we would never take from people who we knew to be in want.

I finished with the schooling at fourteen and started in right away helping in the house. (In those days there was no going on to further schooling unless you were of the gentry.) There was not a day that yielded too many idle moments; each of us had our work to do, and sometimes there seemed no end to it.

I remember often feeling alone and forsaken in those times. Most of the girls I knew and had gone to school with were gone. Some of my friends who lived close by – Mary O'Connor and Lily O'Brien and others who came from big families – left as soon as they got to fifteen or sixteen years of age to take up service in the great houses in Limerick or Dublin. A great many left to take the sailing ship to join their relations in America.

I remember the gatherings of us young people under the old chestnut tree by the crossroads on summer evenings and hearing this one or that one tell of their plans to emigrate to join their sisters or brothers in the great cities of Canada or the Americas; mostly they went to the Americas. It seemed to me there was not a single family in the land who did not have relations in Boston, New York, Philadelphia or Chicago.

There was great excitement then, great hope and great dreams too, as those men and women looked to a better future on those distant shores. Later, under the same chestnut tree at the crossroads, I would witness the leave-taking and the tears, the banshee wails and terrible sobbing of mothers, aunts and sisters as they clung for one moment more to the heartbroken leavetakers. Silent fathers and other kinfolk stricken with grief would stand like ghosts wishing that time would stop – or at least pass more slowly – so as to delay that awful moment and the saying of their last, fond farewells to their departing strapping young sons or daughters. I myself stood at this crossroads of tears with all our family and neighbours gathered there to bid our fond and final farewells to our lovely brother Frank and his young wife Margaret, who took the ship for Australia, never again to be seen by us.

What sadness! What grief! What heartbreak suffered by those departing and by those left behind! To return home to their humble cottages and know that they would never again lay eyes on their loved ones on this earth. You cannot begin to understand the pain, till you have suffered it yourself. And I pray God you never do.

As the years passed, our little community grew smaller and smaller as, one by one, the pals and acquaintances of my childhood and youth died from consumption or departed the land forever. Few ever returned. Some – mainly the womenfolk – kept up contact for a period of some years with letters and money and packages, and news of marriages and births and even deaths. Then, sometimes for no given reason, the letters would stop and no word might ever again be heard by their loved ones on this side of the ocean. I suppose they had aged, or died, and their American sons and daughters allowed the link with their blood at home in the Emerald Isle to be broken.

Few returned home, and those who did return home, such as Mary Mulqueen and Jane Reilly, came home to die and to be laid to rest in Irish soil. Mary Mulqueen returned after half a lifetime of servitude in Boston and she came home to die from a terrible cancer. Poor Mary, she was one of my dearest friends.

When the time for parting with our friends and companions came, we would go to the American wakes held in the houses on the night before the leave-taking. In those days when a body left for America it was considered as a death in the family. And for those left behind, the grieving was as for a death. The terrible pain of those partings still cuts into my heart. So much sorrow . . . so much heartbreak. . . the shedding of so many bitter tears. If sorrow and grief brought wealth, then this old land would grow emeralds from the tear-wet earth and gold from the hazel bushes.

Of course, there were some who departed against their will, forced to do so in shackles and chains in the hold of the convict prison ships. There were many such poor unfortunates who were banished to Van Diemen's Land for the remainder of their days. My own cousin Hannah was no more than a lass when she sailed away on a convict ship with so many others whose bones now lie under foreign skies.

But there was no shame in it. Deportation was one method used by the English to clear the land of those poor, impoverished and unwanted souls and populate those faraway, godforsaken spots! I heard later that the English did the same when the landlords cleared the crofters and the poor from the Scottish highlands.

Hannah was sentenced at the Ennistymon Quarter Session Assizes; her only "crime" – so she was accused – was that she stole a loaf of bread to feed her hungry baby. She was sentenced to deportation to serve seven years' labour in Australia. Others such as Margaret Daly, Robin Duane and John Galvin were also sentenced for sheep-stealing at the Ennis Assizes and deported to Botany Bay for seven or ten years' prison labour or indentured service. Many never survived the terrible sea journey and their bones rest in watery graves.

Those who did survive never again returned to the land of their birth.

Hannah was only eighteen or nineteen years old, and she sailed away from the Cobh of Cork on Her Majesty's convict transport ship, *China*, never to be heard from again. Her cruel judge – a hated tyrant called Baron Richards, may his soul never find peace – grew fat and rich and powerful on the sweat and blood of those of us who remained on the land.

It was pitiful. Hannah's people did all in their power to have the sentence annulled or at least reduced due to her youth and condition. Hannah's mother wrote a letter to Queen Victoria herself – as one mother to another – to plead mercy for her daughter. She asked that Her Majesty take into account Hannah's tender age, her impoverished condition due to the severity of the famine in Clare and – above all else – for the sake of her suckling baby whose only crime was to be born to an innocent girl and in such a hard place, in a hard time.

But she never got a letter of reply. Neither queen nor the courts nor our overlords showed a jot of mercy or compassion or Christian relief. They rarely did in dealing with the common working people, and so Hannah – branded a common criminal for her so-called crime – and her babe-in-arms sailed away in that convict transport ship never again to set foot on, or lay eyes on, her native land.

So it was the seasons came and seasons went and I grew out of my girlish clothes. One day, when I was about fifteen or sixteen, we had a visit from old Jamsie Nestor. Settled by the turf fire, sipping from a cup of hot sweet tea – between puffs on his clay pipe – Jamsie, who had not visited the house in several months, said to me, "Well, Mariah. Look at how you've grown! You were but a girleen the last time I laid eyes on you."

He turned to my father, "Michael, you've got a young woman in your house now. We will soon have to start looking out for a husband for her."

He beamed a toothy smile in my direction.

So, this was the reason of his visiting! Looking for to make a suitable match for me. I reddened, turned my face from the company and made no reply. I knew what was behind his comments. Old Jamsie was the local matchmaker, and his visiting a house other than his near neighbours could mean only one thing: he was looking to see if there was an eligible girl in the house who might make a good bride for one of the many bachelor clients on his books. The wiley old scoundrel! Now, that I was coming up to marrying age – sixteen in those days – he was in our house looking at the lie of the land to see if my father had a mind to marry me off.

As was the tradition of the time, daughters of marriageable age were found suitable husbands by the parents or the local matchmaker and once the size of the dowry to be paid was negotiated and agreed by both parties, the poor girl often had no say in the matter of choice.

But I most definitely had no desire to be married off to a man not of my choosing. At the tender age I was then, I simply had no desire to marry! Nor was I happy not be allowed a single opinion or say in any nuptial arrangement that might sever me from my single life. Especially if it meant being wed to some crusty old farmer desperate for a wife and becoming like many other slips of girls who, against their wishes, became no more than unpaid slaves or breeding stock to their loveless, miserly husbands.

I remember Peg Carey, who was in my class at school, who was married off at seventeen to a sixty-five-year-old widower from east Galway. The farmer was a well-to-do old bachelor with close to fifty acres of well-stocked grazing land and gardens.

Jamsie it was who offered Peg's mother and father a good

match for that pairing and, being not well-to-do, they accepted on her behalf. So it was, young Peg had no choice but to walk the bridal path with the farmer – an aged man with one wife already in her grave and he then old enough to be her grandfather! The people all around gossiped and tut-tutted, some laughed and made jokes, and all waited for the old man to die. Then Peg would be mistress of his farm and lands and still be young enough to take a husband closer to her own age.

That may have been the plan. But life has its own plan, and events didn't turn out like that. The old man was as healthy as a bog snipe, and in the years they were together they had two healthy children – a boy and a girl. The old codger lived well into his eighties, and it was said they both were as happy as any young couple could be. Peg herself followed him to the grave of a heart condition only ten or so years later. The surviving children left for America and the farm got divided.

Like all parents of the time, I suppose my father and mother had their dreams that they (or I) might one day find a well-to-do honest, decent farmer with youth still on his side who would make a good husband for me and that the match might please both them and me.

But life had a different way mapped out for me. Few girls of any age in those days had the freedom to choose husbands for themselves. Neither the parents, nor the matchmaker, nor the church would allow a couple to do such a thing. And woe betide a couple that would break with that tradition! Those that did caused open scandal to themselves and their families and had to run to America or England to marry.

Old Jamsie called to the house many times after that, but his trips were all in vain. I was not for marrying – and most certainly not to one of his prospective bachelor hill-farmer husbands. I had seen a few of them look at me from under their Sunday peaked caps as they would a brood mare or heifer they were of a mind to purchase. I would see Jamsie and my father in deep out-of-hearing conversation by the hayrick, or at the garden gate, or by the cow-house wall. I could also see from a distance that the matchmaker was less than pleased with how negotiations were progressing.

My father never spoke to me of anything that passed between the two men, and I never inquired, though I was desperate to learn the names of the suitors suggested by Jamsie as possible husbands for the only and eligible daughter of the local healer.

Father knew my mind. They both knew that I would never agree to a made marriage, unless it was to a lad of my own choosing and in my own time. That was what my mother wanted for me, too. So I was happy not to witness any further visits from old Jamsie, but knew it was just a matter of time before the subject of my marriage came up for discussion yet again.

Life can be as a fragile boat on a stormy sea. No matter how we sail and control its course, we can get buffeted and tossed about and driven hither and thither and oftentimes cast up on strange and unfriendly shores that are neither in our plans nor to our liking.

I suppose I continued to dream my innocent dreams of what life might bring and what I might yet make of my life. Not that I had much time to dream – except in my bed asleep, where dreams came freely and unbidden.

And what of my days? Well, as I said, in those distant times, my days were much too busy and full with the business of living to wait for the sky – or a flight of larks for that matter – to fall in my lap.

CHAPTER EIGHT

EVEN NOW, WHEN my mind returns to that long-ago time, the blade of bitter memory pierces my heart and my tears flow as they did on that accursed August day over seventy long years ago.

I was a young woman of but twenty in that year of 1878, living only for the days as they unfolded and, being innocent to the cruelties of the world, lived that year with not a worry or care in my young head or innocent heart.

It was a year I will never forget. It was a year of emotional extremes; a year which saw the flame of love come alight within me. I watched as it grew from a light to a flame through that spring and summer. It burned even as my love was snatched from me in autumn. But still it burned and, all these years later, it burns yet!

It was, you see, the year of my meeting the man who was to be my one and only true love. The intensity of my love all that summer was matched only by the intensity of a most unnatural spell of heat and drought that settled on the land.

Even the birds of the air stayed close to the shade of their trees and hedges. Laying hens, geese and turkeys dug deep ruts in the cooling, dusty earth at the edge of the vegetable garden. The air was so still and quiet we would hear cows bellowing on the hillside beyond the lake, five miles away. Sometimes, in the dead of night, we could hear the deep rumble and crash of the ocean waves rolling in on the shores, turning pebbles into sand, a dozen or more miles to the west.

Water – or I should say the lack of it – was the sole topic of conversation among the people all about us.

The world seemed that summer to have stopped its turning. All through June the air was perfumed by the scent of cut grass, wild garlic and meadowsweet. July brought with it the sour scent of burned nettle and withering potato stalks. The summer sun seemed content to rise and set, and the long days passed in a sort of hazy, sky-blue dream.

One morning in late July, Mrs Hennessy, a stout, red-faced woman, came rushing into our yard. Father and some men were seated outside the forge, busy edging reaping scythes.

"I'm lost! I'm lost!" she cried out. The poor woman appeared to be in some considerable agitation and started to wail and lament as if she had witnessed some terrible event.

"Calm yourself, Biddy," my father said. "What ails you?"

Biddy Hennessy was a nervous sort of woman, who almost every day saw fresh signs and portents all about her that the world was about to end. Now, in between choking sobs and sighs, she swore that in the deep of the hot night she had clearly heard the ghost bell ringing its song of doom deep beneath the waves in the sunken village a mile or so off the Liscannor coast.

The ghost bell! Though the day was hot and a sweat tickled the back of my neck, a shiver ran down my spine. The ghost bell's pealing signalled danger for whatever poor soul should hear it toll.

"A terrible sign! A terrible sign!" Bridie wrung her hands and looked grieved and anxious as she sobbed out her troubling experience to my father.

"And why is that, Bridie?" Michael asked, drawing her out.

"You know the why as well as I do, Michael!" Her eyes were like saucers. "It's terrible bad news for those that hear the ghost bell ring; it's a sure thing their days are numbered. That's what the old people said, and they were rarely wrong. And now I myself have heard the ghost bell ring out in the middle of the night. God have mercy on my soul, I will not live to see the year out!"

"Oh, that's just another old *piseog*. There's no truth in most of those old sayings. Banish it entirely from your mind," somebody answered her nervously.

This was all very well to make such a comment in the full light of day.

"Some things happen that are not true, and some don't happen that are," my father said in a low voice and puffed hard on his pipe.

Some things are both true and untrue at the same time. If you ask me, these are the real mysteries of life.

But back to my story of Bridie Hennessy and the ghost bell.

It was said that any poor soul who heard the bell of the sunken village ring would themselves fall ill and die before a year had passed. It was told that several hundred years ago, without warning, the entire land shook and trembled as if the final day had come, and an entire village, which sat west of where Liscannor sits today, disappeared beneath the waves, never to be seen again. The church, the houses, the animals, living men, women and children sank and disappeared forever without trace!

Sometimes, though, on certain nights, the spire of that sunken village church would rise up above the sea from its watery grave and toll its ghostly bell. The old people came to believe that any poor soul who chanced to see the spire or hear its bell ring out across the waves would not live to see another year through. When the moon shone down to light a road of gold across the calmed sea, that was a time when all good folk would stay indoors in fear that they might catch sight of that spire floating above the waters or hear its bell of doom.

It was often said that when the great inventor, John Philip Holland, born in Liscannor, was a young lad, he listened to the tale of the sunken village and dreamed of a way to go under the waves to see for himself this amazing village, to float beneath the waves with the fishes and sail down those sunken streets.

On summer days he was often seen rowing a small boat out on the sea to peer down into the murky depths in the hope he would catch sight of the roofs or the church spire of the sunken village. He spent many a day and night staring out to sea and finally dreamed of building a sea-faring contraption that could carry him safely down beneath the waters to witness this spectacle for himself. He never did get to see the underwater village, but his dream stayed with him. He travelled far and one day invented and built the very first submarine.

It was said that before he died in America he dreamed that he – in his underwater iron boat – visited the sunken village not a mile out to sea from the place of his birth and sailed down the cobble-stone streets and looked through the open doors and windows where now the fishes and the ghosts of drowned fishermen lived.

He dreamed, too, that he heard the tolling of that sad old ghost bell.

Mrs Hennessy was beside herself with worry at what the signs had foretold for her. She had heard that bell ring out, and that meant only one thing: her time on this earth was short.

"You're imagining things, Mrs Hennessy. That's only an old superstition, an old *piseog*. It's this great heat playing tricks on your – on all of our minds. It may have been the Ennistymon church bell ringing out for mass or a funeral. Pay no heed to it. Aren't you as hale, hearty and healthy as a woman half your age, and didn't all your people live to ripe old ages? You will outlive us all." My father thought it wise to console her.

But poor Mrs Hennessy could not be consoled. Though my father tried to ease her mind, he, like everybody else, believed that if a person heard the ringing of the sunken ghost bell, his or her days left on earth were few indeed. As far as she was concerned, she had indeed heard the ghost bell tolling loud and clear from its sunken bell tower and her grief was heart-rending to witness. As far she was concerned, this sign had but one meaning: that she would not live to see another Midsummer's Day.

As she walked away from our yard that morning, wringing her hands and with stooped shoulders, my blood ran cold, for I saw about her a whitish glow and by her side walked two of the pale people.

Had she really heard that ghost bell ring from deep underneath the sea? Did she – or we – truly believe that old *piseog*? We did – and did not – believe!

"Funny," Father said later, "how we are all unbelievers in such superstitions in the light of day, yet become true believers in the black of night!"

Superstition or not, strange to say, poor Biddy Hennessy died following a bad bout of the flu in the early spring of the following year. At her funeral, not a soul mentioned a word about her having heard the ghost bell ring out the numbering of her days. As they let her coffin down, I couldn't help but recall her visit less than a year before and the fearful words she spoke that day. The day after her funeral, a fisherman said he saw a shimmering light move beneath the waves off the Liscannor shore.

When we stood out in the twilight of the late evening to hear the crashing of the great waves on the shore away to the west of

Mount Callan, I felt a tremble of fear run down my spine. If the wind turns to the north-west, I might hear – above the rumbling of the sea – the sound of that ghost bell ringing out its terrible truth.

But all I heard was the sigh of the night wind and the crash of wave against distant rock and shore.

In the early weeks of the dry spell, farmers far and wide were delighted and gave thanks for the fine weather so they could cut and save the turf for the dark months to come. The hayfields were bursting with growth and soon grew fat with haycocks. The cornfields were turning to bright gold, and the potato and vegetable gardens thrived as they had not done since before Black '47.

But as the days and weeks passed, the rivers and wells all up and down the country dried, and so the animals had to be driven to lakes for water. Even our own well, never dry in living memory, began to go so low we had to ration our water. After three months without as much as a single drop from the heavens, the people began to pray for rain as the very green of the fields turned to brown, leaves no longer green and fresh burned dry on the branch, and cracks lined the dried-up river beds and the earth all around had a parched, thirsty look about it.

After ten weeks of this drought, the people prayed to their saints and the priest prayed to Jesus and his mother, and still the sun burned in the sky and the rains did not fall. Nobody – neither those who had survived the Great Hunger nor even the eldest man or woman living in the three parishes – could remember a summer so hot or so dry.

"This terrible drought we suffer is a punishment sent from God above," the priest regularly sermoned the people at Sunday mass. "Unless you repent your sins, you and your children will suffer and you will crave water as would the burning souls in Purgatory! Repent! And ask God for forgiveness and He will cause the rains to return."

The older people smiled knowingly but remained silent, for no one ever disagreed with what a priest might utter from the altar. They had lived long and seen strange things and hard days and had seen other years when the clouds abandoned the skies and knew that the rains must surely soon return.

In the final days of July, there was talk of signs of change. The fisherfolk from the coast, who sold their herrings, trout and mulletfish in the village on Fridays, had reported that the sea-weed and seabirds were beginning to show all the signs of change and that a break in the weather was close.

There were other signs, too. The northern lights danced in the midnight sky and were seen each and every night. The sound of distant thunder rumbled away to the north-west, and sudden gusts of the *sí gaoithe* blew loose hay and road dust high into the air in swirling spirals, panicked a few highly strung horses and blew Tommy Tierney, who was mending his thatch roof, off his ladder.

On St John's Eve, Midsummer night, just after the running of the cattle through the St John's bonfires, a strange shower of red dust fell all over the land and covered the stones like coloured icing on a Christmas cake. Somebody swore that in that strange fall from the skies, they found a toad the likes of which nobody around here had ever laid eyes on before.

The skies were busy; that was plain for all to see. Clouds, the colour of wet stone, began to gather in great black-topped tow-ers away to the west. As the first Sunday in August drew near, the air became as heavy as treacle, and the skies pressed down on the heated land, causing sleepless nights and restless days for both man and beast.

I recall my mother being in great discomfort during these heavy, hot, airless days. So was I. During the day my skin prickled with heat rash and skin itch, and at night it seemed as if my blood was boiling inside my veins and my brain. It seemed as if every living and growing thing cried out for relief; and now it seemed as if relief might be on hand as the skies filled with weighty dark-edged clouds. The drought now seemed to be the sole topic of conversation.

"This can't last. It will break any day now," a neighbour would say.

"Let's pray that it does," Father would nod in agreement, and would laugh, "and all our tempers will greatly improve. Then after a week or two we can get back to giving out about the wet and damp and praying that the rain will stop."

As I mentioned, my own temper had been on edge for weeks. I was not a person who thrived in the heat. I could never live in India or any of those hot eastern countries. I preferred the dark and gloom and doleful mystery of short, grey winter days. I longed for the softening days of autumn and long winter evenings spent talking or just lost in my thoughts while huddling as close as I might beside the glowing open wood or turf fire.

Still, all through the days and weeks of this great drought, I lived each day as happy as I had ever been in my life. There was, as I mentioned, now romance and love in my life, and I saw no reason as to why – or how – it could end or be taken from me. Nevertheless, deep in my mind some nagging feeling that I could not reason troubled me. As the days passed, my moods were like a pendulum as they swung between some deep, unnamed sorrow and such great happiness as I had not experienced before in my life. I was twenty years old and in my prime, and there was every good reason that year for my being happy.

For, you see, I had met and was seeing a young man. A striking handsome man he was, barely four summers older than I, and who soon after we had met in the mid-March of that year would court me as he would a queen of the land.

I cannot recall ever a time, before or since, being as happy as I was then. Many an evening would find me sitting alone by the lightning tree while I whispered to it of my joy of living and being alive – of my first great love.

CHAPTER NINE

As I REMEMBER, it all began about a week before St Patrick's Day in about 1878, the year of the great drought. The weather that early March was typically hard and dry: nights of crisp, hard frost and piercing star-filled skies. Daytime saw a cold east wind snapping at our heels and on the land; the ash, beech and chestnut trees were all yet bare.

I was making butter at the churn outside in the yard dairy when Mattie Connors rode a sleek, dappled mare into our yard to deliver a letter to my father. Mattie was a big, red-faced, wild-looking man in his mid-twenties with hands like shovels and the dangerous darting eyes of a trapped ferret. Like his father before him, he was a hired workman for the Butler family – all long since departed – who lived in the big house across the lake. The Butlers were local landlords, though it has to be said that as overlords they were not as bad as many others of their ilk in those hard old times. Many treated their tenants no better than their livestock, but the Butlers were humane, fair and honest in their dealings with all.

Mattie dismounted, and leaving his horse to drink at the water trough by the barn door, called out to me,

"Is Michael at home?"

"My father is within," I answered, as coolly and as distant as I could. I looked away and went back to my work, not wanting to converse any further with this man. He did not move, and I could feel those cold eyes of his on my back as I worked. I heard him sneer as he walked to the house door to hail my father. "Good day to all here. Is Michael within?"

I had learned a month or so earlier that this same man now standing in the doorway was one of the single men whom Jamsie the Matchmaker considered as a suitable match and a possible husband for me.

I had seen Mattie – usually red-eyed drunk on rough whiskey or *poitín* – a few times at a few house dance, *céilís* and funerals in the parish, but I had no interest in him as a possible suitor. In a way I could not yet explain, I was repulsed by him, and my spirit was bothered whenever he came in sight. I had always noted the dark glow that constantly shimmered in a troubled way about his person, and it sent a cold shiver down my spine.

No! I knew in my heart even then that whosoever might eventually win my hand in marriage, if indeed marriage was to be my fate, it would be a man I had not yet laid eyes on, and would never be this Mattie Connors. But what was I to do or say if my father decided that a match was to be made? It was rarely a daughter refused or went against the wish or decision of a father, however repugnant that wish might be.

I decided there and then that I would leave the land if such a thing were to come to pass. Rather than accept a forced match, I would go anywhere to escape such a fate: to England, Australia or to the Americas. Letters from Mary Mulqueen in America spoke of single women in that country being of such independence of body and mind as to form relationships as and when they pleased and marry husbands of their own choosing. I decided I would go there rather than marry a man not of my choosing. To my great relief, neither Father nor Mother would give Jamsie's proposal a minute's consideration. In their opinion, Mattie was a man of little worth: landless, feckless, penniless and, worst of all in their eyes, without breeding. But I discovered this only later.

As I worked at the churn with my head down and determined not to give him even a single glance that he might see as encouragement, I went cold at the thought that perhaps Mattie, on the urging of old Jamsie, had now come to ask my father for my hand in marriage. My heart raced. What if Father might agree to such a match without any consultation with me? I resolved to make my feelings towards this man known to Father right away.

But on this occasion, Mattie's mission to the house, as I learned after he had departed the yard, was but that of messenger boy for his employer, old Richard Butler of the big house.

As he mounted his horse, he called out to me in a grating, sneering voice, "I'll be no doubt seeing you at the big soirée next week. I'll expect a dance or two from you?"

At that stage, I had no idea what party he spoke of, and though he awaited, I made no response nor gave a glance in his direction and continued to concentrate on my work. I heard him give a snort and a "gee-up" to his horse, his whip falling hard on the horse's rump and the animal snorting and chomping on his bit before galloping out of the yard. I immediately halted my work at the butter churn and went inside the house to find my father waving an envelope in the air. There was a grin on his face.

"Mariah, we've been invited to attend a soirée! This letter is from the Colonel and Mrs Butler, inviting the family to attend a party at their house on Patrick's Night. The Butlers inviting us to an evening soirée! Now doesn't that beat Bannaher!"

I breathed a sigh of relief. Mattie's visit was on business other than that which I feared.

Father was as pleased as he could be and stared at the letter for some while before handing it to my mother to read for herself.

Other than their close friends and relations – such as those in high office, wealthy merchants from Ennis and the other well-to-do Protestant landlords and gentry of the area – few locals or tenants, outside their own employees, were ever invited by the Butler family to social occasions at the big house.

But it was well known that old Colonel Butler, the master of the house, had great *meas* on my father, as he had cured many a valued horse for the Butlers – and indeed many human ailments suffered by the family over the years.

This invitation to attend a St Patrick's Day soirée at their home was no doubt old man Butler's way of saying thanks to our family – and to my father in particular – for these many services rendered free of charge down the years.

Later that night it was decided that only my father, my mother and I would attend this big do; Brian and Robin never much cared for soirées or do's. Brian said he had a card game to attend. Robin was to keep watch over a cow that was about to calf and a difficult birth was expected.

In the days and nights preceding St Patrick's Day, there was a quiet excitement in our house as preparations were made for the night at the big house. We had, after all, to look our best for this affair, and we worked hard to see to it that we were well turned out for the occasion. Mother and I sat late into the night sewing hems for the dresses she and I were to wear for the evening. These were our Sunday dresses – a plain black for my mother; I was to wear an ankle-length, dark-green gown with a wine-coloured satin collar and cuffs worn over a starched-collar white blouse, clasped at the throat with a large ruby stone set in a gold brooch which came with Mother's dowry when she married Father.

This finery – such as it was – was all we owned apart from our daily working clothes. My father's only good suit – once worn by his father before him and in mothballs since its last outing on

Christmas Day – was taken from the old chest in the bedroom and ironed and hung out to air to rid it of stale air and the scent of camphor balls.

"We will look as well as any of the gentry." My mother put on her "grande" voice. "Especially you, Mariah. You'll be the belle of the ball."

I blushed, yet I wanted to believe her words.

My mother smiled to herself as she continued to work on my shawl: deep, soft, crimson velvet it was, studded with yellow pearls and white lace frills. It still hangs in my bedroom wardrobe, though I never again wore it after that night.

The house had not seen so much excitement in years. Parties, or indeed *any* house celebration in those hard times, other than a wedding, or a Christening perhaps, were rare events in the parish. Only the gentry could afford to give "nights" in those days as, God knows, the people found it hard enough to feed themselves from day to day.

I recall St Patrick's Day fell on a Sunday that year. After early mass, my father busied himself for most of the day cleaning the pony-trap brass, polishing the pony tackle and brushing and tail-combing our old pony Paudie, who was also to look his very best for the outing. All that day I could hardly eat with excitement, and could you blame me? This, after all, was to be the most important social occasion I had so far ever attended in my adult life.

It was almost dusk when we finally prepared to depart for the big event. And so we set out – the three of us bedecked in all our finery and even Paudie looking smart and proud in his gleaming harness – on the three-mile journey to the Butlers' house at the far end of the lake.

"It's going to be a hardy, frosty evening, thank God," Father said, looking at the sky as we climbed aboard the trap. "It will stay dry for our journey there and back. But there will be a nip in the air, so stay well wrapped up."

Mother and I climbed aboard the trap, followed by Father, who took the pony reins and, placing a heavy rug on Mother's lap, "gee'ed" Paudie into motion.

"Amn't I the lucky man tonight?" He smiled at the both of us and placed a spring lily in both our laps. "To be off to a great ball in a grand house with two lovely ladies at my side."

At this I saw my mother blush, though she smiled and looked as happy and contented as I had seen her in a long while. I looked at Father – really looked at him then – and realised what a fine, handsome man he was; especially on this night seated at the front of the trap as if it was a grand coach and he a man of station and wealth. Looking tall, dignified and proud in his best blue suit, which still whiffed of camphor balls, his grey beard and hair trimmed and neat, he could, I thought then, pass for gentry. So, I thought, would my mother, who now busied herself pinning the yellow lily on her shawl and spreading the warm, plaid rug across both our laps.

Father decided to take the Wood Road around the lake to the big house, it being the shorter of the two routes. With the moon just rising over stony Mullaghmore hill away to the east, the slate-coloured lake lay below us, utterly calm and still, Clifden's dark hill rising to our right. With the music of Paudie's polished harness jangling like sleigh-bells in the crisp evening air, I felt like some great lady being transported to her first grand ball in a golden coach and four.

CHAPTER TEN

STRANGE, ISN'T IT, how we sometimes cannot recall things which we strive so hard to recall . . . scenes from our past which we long to recall. . . which we should recall. . . but we cannot? Yet we daily remember events which are often best banished from our memories. We gather some memories and store them like we would precious pieces of jewellery, and yet when we return to enjoy or examine them, we find them mislaid or lost or – worse – stolen by the silent thief of time. We then spend much of the rest of our lives searching for those lost jewels.

That's the way it is with me when I try to live again in the full memory of that night all those years ago. Try as I might, I can remember only snatches of that evening's events. Like some half-forgotten song, poem or story, the memory of the moments present themselves at odd times, and the most we can do is thread them together as best we can. Little less than a week after, the events of the actual night had become but a ragged patchwork of images.

I do remember with great clarity the pony-trap drive and our arrival amid the magical flaming glow of the barrel torches that lit both sides of the driveway past the mill to the house. I remember gazing with amazement at each window ablaze with candlelight as if it was Christmas Eve night, and I remember the welcoming atmosphere of warmth, light and laughter that flowed out to meet us from within the house as we entered the warm glow of the decorated parlour. I remember old Colonel Butler, like some great genial lord, his white beard trimmed and pointed, dressed in a fine tweed suit and sporting a large cigar. I recall Mrs Butler in her wonderful green velvet dress and the throng of happy, laughing guests already milling about the hallway and parlour. I remember gazing, too, in amazement at the long tables laden with all manner of foodstuffs: cooked chicken, quail, duck and turkey. The sideboards, too, were covered with bottles, jugs, tumblers, wineglasses and gleaming, polished silverware. Under a gleaming silver candelabrum holding seven lighted red candles, a huge cut-glass punchbowl, filled to the brim with a golden liquid, sat in the centre of one side table.

It was around this table, amidst an air of great merriment and clinking of glasses, that most of the men present were gathered. I try to remember as much of that night as I can: the music and song, the gaiety, the conversation and the laughter.

Soon after stepping inside the house and our greetings made to the hosts, Father became engaged in deep conversation with Colonel Butler and some other pipe-smoking men.

"Horse talk. I'll bet money on it. It's all those men care about in the world. Horses! Whether they be racing thoroughbreds of working nags," Mother smiled and whispered to me before moving off to make small talk with Mrs Butler and to be introduced to some other elderly ladies seated by the large bookcase that ran almost the entire length of the room side wall. To the side of the bookcase at the centre of the great room was the huge open fireplace, within which blazed a huge log fire that even under the canopy of light cast by the many lanterns and candles cast dancing shadows on the walls about the room.

I looked all about me. Some of the ladies present I knew by sight; some I didn't know. But all, undoubtedly, were Protestant well-to-do ladies and the wives of the local gentry. Being young and not used to attending such gatherings, I suddenly felt awkward and out of place in their presence. What would I say to them if engaged in conversation? How was I to behave? As there were no other women, single or married, of my age in the room, I found myself sitting alone at the edge of a group of women.

After making small talk with Mrs Butler, a gentle, frail lady with a slight lisp, and her friend, a Mrs Dalton from Ennis, I settled and looked about me.

Standing with his back to the great bookcase, the Reverend Hastings Allen, Protestant minister to the locality, was explaining to two gentlemen I did not recognise how his weekly church collection was distributed to the poor, the needy and the destitute.

"It is sometimes difficult to ensure that the truly needy person is not turned away from my door. And there can sometimes be as many as thirty or forty such poor wretches a day who come pleading alms," he said. "I do what I can with the two to three shillings I collect at Sunday service that I have at my disposal. That sum is divided as best I can: to the Sweeneys, who are fatherless, the sum of 6 pence a week; to Madigan, a distressed weaver, 6 pence a week; to Mulvaney, a poor man, with ten in family, 6 pence a week, and many more. Any surplus on hand, collected on Sacrament Sundays, I keep until it amounts to one pound, and then I give it in sums of half-a-crown each to the most distressed persons – chiefly to widows. It is true there is still great poverty out there to be coped with on a daily basis." He shook his head as if in disgust.

"Great physical poverty to be sure, Reverend, and great spiritual poverty, too," answered John Cawley, a grain merchant from the town.

"Just so, Mr Cawley," the Reverend Allen replied. "But consider how difficult it is to nourish the spirit if one cannot nourish one's body or one's own family. To have to live on 4 pence for a day's labour, and most working men cannot receive a single day's paid employment from December to March . . . sometimes for a great deal longer!"

"Now, now, gentlemen," Colonel Butler gently interrupted. "Let us hear no more talk of hardship or troubled times on this day of all days, our national holiday, St Patrick's Day. Fill your glasses, gentlemen, and raise them to life and the living of it."

The group of men nodded full agreement, raised their whiskey and claret glasses and loudly toasted, "To Saint Patrick!"

"St Patrick never set foot in Clare. Never crossed the Shannon," Mr Cawley stated to the gathering.

"But he must have visited Killaloe," one of the group added. "Do you not remember the old ballad?

> *A hundred thousand vipers blue*
> *Patrick charmed with sweet discourses*
> *And lunched on them at Killaloe*
> *With soups and second courses.*

There was loud laughter from the circle of men. Glasses were raised yet again.

"To Saint Patrick!"

"And Ireland Free!" a voice muttered from another part of the room. A moment of sharp silence fell on the gathering.

In the far corner, in the shadows by the kitchen door, I spotted a dour-looking Mattie Connors. I knew the remark had come from him or one of his companions. Decked out in his Sunday clothes, Mattie was in deep and whispered conversation with a group of young men, all huddled in a corner like a herd of nervous goats. They were clearly uncomfortable and uneasy at being inside the house of their employer as guests, yet trying to act and behave as though they were as familiar with their surroundings as if they were gentry themselves.

And, to be truthful, I suppose we, too, were trying just as hard to fit in with these unfamiliar, luxurious surroundings. I was barely able to raise my eyes or my voice, such was my state of nervousness at being in such a grand drawing room among such wealth and finery.

After an embarrassed moment of silence, conversation began to bubble up slowly once again.

I caught Mattie's gimlet eye fall on me from across the room and felt a cold shiver run down my spine. Turning away, I pretended to examine some books lying on a table close by while sipping a glass of ginger-flavoured cordial. I was praying that he would not find the courage to cross the floor of the room to strike up a conversation or, later when the music started, ask me to dance. When I next threw a quick glance in his direction, I saw Mattie and his friends standing with backs to the wall, flowing drinks in hand and staring sullenly at the rest of the guests. A few others stood apart, whispering together as if they were hatching some desperate plot or other.

The sounding of a gong summed all to attention.

"Ladies and gentlemen." Mrs Butler moved to the centre of the room and clapped her hands. "Do fill your plates and top your glasses. Otherwise Cook will be distressed that the food she worked so hard to prepare is not appreciated. Let us eat."

Some time later, after plates of food had been served from a buffet table, wine and beer glasses had been filled and refilled and amid laughter and loud conversation, three musicians hired for the evening's entertainment, two local fiddlers and a famous blind piper from Inagh – Garret Barry was his name, so I was informed – started to tune their instruments and commence to play.

In no time there were several laughing couples taking to the floor to step it out in time to the wonderful, swirling music – reels and jigs, hornpipes, quadrilles, mazurkas, flings and polkas – which filled the room and every heart with lightness and joy.

Not being a good dancer myself, I shyly placed myself at a good and safe distance from the dancers on the floor. This was as much to avoid being asked out on the floor by Mattie Connors as anything else. I had seen him look several times in my direction and knew he was probably trying to drum up the courage to cross the floor. I figured that as soon as he had drunk enough of the strong punch on offer to all the guests, he would more than likely approach and ask me for a dance.

Could I refuse him? Would I turn away from him and insult him in front of his companions? A moment of panic seized my heart. I turned from the floor toward the great stone fireplace and held my breath.

"Will ye do me the honour of a dance, Miss Mariah?"

The deep-sounding, accented – though soft – voice gave me quite a start. I instantly knew it wasn't Mattie's voice and slowly turned to face the speaker. Before me stood a stranger to my eyes, a tall, smiling, young man with fair hair. Even in the glow of lamp and firelight, I could see he had the bluest eyes I had ever seen.

From that moment on, my memory of what happened next is as fuzzy as if I was drunk. I don't remember saying yes to his request any more than I can now recall the exact details of his features at that moment of our meeting. All I know is, in a trice, I was on the floor in the arms of this stranger and dancing several sets of the "Siege of Ennis", "The Gay Gordons", followed by a reel, a quadrille and a jig and a waltz. Suddenly, all about me in that room melted away, and there was nobody in this room save this stranger and me.

"How do you know my name?" I finally ventured to ask my dancing partner as we swung about the deep-waxed, wooden dining-room floor. "For I know not yours."

The stranger smiled and said, "Alexander McNeil – Alex to my friends – at your service, Miss Mariah."

His accent was not of this county, or of this country. "And how do I know your name?" He smiled a broad smile. "Why, I inquired of Mrs Butler, of course. The moment you entered the room, I had to learn your name. I'm actually staying here with the Butlers at present, and as she made no effort to introduce me to you, I decided I had to do it for myself . . . and so, here we are."

In between the dances – and God knows we danced almost every dance together that night – I saw, from the corner of my eye, the black scowl of a look that Mattie Connors threw in the direction of me and my dancing partner as we swept by him and his drunken friends, still huddled by the parlour door. As we waltzed by the group of ladies seated by the fire, I caught Mother's eye. She gave me a smile and just nodded to herself.

After a final lively "Siege of Ennis", my dancing partner escorted me back to the group of women by the fireplace before joining the men drinking and in raucous conversation at the large table at the other end of the room. Miss Walsh, a sprightly spinster who lived in a big house near by and was renowned for her lovely voice, was called on to sing. As she stepped to the centre of the floor, her clear voice soon stilled the entire room with her rendition of a song she announced to be a Thomas Moore song titled "Oft in the Stilly Night".

> *Oft, in the stilly night,*
> *Ere Slumber's chain has bound me,*
> *Fond memory brings the light*
> *Of other days around me!*

Then it was the turn of Reverend Allen, who stepped forward and, in a voice shaking with both emotion and nervousness, gave a heartfelt rendering of "A Lament for Kilcash".

> *Oh Sorrow the saddest and sorest!*
> *Kilcash's attractions are fled –*
> *Felled lie the high trees of its forest,*
> *And its bells hang silent and dead...*

For his effort, the Reverend, too, was rewarded with a great round of applause and more than a few sniffles from other damp-eyed listeners, obviously moved by the song's sentiments.

Not to be bettered in his own house and at his own hearth, Colonel Butler followed with what I heard was his regular party piece, a rousing rendition of "The Charge of the Light Brigade". With the exception of his close family, who applauded loudly, his reciting of this recently written poem was met with a muted response from the gathering. Indeed, as the story and content of the poem began to unfold, there were whispered mutterings and grumblings from Mattie Connors' group huddled by a doorway to the pantry.

"Up the Fenians!" called one of the drunken party.

"Down with the Empire! Long Live Parnell," cried another.

Another strangely uncomfortable silence descended on the gathering. A few nervous coughs could be heard, and you could have cut the atmosphere with a blunt axe.

"Piper!" called out Colonel Butler, quickly sizing up the grow-ing tension and strained atmosphere. "Play up. I have heard there is no finer piper in the whole of Munster. Show us your mettle. Blow up your bags and bellows, my good fellow, and play us your best tune."

The strained mood in the room was eased almost immediately as the white-haired, blind piper nodded and smiled, settled his ebony wood and silver-keyed instrument on his lap, tucked his bellows under his arm, blew up his bag and drones and chanter and commenced to play.

Very soon the sound of his *uilleann* pipes filled the room as he proceeded to enthral and enchant all present with a rendition of "The Fox Chase". His fingers danced on his instrument and ren-dered a sound so realistic you might think the hunting horses and dogs, the bugles, the hens, geese and ganders and even the poor dying fox were all gathered here amongst us in the room as his pipes conjured up the excitement and atmosphere of a fox-hunt in full spate. To gasps of amazement, the piper brought the hunt to an end with the baying of the beagles in full chase, the killing of the fox and the horses galloping home with their prize.

The piece ended with the entire room on their feet giving the piper a lengthy and well-deserved round of applause. A few gentlemen moved forward and tossed silver coins in the instrument case lying by his feet. Colonel Butler, all credit to the old gentleman, shoved a one-pound note in the piper's hand, acclaiming the piper to be "as great a virtuoso as could be found in the length and breadth of the country!"

While the piper took some refreshment from the whiskey-punch bowl, the fiddlers put their bows to work. Soon the echoes of fiddle notes were ringing off ceiling, wall and floor, and there was not an unsmiling or unhappy face to be seen in the room for what remained of this happy, carefree evening.

All too soon – it being close to the midnight hour – the night drew to an end, as guests began to take their leave. So, too, was it time for us to gather our hats, gloves, wraps and shawls and offer our thanks to our generous hosts to say our goodnights to the other guests and prepare for our long journey home.

While Father lit a lantern and went to the stables to harness Paudie to the trap, I stepped out on the front porch into the sharp night air and gazed up at the million stars twinkling across the clear night sky. There was the sound of a footfall close by. In a moment my dancing partner suddenly appeared at my side.

"Miss Mariah," the tall stranger said softly, "I wanted to say a goodnight to you. I wanted to say goodnight in the hope that it will not be a goodbye, as I hope that we can see each other again . . . soon. Perhaps we could step out together one evening soon? Perhaps I could call on you? Or write you?"

I don't recall what my answer was, as my head, and my eyes, were full of stars. I must have agreed – I truly cannot recall my response – but I do remember he smiled, leaned forward, took my hand in his, raised it to his lips and gently kissed my gloved fingers.

I felt a single star fall to explode inside my heart.

CHAPTER ELEVEN

F ATHER HAD OFTEN mentioned that, as far back as the 1860s, there had been much talk and great speculation among the people about the planning and building of a great railway line to run beyond Ennis to the north, west and south of the county on which would run a mighty steam-driven engine! A truly marvellous and historic achievement, so they said it would be. Most people in the county, myself included, had never laid eyes on a train, let alone ridden on one.

For several years it looked as if it would never come to pass. Now, suddenly, there was fresh talk everywhere of us at last having our very own steam-train railway that would run each and every day carrying passengers and goods the length and breadth of the county.

And that is how it came to be that one of the many railway engineers and sappers to come in from abroad to plot and plan and survey the route of the proposed railway line was the man who led me through most of the dances at that St Patrick's Night soirée, a handsome, fair-haired Scottish Highlander engineer by the name of Alexander McNeil.

Alexander McNeil! I still sometimes say the name aloud to myself . . . just so's I can hear the sound of it in my head or feel it linger for a brief moment, as would a kiss on my lips. *Alexander McNeil.*

Two or three days passed. I counted the minutes and hours as they dragged slowly by and waited – for what exactly? I was not entirely sure. The memories of the ball at the big house and the meeting with Alexander all now seemed as some fantastic fairy tale. Only my mother's comment as she baked a cake one evening made me realise it was not my imagination: that it all had actually happened as I remembered it.

"That seemed a nice young man you were dancing with, Mariah."

She looked at me sideways and smiled a knowing smile. I blushed and didn't respond.

One evening, having been away from the house for several hours, I returned home and sat down to rest my feet and take a cup of hot tea.

"Mariah, there's a note on the kitchen table for you. It's just been delivered," Mother said with a smile.

"Who's it from?" I enquired.

"Well, that's for you to find out. Open it and see." I reached for the envelope as Mother added. "That Mattie Connors – and a sour bucko that one is! – rode up here about an hour ago. He said Mr Alexander – Colonel Butler's houseguest – had instructed him to deliver this note and ensure that it was put into your hands. I said you were away but you would get it by-and-by. He threw the letter on the table and departed without a word. He did not look like a man who enjoyed his task as messenger boy."

I opened the letter and read the finely scripted words. My heart leaped in my breast. It was, as Mother had said, from Alexander McNeil.

The note was brief and formal. Alexander hoped – so the letter read – that I remembered our meeting at Butlers' house the previous Sunday evening; he reminded me of my agreeing to meet him and said that he was counting the days till then. He looked forward to the coming weekend when he intended to visit me and formally introduce himself to my father and mother.

I had to read and then reread the letter, and such was my excitement I could hardly keep my hands from trembling.

"What is it, child?" Mother asked. "Is it bad news?"

"No, Mother." My heart was beating so loudly, I could barely get the words out. "It's news I longed to hear."

I arose from the table and rushed to the bedroom to read again the words that made my heart soar with joy.

I still have that note.

The days that followed were the longest in my life. No sooner had he returned from his railway survey work the very next Saturday than Alexander, as his note had promised, came directly to our house to introduce himself and let both Father and Mother know of his intentions and to ask their permission that I be allowed step out with him.

Of course, it came as no surprise to my mother, who I think was secretly pleased that I should have found myself such a handsome and dignified beau. Though I think that, at that time, Father would have preferred if I had eyes for a local lad and not this foreign stranger, who was not of our knowing and shared neither our religion nor the ways and customs of this place. If he had these thoughts, he certainly did not express them to me then or any time in the future.

I well knew the problems that would arise from any such association an unmarried, single woman might have, or even entertain, with any stranger or outsider – let alone a Protestant outsider. I well knew that if I should enter into a relationship, however innocent or casual, with this man, tongues would wag, gossip would gain legs and great pressures would be brought to bear on ending such a relationship. For a Catholic man or woman to form a relationship with a Protestant was (and still is) something that would not – could not! – be tolerated by either parent, priest or the people. I had heard of many a heartbreaking story of women who were forced to elope with their beaus to England or America and break all contact with family, friends and country.

But my parents were kindly, caring souls. Both knew very well that to refuse this gentleman stranger his request would have broken my heart and caused us to perhaps continue to meet in secret.

And so I began to see Alexander as often as his work on the railway survey would allow. Initially, he would visit the house on a Saturday evening and sit with us, taking tea while charming Mary Ellen with high praise for her fresh-baked scones or rhubarb tarts. After some weeks had passed, I began to meet with him outside the house. I lived for those moments at the end of each week when I would rush to meet him by the lakeside, by the old mill on the river, or the Wood Road where we would stroll and converse and court without a care in the world. Alex loved to talk, and during those walks together, I learned how different our backgrounds were. Both his parents now lived in Edinburgh. His father was a retired major in the Royal Scottish Engineers and had spent most of his life in India, where Alex had been born. He spoke of Edinburgh with a passion in the voice.

"A great royal city of granite with a great castle perched on a rock looking down on it all," he said with pride in his voice. "How you would love the city, Mariah. It's as fine as any to be seen from Italy to India. I'll take you there one day. You will love it as I do."

While part of my heart soared with him to view his beautiful home city, yet another part of me knew that I would be pained to have to leave this place. What if, I thought, he should ask for my hand in marriage? If I truly loved him, would I not have to leave this place and go with him wherever his work might take him? But it was enough then that for these golden days I should be with him here in my homeplace.

In those days it was not considered seemly for an unmarried man and woman to be seen out together, whether at a crossroads *céilí* or just innocently strolling the roads alone together. As we walked out at the races of Coad in early July, I was well aware of the many disapproving eyes cast in our direction.

"Stepping out with a Sassenach."

"No local lad good enough for her?"

"And he a Protestant."

I could not help overhearing many such whispered comments from those wagging tongues we might encounter as we strolled about the field together.

I reddened with anger. I wanted to scream at them that Alexander was a decent man, and that he was not a Sassenach, but a Scot with Celtic blood flowing in his veins, and that it mattered little to me that he was not of my faith. The barbed, snide comments hurt Alex, too, I know, but he laughed and brushed them aside.

"I've had worse said about me," he said as we walked home that evening. "Pay them no heed, Mariah. Their words are only words, the words of the ignorant and those who know not love nor have it in their lives. In any case, I care only that we are together."

At that moment, I think I felt as if there was no one alive as happy and as carefree as the both of us, and I revelled in that happy state and thought of naught but that this would last forever.

Life was giving me more than I had ever expected of it and, being young, I gave no thought to the future.

I lived only for each day and what that day might bring and

for time to quickly pass and Sunday come and bring Alexander to my side.

What mattered now – more than anything in my life – was our being together.

CHAPTER TWELVE

NOBODY IN THE three parishes had ever lived through or even remembered hearing about three long, unbroken months of sunshine, cloudless skies, heat and drought, like that summer of '78. For much of May and the entire months of June and July of that year, not a drop of rain kissed the parched, cracked earth. In the early weeks, everything thrived; pastures, animals, people. As June reached its midsummer peak, the sun shone from dawn to dusk with such ferocity that the cattle and horses and other animals struggled to find whatever shade and water they could, as they might on the plains and deserts of Africa or the American prairies.

While the ashes of the St John's Eve Midsummer's bonfires still burned red, we watched, helpless, as the swollen rivers of spring turned to parched riverbeds, leaving fish stranded and gasping their last as they, too, struggled to find their way back to the retreating waters. Rivers and lakes all about us continued to shrink – some disappearing altogether!

"It will break today," Father said quietly one Sunday in August as he returned with a bucket of brackish water from the only well still striving to push its liquid life-force above the surface. "The air is heavy and there are storm clouds to the west. It is bound to break before this day is out. I feel it in my bones. The animals know it, too. Mark my words, the swallows are flying low and I saw a family of bats huddle together in the barn. It's a sure sign. There will be rains before the sun sets today."

"I hope you're right, Michael." My mother poured the brackish water into the old iron kettle and hung it over the open, freshly lit fire. "May it please God that this drought ends and gives us all ease."

A cricket hidden in the wall behind the fireplace began to chirp. In those days it was believed that a cricket coming into a house foretold a death. Mother crossed herself and whispered a prayer. "May God be about us this day."

Later that morning, after mass, there was great excitement and talk among the people of a definite change in the air. Mrs Daly told of a fisherman's wife she had met in the village promising rains very soon.

"According to the woman, the seaweed is sweating and there are large herring shoals gathering off Liscannor. All these are sure signs, she says, of a break any day now. The fisherfolk can tell by the fish scales if rain is nigh. The signs are all good and all showing a break in the weather, and the signs from the sea are never wrong. So the fisherwoman says."

By midday the heat was oppressive. Skies the colour of buttermilk pressed down on the land like some overheated oven lid, and it seemed as if the stones themselves groaned under this great, unwanted weight.

I sat listless as a dry twig on the grass by the dairy barn, drops of sweat making my neck and back itch and tickle, and stared at the thick sky. I had little to do that day except wait to prepare to meet Alexander at our usual rendezvous by the lake.

I was restless. I had not seen Alex since last Sunday and I was missing him and yearning to see his face. That day being Garland Sunday was the day we had gone to the horse races at Coad together, more to let everybody know we were a courting couple than anything else. On this particular Sunday we had agreed to meet later than we normally would as Alex had promised Richard Butler to join him on an afternoon fishing trip and picnic on the lake. I would have had it different and was unhappy with having to wait the extra hours, but Alex explained.

"Look, Mariah," he said. "I'm truly sorry. I wish I had the entire day free to be with you, but I'm a guest in the Butlers' house. I cannot refuse the old man this one favour. I have to go with him. It would be just plain bad manners not to. In any case, I'll be off the lake by six o'clock and with you at seven, and we can be together for the remainder of the evening."

As we parted, he drew from his inside coat pocket a gaily coloured feather that glistened and shimmered in the late evening sunshine, and handed it to me.

When later I proudly showed it to Mother, her face darkened and she said in a voice that I would never forget, "Mariah, it's lovely, but don't you know that it's said to be bad luck to bring a peacock feather into the house? What was it Grandma Maudie always said? 'A death follows a peacock feather into a house.' Please put it outside, there's a good child."

She shook her head and turned back to her work.

"It's only a feather, Mother," I said, sourly. "It's only a bird's feather! What harm in a bird's feather?"

I thought nothing more of what she had said. Rather than leave it outside the house, I put the beautiful silken feather in a vase and placed it on the table by my bed.

A single magpie sat on the gatepost and flapped its wings in an attempt to circulate a cool flow of air over its feathers.

"One for sorrow," I saluted, as is the custom, and my spoken words were as waves of sound to disturb the air about the bird, who flapped heavily away into the thick air to sit on a nearby tree branch. I lay back on the burned, crisp grass in the shade of the red-blossomed fuchsia and continued to stare up at the troubled, thickening clouds. I noticed their colour was now a deep, slate-blue grey and that they seemed to be pressing even closer than before.

I decided then to return to the cool indoors to drink a cup of sour buttermilk, the spring-water being so scarce and brackish, but the bitter taste could not salve the growing unease inside me.

"Stop fretting, Mariah. Fretting won't bring him to your side. Love has to be endured; you will have to learn that," Mary Ellen said, looking up from her knitting. "Keep busy is my advice. Do something with your hands; the devil finds lots to do for idle hands. There's buttons to be sown on shirts and dresses. Sit with me to while away this noon heat."

She handed me the needle box and pointed to some garments on the settle bed.

I was sowing a bone button on one of Father's Sunday shirts when I heard voices in the yard. I glanced out to see my brother Brian talking loudly and with great excitement to Father and both of them looking towards the house.

"Mary Ellen! Mary Ellen! Can you come out?" Father called.

Mother arose from her knitting and went to join the two men in the yard; both of them commenced to talk with great animation and both at the same time in their haste to give her some important news.

I could not hear the words they spoke to her, but I saw her body stiffen and her hands fly to her face and heard the words that flew like darts to my ears and heart.

"Dear Jesus! Don't say this is true. No! NO!"

She crossed herself several times, her whole body slumped and she began to sob.

I saw my mother approach me. I saw her face, a deathly pale

and sad mask of a face, and saw – but did not hear – the words she spoke to me. Though at the same time, I must have heard her speak those terrible words because they burned like red-hot pokers into my heart and soul and wrenched them both from me in that instant.

"Mariah . . . oh Mariah, *a ghrá*!" Mother gathered my swooning, empty body in her arms then and I heard her voice as if coming from afar. "He's gone . . . he's gone. It's that lovely Scots lad, Mariah. It's Alexander. The poor boy is gone from us. God above have mercy. Dear Jesus, have mercy."

Her words fell on my ears like heavy blows that rendered me beyond words, beyond feeling, beyond life itself. I let myself plunge deep into a great emptiness opening up inside me. I fell towards the swirling, emptiness that closed over my head, and I became lost to the world.

The cold facts of the tragedy were printed – in all their bleak precision – in the *Clare Champion* the following week.

Paddy Keneely and his son Sean – both keen fishermen from the next parish – had gone to the lake at about four-thirty in the hope of getting out on the water in good time to cast their lines and catch some of the early-evening feeding trout. As they rowed their boat out past the Slatey Island, they spied, beyond the Woody Island to the west, a blue and white painted rowboat on the water. As they drew closer, they could see the boat was overturned and drifting and without oarsmen. The men immediately recognised the boat as belonging to the Butler family.

As they drew alongside the upturned boat, they found not a soul under or anywhere in the water about it.

They circled the abandoned boat for a time, loudly calling out across the silent lake. Not a single bird or fish disturbed the waters, while only the echo of their calls answered them across the stilled lake, so they said.

Something was dreadfully wrong here – they knew it! They immediately decided to row ashore towing the abandoned boat behind them and go directly for help and report their findings to the Butler household.

As they beached their boat, they saw, some distance away and half hidden in the tall reeds, a body lying face down in the shallow water. As speedily as they could, they ran and frantically waded out to the spot where the figure lay. With their hearts in their mouths, they lifted the body as gently as they could from the water, carried it ashore and laid it on the grass. It was obvious to both the men that there was nothing that could be done for the wretched drowned man laid on the ground at their feet. They both instantly recognised the body as being that of the stranger who lodged at the Butlers' big house, the Scottish engineer, Alexander McNeil.

Colonel and Mrs Butler were beside themselves with shock and grief, for they loved Alexander as they would a favourite son.

Yes, I can speak of all this now. I can talk of how Father and Brian helped me to my bed following the breaking of the news to Mother and me. I can speak now of how, for several hours, they feared that I would slip from this life as my swoon deepened and my breathing faded so much that Father feared for my life and forced several spoonfuls of one of his most potent mixtures down my throat.

I can now talk and relate of how I awoke from my coma several hours later. As if in a waking dream, I arose from my bed and left the house in the dead of night to make my way to the nearby field beyond the dairy to stand motionless by the old lightning tree. And I can talk now of how I fell on my knees and covered my hair and face and clothes in the dust at the foot of the rotted tree-stump. I wrapped my arms about the tree and pressed my cheek to the dry bark and pounded my fists on its black skin and called and cried and shrieked out to God and to the skies to send another bolt of lightning to strike again the lightning tree, as it had done all those years before, and burn it – and me – to a cinder.

I can talk now of how, as I called for release from my purgatory, it seemed as if God had heard my cries and answered my prayer. A crack so loud as was never heard before split the sky in two and, as a curtain might be drawn across the night sky, the rain began to fall.

At first it fell in great single drops beating the earth like huge fingers on a dry drum skin, then in a sizzling sheet and finally in a great raging torrent of waters pouring from the skies.

And I can talk now of how then my own tears flowed in a salty torrent from some deep well within me, to mix with the falling rainwaters and to spill and flow on the parched earth beneath my feet at the foot of the lightning tree.

With the storm still raging and the rains still falling in great silver sheets, they finally found me. I lay face-down at the base of the tree, drenched and shivering, my face and hair caked with mud, in the rain and mud in a shallow grave I had dug with my bare hands beneath the stump of the lightning tree.

It was Father who gathered my drenched and muddy body from the soaked earth and carried me home in his arms.

Though I was in that fever, a part of me – still lucid, still watchful – had no wish or desire to return to the world I had retreated from. I wanted to die. I wanted to become as mist or air and leave behind this cruel, terrible world that had robbed me of my reason to live. I wanted then with all my heart to follow and join Alex far beyond this vale of tears.

CHAPTER THIRTEEN

COLONEL BUTLER HAD decided earlier that day not to accompany Alex on the water, as he had come down with a severe attack of the gout. Robin related how old man Butler, in a choked and emotional voice, explained how poor Alex had agreed the week before to go out on the water with him for a day's fishing. Notwithstanding the Colonel's condition and not wishing to spoil a good day on the lake, Alex had decided that directly after an early lunch he would put out to water for a few hours.

"It will while away a few hours, and in any case it will be cooler on the water than here on the shore," Alex had said and laughed when he also mentioned to Colonel Butler and his gillie that he had a date with a young lady at seven of the clock and had no intention of being a minute late.

His gillie on that day? None other than Mattie Connors, who was now also missing, presumed drowned.

All through the rest of that day and evening and into the night, under the light of lanterns on long poles, the search party put all available boats on the lake to scout the waters and comb the shorelines in search of Connors' body. After many hours on the lake waters, the exhausted search party called a halt for the night. They resumed the search at first light, scouring afresh the shoreline and keeping watch on the waters, but of Mattie Connors not a trace could be found.

After two long days and nights of such searching with no success, it was accepted that the lake had claimed the gillie for herself and when she was ready she would deliver the poor wretch back to the land for a decent burial.

The story might have ended there, but it did not.

A week or so later, with my love lying still and cold in his coffin, astonishing news quickly spread in the village. The self-same Mattie Connors, presumed drowned but now as alive as you or me, had surfaced and had been recognised in a pub in Kilrush. In a drunken, aggressive state, he had bragged to anybody who would listen of how he had been wronged in love by a faithless hussy who had chosen a foreigner, an outsider – a damn *Sassenach* at that – over him. He also proudly boasted that he had rid the parish and the county of the "unwanted foreign intruder" who had stolen his "wife-to-be".

A short time later – so it was also reported – the miserable wretch was seen boarding a coal steamer cargo-ship from Cappagh Pier heading down the Shannon River to Limerick City.

From there, there was no more news on Mattie Connors. He had simply disappeared from sight. And though the police set up the hue-and-cry for the scoundrel, nothing more was heard of the wretch whose jealous hatred, it was now widely believed, had claimed the young life of a good and noble spirit and who had brought grief and sorrow into my young life.

I now firmly believe that his hateful, spiteful and murderous actions that day sentenced me to the life of a spinster. But worst of all, he had taken the life of an innocent man and condemned his own soul to eternal damnation.

I said that no more was heard of Mattie Connors. Not, that is, until a few years later, when Liam Kelly returned from working in England with news that spread like a fire across the three parishes. Liam had been working as a labouring navvy on a railway-tunnelling site not far from Liverpool, and whom should he bump into one winter's night in a shebeen in Manchester but Mattie Connors himself.

At first he did not recognise the man, so changed and ravaged was he of countenance and appearance.

"He looked like a man of twice his age. The years of hardships and drunkenness could be seen in his face. The poor bastard had a starved and haunted look about him. He was but a beggar and without a shilling to his name."

That was how Kelly described Mattie's appearance to Brian and Robin.

"He looked as if he had been to hell and back," he said.

And back to hell he soon went. Liam went into great detail describing how Mattie met his end at the end of a hunting knife in a bar-room fight in Manchester, not a week or so after meeting him. According to Liam, Mattie's belligerent behaviour had provoked the fight that ended with his woeful death. His killer turned out to have been a huge Scotsman who could take no more of the provocations, slurs and insults hurled in his direction by this wild-eyed, drunken Irishman. One insult led to another. A fight erupted; a blade was drawn and plunged into flesh. A body that Liam recognised as that of Mattie Connors lay on the bar-room floor. Mortally wounded and as his lifeblood spilled out of his body, Mattie's last words on this earth were, "McNeil! McNeil! I'll see you in hell!"

Nobody in the bar knew of whom the poor wretch spoke. A few days later, they buried Mattie Connors – to them just another nameless, itinerant Irish labourer – in an unmarked grave by the side of the road, and there he will lie till he meets his Maker and is judged.

I have no words to tell you how it was for me in the weeks and months that followed Alexander's drowning. How I stumbled from one shapeless day to the next, blind to all life and without hope. How I continued to move from one day to the next as a shadow of a living person. How I could simply breath in and breath out, I cannot know.

How I did not cut the bonds to this earth and follow Alex to the grave, only God knows the answer. And God knows, too, that not a single day passed in that bitter year that followed without me considering going to that same black lake and disappearing forever under the same evil waters that took my love from me.

Though I have pulled a veil of memory across much of that year, I cannot forget the cut and sting of the sharp blade of loss, which lodged deep inside my heart, nor drive from my memory this great weight of grief, which I wore wrapped about me as I would a cloak.

Yet time is a great healer and time was to be the salve that eventually healed the wound that was my broken heart.

I have come to believe that old Mother Nature, in her wisdom, knows not to visit us with a burden so great that it cannot be borne. I was young and had not learned that hard lesson. Wisdom can be gained only through accepting the bad with the good, through suffering and in the living of daily life, no matter what it brings.

And so I walked as a ghost through my empty days and lived only for the night and sleep so to join once again my dead love and to be with him at his side in my dreams. But with the coming of each dawn, I arose to drink again from the bitter cup placed before me.

In the days that followed Alex's drowning, I hovered in some dark place between both worlds, between life and death. Even if I wished it, I could not have attended what passed for his wake

113

while his body still rested in the parlour of Clifden House, the very room where we had met and danced only a few short months before. Alexander was a Protestant, and no Catholic man or woman, under pain of mortal sin, could attend a Protestant service, either within or without a Protestant church, without incurring the wrath of the priests.

I well recall two men of this parish – still alive – who sometime in the early 1930s were ordered by the local priest to go to the bishop to confess a sin so grievous the priest could not give them absolution, only the bishop. What was this great sin? What was this unforgivable transgression that these two good, honest men had committed to warrant such a journey to the bishop's palace?

Nothing more than the simple Christian act of attending a funeral of a good friend and neighbour of theirs, who happened to be a Protestant. By the very act of witnessing a Protestant service, the two men merited the stain on their souls of a sin so grievous that they had to kneel at the feet of their bishop in his palace to have this sin forgiven and gain his absolution.

Outside of the Butlers and some Protestant friends, there were no locals in attendance to wake Alexander; no whiskey or pipes or strong tobacco; no stories or songs or women keening.

When I finally came out of my deep sleep, my first words were, "What has happened to Alexander?"

Mother sat beside my bed and took my hand in hers and gently informed me that poor Alex's body, after it had been waked in the big house, had been transported to journey the great distance home to Scotland.

"There were many people who lined the village street as the death coach, with his body on board, drove by on his way to the city. They took him back to his own place to be buried and to rest with the ashes of his forefathers in his native Scottish earth," Mother said.

With those words it was as if his very existence here had been washed away. No living soul has ever uttered his name to my face from that day to this, and now there is nobody alive other than myself who will recall his passing or even his having existed on this earth.

It was as if he had not lived a single day among us in this place. It was as if he and I had never met or spoken, or danced together, or walked together through scented woods of hazel and summer fields awash with the scent of honeysuckle or fresh-mown hay. It was as if we had not ever strolled at twilight by river-banks and streams or stood and gazed out across the very lake water that was to rob me of him.

Like the water that closed over his body, the events of day-to-day living closed over the memory of his having been among us in this place. But I did not – could not! – forget, nor put aside a single moment or memory of our time together. To have him wrenched from me without a goodbye or farewell filled me with sadness that almost overwhelmed me.

And so I was left to endure alone the full weight of my grief. I had no option but to accept the pain of the days ahead in the sure knowledge that Alexander McNeill would not share with me a single moment of them.

The days that immediately followed that terrible event held no true pattern or purpose for me. I could no longer see a single good reason why I should arise in the morning or eat food I had no taste for. Nor could I find reason to breath the air I had no longing to take into my body. I have no count of the days and nights I stumbled as a ghost down this dark, empty and pointless road.

But the days passed, as all days must, and the seasons came to mirror those of my heart. The August rains that broke the awful summer drought had drenched the fields and flooded the rivers and wells and the low marshy places till only those on horseback could ford the great floods to travel from parish to parish.

September brought gales, and darkening evenings brought signs of an early winter. Great swans bobbed up and down on the waves of the small lake recently created by the floods in the *riasc*, and great flights of crows swooped low over apple orchards and wheat fields now flattened by the driving rain.

By the time October arrived, the swifts and swallows had long departed southward, and the blustery winds, which had shifted to the north-west, turned to salty gales, which turned to fierce storms blowing in from the wild Atlantic.

What little corn and oats was left standing in the fields after the heavy September rains fell to those terrible October storms. As every old and rotting tree and insecure roof or thatching fell like rushes to a scythe, the old people got to fearing that we would might again suffer another *Oíche na Gaoithe Móire*.

This great wind near ruined the land when it blew in from the sea back in 1839, twenty-odd years before I was born. So terrible a night it was that many believed they would perish. So terrible a night it was that many believed it to be Lucifer and his demon horde that rode down on this terrifying howling wind to punish the people and purge the land. The memory of that great storm still haunted those who had lived through and remembered that terrible night.

Hallowe'en ushered in November and came as a bleak, forlorn and lonesome a night, as I have not witnessed before or since. The winds shifted further north-west in mid-November, bringing with it the killing night frosts which fell like a scalding curse on grass and remaining leaf, rotting the pitted potatoes, carrots, onions and other vegetables. The farmers all about thought it wise to put in canvas sacks what root vegetables the frosts had not destroyed and move them, along with most of the animals, indoors to house and barn to see out the cold spell.

"This weather would skin a snipe, but the new moon is bound to bring a thaw." So the old people said.

The new moon came, but it did not bring a change, as expected, in the severe cold. The sun dulled and continued to slip and fall low in the winter sky. The hours of daylight shortened, and the winter turned so flinty hard that even the crows, rooks and magpies deserted the air to take refuge in secret places out of the raw wind and bitter cold.

As Christmas drew near, the hard frosts had not released their grip on the land. The lakes and rivers were solid ice, and it was said that the sea off Lahinch and Liscannor and Spanish Point had frozen solid, trapping seabirds and swans in its steely grip, and that icicles one hundred feet long hung as dangling spears of silver from the edges of the Cliffs of Moher.

All through that Christmas and New Year, the hard weather continued. Nobody in the parish, not even the oldest man or woman alive, could remember a winter so bitter; nor was there a winter since the Great Hunger which visited so much hardship and suffering on us all.

In early January the winds swung to the north-east, and on the morning of *Nollaig na mBan*, we awoke to find the land all about us covered in a thick white blanket of glistening snow.

The snows brought no ease to the bitter nightly frosts. So cruel were they, many old people gave up the ghost and closed their eyes to the hardships of life. They just let go of life, I suppose, there being no heat remaining in their old blood. Even the running blood of youth could not fight off the grasping, killing fingers of Jack Frost, which reached into our houses through our doors and windows and chimneys and into our very beds and into our very bloodstreams.

Cornelius Kenny and Kitty Callaghan died within days of each other. So cold was it at that time, their coffins had to lie above ground for nigh on a week, within the walls of the church, till the menfolk could sink a pick or push a shovel into the frozen earth to dig their graves.

While all about suffered and endured the hardships visited on them by this never-ending winter, I looked out on this frozen world as if through some window: safe yet detached from it all. To my thinking, what this cruel season had brought to the land and the people was no more than the overflow from the bitter, icy season that had taken possession of my broken heart.

The cold! The cold! It had taken up residence and lived now inside the marrow of our bones. In the end I began to fear that it would never end and that my selfish grief was the cause of it all.

Then when it seemed as if we were destined to live in a permanent winter, on one bright moonlight night with the waxing of a March moon, the thaw finally set in.

From my bed I heard the wings of a flight of wild geese cutting a pathway through the frozen sky to the north lands. It sounded like the snapping and cracking of ice, and to my ears it was the most welcome, beautiful music I had ever heard.

The wild geese had returned. The winter was over.

The thaw was about to free the land for the arrival of spring. But how to bring about a thaw to my frozen heart I could not know.

And so, like those all about me, I had endured and lived through that hard winter. Each day lengthened by a cock's step, and in no time the first daffodils were waving their yellow heads at the watery sun. It was as if the land was smiling. There was a quality of lightness in the air and a quiet joy and a quickening of the hearts of the people. I, too, as best I could, rejoiced in the lengthening of the days and the arrival of this longed-for spring. Yet I dreaded the coming soon of St Patrick's Day and the flood of memories it would bring. Could it be that a year, a whole year of three hundred and sixty-five long and separate days, had passed since the Butlers' soirée and my first laying eyes on Alexander McNeil?

For the first time in so many years, the Butlers did not – as had been their yearly custom – open their house that St Patrick's night for a soirée. It was said that old Richard Butler was ailing, and no comments were passed either by Mother or Father.

St Patrick's Day was celebrated nevertheless. Thick bunches of green shamrock, collected at dawn by Father, awaited each of us on the table as we sat down to breakfast. Mother had baked a fine sweet loaf to celebrate the day and throughout all that day was as gentle and as caring to me as she could be. Yet neither she nor Father once mentioned the events of that night but one short year ago. Neither did they make mention of what we had lived through and shared in the year gone by.

As the sun set on that day, I went to sit alone by the lightning tree to be with my thoughts. I wrapped my arms about the tree, pressed my cheek against its withered bark and again shed salty tears I did not think I had within me to shed.

Soon after that, to the great ease of all, a full thaw set in, and in no time at all the spring swept down to fill the fields and gardens, trees and hedges with blossom and colour, and the dawns and twilights were filled to the brim with birdsong.

Not that we had much spare time to relish or appreciate the gifts that springtime had brought with it. Now that the long winter had been driven away, there was a quickening of the pace of life, with much work to be done in the bog, gardens and meadows. Father and Robin were busy preparing the gardens for ploughing and early potato setting, while Brian and Willie Keane were out before dawn to prepare the bog for turf cutting. While they were away at their work, Mother and I set about readying the kitchen garden for vegetable-sowing, as well as doing all the other household chores which kept us busy from first to last light.

Once, she caught me frozen where I stood, as if in a trance, staring at the cabbage plant I had just stuck into the warm earth. She laid her hand on mine and in a soft voice said, "Mariah, you are young, with your whole life ahead of you. It is not good to hold on to your grief and nurse it at your breast. The pain you yet feel will pass, unless you make a home for it in your heart. Let it go, *alanna*. Let him go. Life is for the living."

On that particular May Day morning I speak of, I was to go, as I now did each year, to collect water from the Healing Well. Before I departed the house and while the night lay dark on the land, Father came down to the kitchen as I was lacing up my boots.

"Mariah, *a ghrá*," he said, as gentle as could be. "Go to the well and collect the healing water, but before you leave that place, lay down all your pain, sorrows and troubles and leave them behind you. You will never carry the cure and pass it on or be of use to others while you carry such pain and trouble inside your heart."

It was the one and only time Father ever alluded to the burden of the soul-pain I still carried within me. I made no answer but set out on my annual journey to the well.

I must have heeded his words, for I returned home that May Day morning with the bottle of healing water and carrying about my heart a strange lightness, such as I had not felt within me for what seemed like a lifetime.

My mother must have noticed my change of mood, but she just smiled that smile of hers and said, "Will you listen to those birds and the songs they sing for us today. Aren't they sent down from Heaven above? Listen to how they sing as if their tiny hearts are fit to burst. And why wouldn't they, when you think of what they have survived this last winter? Even they know that there is an end to their suffering if it's born bravely and endured with acceptance."

At that time I didn't rightly know the full meaning of her

words. I had yet to learn that if we continue to carry all the hurts and pains and troubles that come to us in our lives, they will in the end drive us to our knees; and so we have to learn to cast them aside, as I had done at the well that morning.

It would be many years before my mother's words would reveal their full meaning to me. Yet at that time, somewhere deep inside, I felt that I had passed some important marker on the crooked old road to that place of acceptance and healing.

Spring gave way to summer, and life flowed and moved to its own rhythms it its usual way. I busied myself with chores both inside and outside the house. I worked with the men in the gardens and in the peat bog and meadows, and as the days grew longer, the work increased to fill each hour. But no matter how long the daylight hours, how hard the work or how weary the bones, at the end of each day I went to the lightning tree to sit alone with my thoughts under its twisted limbs. There I sometimes poured out my thoughts to the charred wood and shed silent tears. Sometimes I would empty my mind and simply listen to the sound of the earth all about me.

I knew now I carried less weight in my heart than I had all though that winter. I knew, too, that I had changed in ways I could not yet understand. I had become a more solitary person and much less outgoing in my ways and habits. I shied away from contact with people. I refused all invitations from my friends and companions to attend local house gatherings. I ceased to attend the regular horse and cattle fairs or hurling matches in the village on summer Sundays. Other than attending the funeral of a neighbour or mass on a Sunday morning and occasionally joining the after-mass gathering under the trees outside the church, I had very little social contact with anybody outside my own family or those who might call to the house for *cuaird* or for cure.

One morning in early August, just as dawn broke, I awoke to hear a soft fluttering and tapping on my windowpane. I arose from my bed, lit my bedside candle, and went to peer out into the half-glow of the early-morning light. There, on the outside window-ledge, lay a poor little sparrow, its little body broken and it beating its last few wing beats of life.

I remembered then that this day was August the fifth, a year to the day since my love was taken from me. A year to the day since my world was turned on its head. A year! Three hundred and sixty-five long days and nights, four seasons and twelve waxing, waning and full moons in the sky since my love was snatched from my arms and my old life ended.

Yet here I was, as alive as I could be and seeing in yet another dawn of another day on this earth without my one true love.

I arose and dressed and went outside. As gently as I could, I took the tiny bird body across the fields to the foot of the lightning tree. As the first rays of the sun touched the hills all around, with my bare hands, I scooped out a small grave in which to place the poor little bird. I had to search hard for a place beneath the tree where the soil was not soured by the salt of the million tears I had shed on this earth in the twelve months gone by.

Before covering over the still-warm body with earth, I gently brushed away my teardrops from its soft downy feathers.

"Rest easy, little sparrow. Fly with your song to my love," I said, wishing whatever pain and hurt still lingered within my crying heart to go down in this grave with this tiny songbird.

I returned to this place later that evening, and twilight found me still there, huddled inside the hollowed-out stump of the tree.

For the first time in a year, I felt I sat in that place with no company save the lightning tree.

For the first time in a year, I did not have as company the Lady Grief and her sister, Sorrow.

CHAPTER FOURTEEN

WHY DO WE dream the dreams that we do? What strange journeys do they take us on? What do they tell us about our waking lives? I've pondered often on what is the purpose – the true purpose – of dreams, other than filling in the dark hours of our sleeping. For the life of me, I still have few answers. You go to your bed and fall asleep, and with no effort you are transported to a world inside ourselves yet outside and beyond anything we could imagine in our normal waking hours. The poor dreamer has no say whatsoever in the affairs and events of dreams.

Think of it: to be whisked away as if on a magic carpet to a place where you can meet and walk and talk with not only the living but also the dead and sometimes with those yet-to-be born. To be allowed to enter strange unknown worlds and view fantastical scenes that can fill us with joy; or be lured to enter shadowy places that are dark and troubled and filled with all manner of unknown dangers lurking in the deepest corners of our minds.

In my youth, and for much of my life, I dreamed a great deal, and on awakening, I would try hard to recall, and sometimes write down, the details of my dream. Usually they melted before my awakening mind could grasp them, to float away like mist in the full light of morning. I would often tell my mother of them and ask what might be their meaning.

"Och, child," she would laugh. "Dreams are what they are . . . just dreams. If it wasn't for our dreams, our souls would leave our sleeping bodies to drift away into the night sky and we might never awake. Dreams are the strings that bind us to our bodies and to the real world."

Maybe Mother was right. As I grew older, I paid more and more attention to my dreams, for they sometimes seemed to me to be but messengers from some unknown place beyond this world to which we should take heed. Mostly my dreams were pleasant enough, though after losing Alexander they became dark and cloudy and offered no solace or light. In one recurring dream, I would see him standing by the lake shore. He would smile and reach out his hand to take mine. I would run to him, but as I reached to take his hand, he would be snatched away by some unseen force. I would next see him on the distant shore and hear his voice calling my name, and then he would be gone and I would feel a great emptiness open up inside me.

Those dark dreams still visit, though not so often now that I am an old woman and soon to become a dream myself.

I still recall one dream that first came to me when I was but a child and visited me often through my life. Of all my dreams, from the sweet and happy to the bleakest of nightmares, this one dream brought about an event in the waking world that caused quite a stir at the time.

Let me tell you how it came about.

I was about six or seven years of age. One night, right out of the blue, I had a dream so real in every way I thought I had risen from my bed and gone out into the moonlight in chase of it. It was the ringing of a bell that first drew my attention. I seemed to know right away that this was not the sound of the bell which hung high in the church bell tower, regularly rung for Sunday mass.

The bell I heard in my dream I knew to be different. How beautiful was the sound of its ringing! Not at all dull and flat-toned like the regular church bell. The bell of my dreams rang peals of golden notes so rich and grand and melodious, you might think they rang from within the very wall of Paradise itself.

As I listened and marvelled at the beautiful sound, I wondered at the same time, "Who is ringing a bell in the graveyard in the dead of night?" I lay very still, waiting for Father or Mother to stir and perhaps venture out to see who it was making this sound that filled the night with its golden tones. Hardly daring to breathe, I lay still in my bed, while all about me in the house nothing stirred, as all slept peacefully and quietly.

Suddenly, the bell fell silent, and I found myself standing outside the door of the house looking towards the old church graveyard. Through the pale, moonlit mist a figure – more a shadow at first – moved slowly in my direction. As the figure neared, I recognised it to be that of a monk, or a friar perhaps, dressed as he was in a dark cowl.

The figure drew ever closer, stopped and looked in my direction. Though I could feel his eyes on me, I could not see a face within the hood. The figure moved even closer. A cold chill coursed through my veins. A wave of panic washed over me as I tried to turn and run back inside the house. But try as I might, I could not move a muscle nor awake from the dream I knew myself to be in. The figure beckoned that I should follow him, and without trying or wishing it, I felt my feet move to follow behind him as he moved down the road, away from the house, towards the bridge and over to the stream and the *riasc* beyond.

Across the stream the shadow stops at the edge of the road.

Turning to me, his cloaked arm rises to point to a spot in the *riasc* a short distance from the roadside.

In that moment, the bell began its tolling. I could now clearly hear that the sound came not from the old graveyard, but from somewhere deep underneath the ground – from the very spot now being pointed out to me by this silent, cloaked figure.

Though I tried to speak to enquire of the figure the meaning of his visitation, my tongue would not obey my mind. In that same moment, even as I struggled to utter my words, I found myself back in my own safe bed trembling from the experience and strength of the dream.

The dream, exact in every detail, returned the following night and the night after that.

I knew then I had to share this vision with another person, and so I related the dream to Mother and told of its visit on three consecutive nights.

While Mother kneaded dough for a soda bread on the kitchen table, she told me the story of the *Clog an Óir*.

"You have had a big dream," she said. "A dream that has visited you to show you where the long-lost golden bell – the *Clog an Óir* – is buried.

"That old ruined graveyard you see there today," Mother said as she slapped the dough. "Well, it wasn't always such. There was a time long, long ago that church was as fine a building with its fine carved doors and windows and a full standing round tower in the yard as to be seen anywhere in the county or indeed in the province of Munster.

"A thousand years ago, before the English came, even before the Normans came, there was a small community of holy women – nuns and penitents – gathered there in a small nunnery. Then came the monks and learned men who cared for the holy place, and people came from near and far to learn and to read and to write in Latin, in Greek and Gaelic. Many came just to meditate and pray. They prospered in those days and lived their simple, holy lives, safe within the walls of their monastery. It was said that, within the strong stone walls of their keep, they held priceless treasures of ancient, leather-bound books, crosses of silver and jewelled chalices and embroidered vestments of the finest cloth."

Mother got so caught up in the telling of her story that she halted her bread kneading.

"But the greatest treasure of all in their keep was the *Clog an Óir*, a wonderful bell wrought, so they say, out of solid gold that hung high in the bell tower above the church. This great bell was rung only at Christmas and Easter time, and the people believed that for as long as it hung there and rang out its song, the land and the monks and the people all about would prosper, safe from war and famine and pestilence, and be free and happy. And so it was for generations the bell rang out peace and freedom from plague and want and hunger."

As I sat enthralled, Mother stopped her bread making and sat herself down by the fire to ready herself for the next part of her tale.

Hardly daring to breathe, I listened as she told of how one day, a few hundred years ago, there was a great battle fought in this very spot between two mighty Burren clans, the McMahons and the O'Briens. In the heat and tumult of battle, the round tower was partly levelled and the church burned to the ground. But before the battle had commenced, the monks had removed all their treasures, including the great bell, and placed them safely beyond the hands of their enemies.

The story goes that as the monks and the local men prepared their swords and spears and defences for the coming attack, their women removed and carried the golden bell away and buried it deep in the *riasc* where the attacking clan would never lay hands on it.

"And there it still lies to this very day," Mary Ellen concluded.

She was to tell the same story to a Mr Westropp, the famous journeyman collector of old tales, who stopped by here in the summer of 1884 to write down all the tales and stories and folk-lore of the parish and the county.

"That was my dream! That is exactly as my dream came to me!" I could hardly hold my excitement. "Where did they bury the *Clog an Óir*?"

"Not a hundred paces from this very spot." Mary Ellen was whispering now, enjoying the telling of her tale. "And it's said that anyone who will dream of the bell three times in a row will learn of its exact hiding place. But the dreamer of the dream will never lay hands on it. They will have to relate its whereabouts to another and that person – though it can never be a woman – must then locate the spot, dig deep in the ground and find the bell. They must then replace it in its rightful place atop the old church tower. When the bell is replaced, the land and the people will be free and once again prosper and be happy, as they were when Fionn and the Fianna ruled the land. That's what the old people say."

I could hardly wait to tell my brothers Brian and Robin about my dream, and before you could say Jack Robinson, we had fetched a spade from the garden and together we went directly to the *riasc* to dig for the mysterious, hidden *Clog an Óir*.

Brian, being the eldest, begun to dig the soggy ground, in the spot I pointed out to him, not ten yards in from the roadside. The ground was wet and marshy, and so his task of digging in the spongy earth was not difficult. He was about two feet down in to the muddy earth when he halted.

"Ah, I've hit water already. Are you sure this is the place you saw in your dreams?"

I answered that this was – or as close as I could determine – the place as shown me in my dream. But I could now see there was no point in trying to dig further as a stream of brown bog water bubbled up out of the hole around our feet.

"You and your dreams. We are the fools to listen to you," is all they said to me as we walked homeward without the treasure that a few moments before had seemed so close to us.

It was about maybe six years later – I was thirteen or fourteen then – when the story of the fabulous bell took a strange turn.

It was a night in late October, when the first signs of winter were to be seen and felt. The night was sharp with an early frost, and all the family were gathered around the fire in the company of Sam Nestor, Timmy Mulqueen and Jack Guirin, three middle-aged bachelors who lived alone and who would regularly visit the house on winter nights on *cuaird*.

It must have been close to Hallowe'en because, on this particular night, the talk soon turned to *púcaí*, ghost coaches, restless ghosts, bad-minded witches, troubled spirits and strange visions and dreams. Such fireside conversations were common around Hallowe'en, and in the flickering of the lanterns, candles and the firelight, the atmosphere was thick with magic and a sense that the other world was but a breath away from us the living. On this occasion I paid great attention to the stories and conversation, as shortly before this night, I had had yet another dream about the lost golden bell.

As Sam Nestor told of the *púca*, who could not cross over running water, I could not contain myself any longer. I had to pipe up and relate my recurring dream and before you could spin a penny in the air, the conversation turned entirely to the lost *Clog an Óir* and those poor souls who had sought it in vain over the centuries.

"They say that anyone who will dream of the bell three times can discover its hiding place," Sam said.

"Well, I have," I said as coolly as you like. "I dreamed of the *Clog an Óir* three times in a row."

The men looked at me in amazement.

"It's true," my mother said. "Mariah did dream those dreams."

That was how the whole affair began, with me relating my recurring dream. Sam, Timmy and Jack got all excited and decided there and then that they could not let the opportunity slip away of being the men who would discover the long-lost treasure and return it to its rightful place over the church.

"We'll do it first thing in the morning." Timmy's eyes were like saucers.

"No, no, ye can't do that," Father interrupted. "It's said that the bell can be retrieved only between midnight and cock-crow of a Sunday morning. Ye'll have to do it this coming Saturday night."

And so it was decided that, as soon as I had pointed out the place in the marsh shown to me in my dream, the three men would prepare to dig in that place for the lost treasure.

I can still recall the hullabaloo in our house the following Saturday night. We were all as excited as if it was Christmas Eve, with everybody talking at once. Sam, Timmy and Jack, in their hats and long, black overcoats – for it was a cold, frosty night – readied themselves for their forthcoming quest as they would for some great adventure. Mother was busy making griddle bread and pouring mugs of hot, sweet tea. Father sat trimming a lantern wick, and we youngsters, caught up in the excitement of it all – were beside ourselves with glee and expectation. You could hear the chatter and babble in the next parish.

Finally, the expedition was ready to depart on its mission.

"Remember now, men," Father said as the three men prepared to leave the house. "Not a spade in the ground till the last stroke of midnight."

Don't worry, Michael. We're the men for this job. The bell is practically in our hands. Wait and see. We'll be back here before an hour passes with the lost *Clog an Óir!*"

With that, and with shovels on shoulders and lantern held high to light the road ahead, the three men stepped out of the house and set off, like the Three Wise Kings following their star, in search of the bell of gold, lost for who-knows-how-long and buried deep in the ground not one hundred steps from this very house.

"Will you look at them," Mother laughed as the three men headed off into the chilly night. "Grown men acting like children on a Christmas night. Off digging for some rusty old bell when they should be at home in their beds. Some men never grow up!"

Father laughed too, but, like the rest of us, he, too, was caught up in the moment and excitement of it all.

"Who knows, Mary Ellen?" Father smiled broadly. "Maybe they will surprise us all and bring back the lost bell. After all, Mariah did have those dreams, did she not?"

"Humph." Mary Ellen prepared to go to her bed. "I'll believe it when I see it."

I was not as much an unbeliever as Mother.

After all, was it not a known fact that there was indeed once a great golden bell? And did that bell not once hang in the old church bell tower? And was it not true that it was removed and buried for safekeeping, and had it not lain in its underground grave these several hundred years? And, as Father said, what harm was there in having a go at discovering its hiding place? Surely the women who buried it all those years ago did not mean that it should remain lost for ever? None of us asked why the bell was not recovered following the battle.

Sam, Timmy and Jack certainly were in full agreement that it was high time it was recovered and that it might as well be they who recovered it as anybody else.

"Sure, we'll go down in history if we find it," Timmy Mulqueen had said.

CHAPTER FIFTEEN

SUNDAY MORNINGS WERE always busy times for us. All in the house arose early as fires had to be set and lit, bread baked, cows foddered and milked, chickens and hens and other fowl fed, and all that work completed in good time to get to first mass at eight o'clock sharp.

I had hardly slept a wink, but I must have finally fallen asleep, for I heard the lost bell ring in my dreams. In my dream I looked in the direction of the old graveyard to see the bell swinging back and forth atop the old bell tower.

I awoke well before first light but tossed and turned in my bed while anxiously awaiting stirrings about the house. I was eager to be up and to hear what news there might be as to how the three treasure hunters had fared the night before.

In the midst of completing my many Sunday morning chores, I forgot about the men and their midnight mission to retrieve the lost bell from the marsh.

It was later, while at mass, that Mother whispered to me, "I see no sign of Timmy, Sam or Jack. Where can they be this morning?"

I scanned the men's side of the church. Sure enough, I could not lay eyes on any one of the men, who usually sat at the back of the church in the same place each Sunday. My imagination raced. One of the men not attending mass, maybe! But all three missing from their usual church pews? I thought that very strange indeed. Was their absence, I wondered, anything to do with their activities in the *riasc* through the night? I could hardly contain myself.

When Father also mentioned their absence when we returned home, we just looked at each other with the same question in mind. Just where were the three men?

"Right!" Father quickly arose from the table and pulled on his hat and overcoat. "Come with me, Mariah."

Straightaway, we set off down the road to the *riasc*, to the Place of the Bell, as I now called it. We soon arrived at the spot only to find two shovels lying by a freshly dug mound of frosted earth and a discarded lantern.

"Off home with you, Mariah," said Father, a worried look on his face. "I'm away off to Timmy's house to get to the bottom of this."

I was for going with him to Timmy Mulqueen's house, but he would not hear of it. This, he insisted, an anxious look on his face, was something he had to do on his own.

An hour or so later, Father was home with a story that had us fairly riveted to the floor. With a cup of hot tea in his hands, he told of what he had discovered.

"The first thing is the good news. Timmy, Sam and Jack are all safe. But what a night they've had, according to Timmy, who's at home in bed with a sore head and an empty whiskey bottle with him for company."

Father then sat down and told his story as related to him by the still-drunken Timmy.

The three treasure-seekers had left our house the night before at a quarter to twelve and had proceeded with lighted lantern, shovels and high hopes to the Place of the Bell. There they had

133

waited till Sam's fob watch read just gone midnight. Now being officially Sunday morning, they commenced to dig in the exact spot I had indicated to them earlier. At least, Timmy and Jack dug while Sam held the lantern and whispered encouragement to the two men.

They had dug no more than three or four feet into the sandy, wet ground when suddenly there was a sharp "clang" as a shovel made contact with a hard, metal object.

"I've struck something solid," said Jack, who began to dig as if his life depended on it.

Clang! "We have it!"

Clang! The shovels rang out again.

"By the hokey," cried Timmy. "We have it! We have the *Clog an Óir*!"

Before a spade could lift another spoonful of earth from the hole, the three men froze in witness to sights and sounds the like of which they never before had experienced. For in that very moment of Timmy's shovel striking that solid object a third time, the air all around them was suddenly filled with a strange glow and the sound of a great bell ringing out its mournful peals across the night sky.

"Saints protect us! It's coming from the hole!" Timmy shouted, jumping backwards.

"It's coming from the sky above us!" Jack pointed towards the heavens.

"No!" said Sam, turning and pointing to the graveyard. "It's coming from the old church. Listen."

They turned and looked up the road towards the church to see it bathed in light, and there in the old bell tower was a huge bell, swinging back and forth and ringing out loud and clear for all the parish to hear.

And if that wasn't enough for the terrified three, there was worse to come.

"Oh Jesus, Mary and Joseph!" Sam fell to his knees and crossed himself. Coming slowly down the road towards the men were two black horses pulling a funeral carriage followed by a large procession of silent mourners led by a hooded monk.

Timmy saw it. He swore to it! Jack also saw it. So, too, did Sam, still on his knees in the wet grass, hands clasped together in prayer.

Without a sound, save for the continued deep ringing tolling of the bell, the silent procession drew nigh and halted on the roadside and the mourners turned their dark, hidden faces toward the three men, frozen to the spot in sheer terror. Then, as suddenly as the tolling of the bell had started, it stopped. When the men looked again, the funeral procession had vanished into the mist rising from the river. With that, and without another word to each other, the three men dropped shovels and the lantern and took to their heels and fled that accursed and haunted Place of the Bell.

That was the terrible story as told to my father by Timmy – still in his bed.

"Timmy's a very shaken man, so he is," Father said solemnly and continued his story.

Leaving Timmy to nurse his whiskey head, Father then hurried across the fields to Jack's house to hear his version of the night's events. He found Jack seated by an unlit fire, looking pale as a ghost, and his account was, more or less, the same as Timmy's. Like Timmy, he had no real memory of what occurred other than what Timmy had already related.

When Father then went to check on Sam, he found his cottage door locked, the curtains drawn on all the windows, and though he called out and loudly knocked, he could not raise a response from Sam. For a moment, he considered breaking down the cottage door to assure himself of Sam's safety, but decided against it. He assumed – rightly, as it happened – that

Sam was probably in his bed sleeping off the stress of his nocturnal adventure.

With that, Father decided to return home satisfied that none were the worse following their extraordinary experiences.

"Needless to say, they never did uncover the lost *Clog an Óir.*" With a twinkle in his eye, Father looked directly at me as he spoke. "Oh, and by the way, Mariah, when we were down on the *riasc* earlier to examine the site, I couldn't help noticing that there was a herd of cows and two horses grazing around and about the freshly dug pit. I can't help but wonder, could they have been that 'funeral' procession seen on the road by the men as they excavated for the bell?"

There was a gleam in his eye as he said this.

He made no effort to explain away the tolling of the bell, which all three swore they heard ringing loud and clear in the moonlight.

It was several weeks before Timmy, Sam or Jack was seen in public again and even longer before they visited our house on a night's *cuaird.*

When they did come, not a word was mentioned about their ghostly experiences, though I was bursting with questions to put to the men. As they left the house, Mother whispered to Father, "Did you notice? Did you see how old and grey they look?"

It was true! All three men, young and fresh before that fateful night, seemed to have aged twenty years or more in a few short weeks. Whatever they had witnessed on the marsh that night – real or imagined – had taken a toll that now clearly showed on their features.

Nary a word did they ever again speak to a living soul regarding their experiences in search of the still-lost *Clog an Óir.*

To the best of my knowledge, in all the years since that time, no person has ever set out to search the marsh or dig there for the golden bell, and I doubt now if anybody ever will.

Some say it's all a fairy tale, that there is no lost bell of gold, but I know it to be there. I know it to be true for I saw it clearly in my dream. I still have that same dream in which that bell rings clear through the night air and the old hooded monk still beckons and tries to lure me away from bed and house to once again point out to me its secret place of rest.

Though many still talk and wonder about it, nobody since then has had the inclination, or the courage, to search for the mysterious golden bell. And so it still lies to this day in its safe and secret place, deep under the earth, waiting to be found and returned to its proper place in the old graveyard church bell tower.

Who knows? Maybe one night soon, you will dream that same dream which will reveal the resting place of that lost bell of gold.

Isn't that a good enough reason to listen to your dreams?

CHAPTER SIXTEEN

"SIT DOWN, MARIAH." Mary Ellen, my mother, poured a mug of hot tea from her best china teapot. "There's something I want to talk to you about."

Mother used her china teapot only for special occasions, such as when we had special visitors on a Sunday or at Christmas, so I knew this had to be about something important.

It was a bright, chilly March morning in 1902. A watery sun hung low over the *riasc*, and a hard gale blowing from the Atlantic carried with it a bitter tang of sea salt.

I knew from Mary Ellen's tone of voice and demeanour that she had more on her mind than engaging me in idle chatter or gossip with so much work to be done both within and without the house.

She placed the tea in front of me on the table and swung the iron kettle over the blazing hearth fire.

"I got a note delivered yesterday," she said, drawing an envelope from her apron pocket. From it she drew a sheet of notepaper and smoothed it on her lap. "It came from Bessie Moran in the village."

I knew Bessie Moran. Everybody knew Bessie, a feisty lady in her seventies who at that time had been a widow for twenty years or so and who owned and ran her public house on the village main street. Bessie was also, if I remember correctly, a second cousin to my father and always made it her business to acknowledge that blood connection whenever we might casually meet on the village street.

"Bessie is talking about retiring and looking for a good reliable manager to run her pub business. She has asked if you would consider the position. She thinks highly of you. How would you feel about taking up that job, Mariah?"

I looked at Mary Ellen in amazement and hardly knew how to respond to her suggestion. Me? Run a public house? I was then in my mid-forties, a spinster of quiet manners and disposition, living here in the house I was born in. More importantly, at that point in my life, I had had no experience that I felt would qualify me in any way for such a responsible post as running a public house.

I was a home bird, a simple housekeeper. I suppose I had to admit that as a healer I had had some experience in dealing directly with people. But, I also had to admit to myself, at that stage of my life, that I had never worked in any business outside the farm and the home, let alone a public house.

I could see Mother was excited at the prospect. According to Mother, Bessie's note, alluding again to the blood relationship between our families, hinted at the possibility that I could very well be in line to inherit her premises on her death.

"There's a good living to be made in the public house business, Mariah. Did you ever see a pub owner short of a shilling or in need or in want?" Mother suggested.

I had to admit I had not. Apart from the few who were among their own best customers, all the other publicans were among the wealthiest businessmen and women in the village.

I looked at my mother. To me, at that moment, she looked old and frail and sad. Since Father's death, just four years before, she had lost interest in life, and I could sense some vital spark had been quenched in her. More and more these days, she would tell us often that her single greatest wish in this life was to see that we, her remaining family, were all healthy, safe and sound, while she awaited and prepared for her own end. Looking at her then, I feared that day might not be too long in coming.

As we sat together that morning, sipping our hot sweet tea, I could see a look in her eyes that silently begged me to accept, or at least to give serious consideration to, Bessie's offer.

"Bessie would never make this offer if she did not believe you to be well capable. Do not let the opportunity pass you by, Mariah. That's all I will say." She folded her hands about her cup for warmth.

They were hard years then, and the coming of the new century had not, as many expected it to, improved our lot. Father had died in 1898 from a bout of pneumonia which swept through the three parishes and which took many of his age. His death left a great empty hole at the middle of our family, and in the years following his passing, everyday life for us was just as great a struggle as it had been in the years following the Hunger.

I remember New Year's Day of 1900, the first day of the new century. As midnight approached, Mother, Brian, Robin and I gathered around the fireplace and the blazing fire of heaped turf and timber root. We stood together by our own hearth to remember those who were no longer with us.

Just as Father used to do on New Year's Eve, Brian, now being the eldest man in the family, raised a glass of whiskey as a toast to the dead and for them threw the contents into the roaring fire. We watched in silence the flames leap up, and as shadows danced all about us, we felt the spirits of the departed to be with us in the room. Then, in renewed and uplifted spirits and with great dreams and hopes and in welcoming in the newly dawned century, we again raised our glasses to drink to happiness and prosperity and freedom from want and ill health.

"A better future for us all in a brighter and better century." Mother's eyes glistened wet as we toasted and raised our glasses to give thanks that we in that room had survived to see in this brand new year of 1900 and this brand new century about to unfold.

That hope and expectation of better days ahead for the Irish people was given a boost in late January of the following year of 1901 with the news in *The Clareman* newspaper of the death of Queen Victoria. For six long decades she had sat as empress and queen on her lofty throne and – some would say – bestowed gifts and shown mercy and compassion to all her subjects. To all except, that is, her pitiful Irish subjects, who were also her nearest neighbours and who, in full view of her faithful servants on this island, lived in great fear, in great need and in great want.

When the news of her death became known, the Anglo-Irish Protestants – the landowners and the merchants in the town – mourned their dead queen by draping their closed premises with black crepe, and held many church services. I heard of one landlord who was so grieved by the news that he painted the horns of his cattle black in sympathy. But I can tell you there were but very few damp Irish eyes at the news of her passing on that grey January day in 1901.

We could not forget. How could we wipe from memory how she abandoned us to our terrible fate? Were we not her closest neighbours, with whom her country had had dealings since Strongbow and his English Normans invaded us hundreds of years before? How cruelly the queen, who saw herself as a mother to her empire, ignored the desperate plight of the starving and destitute Irish in that time of the Great Hunger. It was reported that she presented a larger sum of money to a home for stray dogs in the city of London than she did to the Irish famine relief.

But now she was dead, and it's wrong to speak ill of the dead, isn't it?

So it was, not many days later, I found myself in Bessie Moran's dark parlour directly above her bar. I sat in an armchair across from her – a glass of brandy in her hands, a glass of sherry in mine – discussing her retirement plans and her hope that I would consider taking over the day-to-day running of her pub.

"I'm seventy-five years old this year," she sprightly announced. "I've run this bar since I married in here in the summer of 1860, and I did a good job, if I say so myself. My poor late husband Jack wasn't a good man behind the bar except to fill too many pints of porter for himself, and so he let me take the business in hand and run the pub. I knew that if I did not make a go of it, we would soon be on the street. So I applied myself as well as I could and, with diligence and hard work, made profits where there were only losses.

"But the years have caught up with me, and I feel it in my bones that it's time I retired. This is a job for a younger woman. A woman like yourself, Mariah: a capable woman and a smart woman at that. You would be more than just a working barmaid; I see you as a co-proprietor . . . . a business partner, so to speak. What do you say to that?"

I thanked her for her unexpected and generous offer and for her confidence in me. However, I felt it only right that I should inform her that I had rarely stepped inside a public house as a customer except in the snug following a christening or a funeral, perhaps, let alone being capable of taking over and managing one. In those days, only the wives of the owners would be seen behind a bar, and only tinker women or a fallen woman would be seen, or allowed, inside the doors of a public house to sit and take drink alongside the men.

"It'll be the making of you, Mariah. You'll take to it like a duck to water, you'll see," Bessie said, topping up her brandy glass. "And," she smiled, "you'll get to meet the people."

How right Bessie was on that score.

CHAPTER SEVENTEEN

BESSIE MORAN'S PUB was little different in style or structure, inside or out, from the other seven public houses that lined both sides of the village street.

The sale of porter, beer, liquors and strong tobacco and a little grocery business on the side comprised the trade carried on here. Entry to the premises from the flagstone pavement through a door of buttermilk-coloured frosted glass panels led you into a long, narrow bar-room with a high ceiling, stained brown from the pipe and turf smoke of the years.

Directly inside the door on the left was the snug, a small room with leather-cushioned seating about the walls, which were lined with smoke-stained walnut timber.

That little snug room was also to become both my office and dispensary in the years to come, a quiet, calming place to which I could retreat and where I could converse in privacy with those men and women who would regularly come to me for the healing cure for various physical and other ailments.

From the snug to the end of the room ran the long, high marble-topped oak bar with eight high barstools tucked up to the boot-rail which ran along the bottom of the bar.

The first thing you would sense when you stepped through into the bar-room was the strong aroma of the bar-room itself. The smell of raw whiskey, stale porter, damp sawdust and paraffin-lamp oil mixed with the smoke of cigar, cheroot, cigarette, pipe and turf. Add to that the smell of cow manure brought in on Wellingtons and hobnailed boots and dog piss delivered by customers' mongrels on the sawdust or turf basket.

All these scents mingled with that of the strong human sweat of unwashed bodies to present the nose with as pungent an aroma as you could get in one small room.

Once your eyes had adjusted to the gloom, they might fall on the well-stocked stack of walnut shelves that ran along the back wall of the bar from floor to ceiling. These were lined and crammed with polished whiskey and single-shot glasses that glistened like crystal in the dim light of a single lantern. Pint and half-pint tumblers sat alongside bottles of dark porter, pale and brown ales, whiskies, sherries, ports, gins, brandies and wines and sweet white lemonade in bottles with glass-marble tops.

Set square at the centre of this array was a weight-wound wall clock with a single pendulum and a large mirror with the words *"Drink 'Irish Arms' Whiskey"* inscribed in gold lettering on the highly polished glass. Underneath this grand centrepiece mirror sat a single oil lamp, which, along with two large wax candles, usually lit only at Christmas and Easter time, was the bar-room's only lighting.

What natural sunlight God allowed through the windows provided daytime lighting. Though should you enter the bar on the brightest summer's day, you would still have to adjust your eyes to the dim light within.

The only source of heating was a small open turf fire at the end of the bar that was kept alight winter and summer.

When the wind came from the north or north-east, as it did in February and March, the chimney smoked and choked and often coughed out its contents to fill the bar with a foul-smelling mist of old soot, wet leaves, damp twigs and crow feathers, driving the complaining customers to the far end of the room.

From the day I walked through the door in the first week of May 1902, this was to be my constant place of work for the next seven years of my life.

There were no more than a dozen or so customers in the bar on that May evening when Bessie, with myself at her side, made the solemn announcement to the drinking men present of her imminent retirement and of my appointment as manageress elect, so to speak, of her establishment from that day forth. You could have heard a butterfly's wing beat half a mile away as the silenced group of men absorbed this surprising, astounding, and possibly unwelcome news without comment. When it came to their drinking habits, Bessie's regulars had long established their individual routines. This news of Bessie's retirement obviously unsettled them greatly.

The deadly hush in the bar following Bessie's bombshell news was broken only when Bessie suggested "a drink on the house for all in the house" to mark this auspicious occasion.

For the rest of the evening and well into the night, until the last customer had been ejected into the dark street (in those days there was no street lighting), Bessie showed me the ropes of bar, and people, management.

There was much to learn, as I soon found out.

Such as the storing and maintenance of the porter and whiskey barrels. She identified for me the various and varied liquors and wines; most were strange and new to me. She showed me the regular Irish and Scotch whiskeys and the top-shelf single malts, American Kentucky bourbons, French brandies and cognacs, German schnapps, Jamaican rums, Bordeaux clarets, Spanish wines, Jerez ports, and an assortment of cordials – the gingers, peppermints and raspberries – while reciting her litany of their respective bar pricings. I tried to absorb all this information as I frantically scribbled all the details into the small notebook I kept with me from that day on.

Porter – to sell at 2½ pence a pint – had to be tapped off into jugs and a tablespoon of soda added to give it a frothy head. Barrelled whiskey was known as unracked whiskey and had to be mixed with water before it was served at 2½ pence a glass. McQuaid's Plug Tobacco cost 3½ pence a quarter, and cigarettes in packets of twenty cost 20 pence and could be sold singly for one penny per cigarette.

My notebook soon filled with facts and prices, and there seemed to be so much to commit to memory, I wondered if I could ever learn all there was to learn about this public house business.

Bessie then introduced me to the most important knowledge any bar server can possess: the art of pulling and filling a good pint of porter. Firstly, there was the correct angle of the glass to the flow of ale from the barrel tap. Otherwise a goodly per cent of the liquid – and therefore profits – would end up in the slop bucket under the tap. Then there was the skimming of the frothy pint head into the slop bucket and the leaving of the glass to stand and settle for the correct period of time until ready to be served to the discerning and demanding customer.

"A pub that serves a good pint of porter," said Bessie, as she expertly skimmed a frothy pint top with a timber spatula, "is a pub that will never be without customers to serve. I like to think I serve up the best in the village."

Finally, and most importantly, she introduced me to each of the dour men seated or standing at the bar.

They did no more than nod in my direction when introduced.

"My most valued customers," Bessie whispered to me as we chatted later that night in the snug. "Without these men, I would be above in the workhouse. I call them 'the twelve apostles'. Daily supplicants at the high altar of Bacchus they are, but rarely at home for their last suppers."

She laughed as she said this, but I only came to understand her meaning in the months that followed. For these twelve apostles, Bessie's bar was a second home, and they spent many more hours seated on the high stool than they ever did by their own firesides with wives or children.

I already knew most of the men, as they were all local, some from the village and some from nearby townlands. Several of the men knew me, having come to our house on occasion for the cure or to consult my father and ask his advice on such-and-such. Bessie then told me of their personal drinking habits and tastes. She also made mention of their changeable humours and varied moods. And God knows, those humours and moods on occasion ranged in the course of a single night from genial and decent to mean and aggressive or downright dull and morose.

"Know your customers. Attend to them, be civil to them, never betray their confidences, neither to their drinking companions nor their wives – *especially* to their wives – but never *EVER* let them forget who's in charge here."

This was Bessie's parting advice to me as she handed over the account ledger along with the keys to the door and the bar till. With that, she filled herself a large glass of brandy and off with her to the comfort of her rooms upstairs.

She was never again seen in the bar.

Even with Bessie on hand for day-to-day advice, my first week was an eye-opener for me, I can tell you! As I faced my second week there, I was nagged with doubts that I had made the right decision to accept this post. Firstly, there was the business of establishing a daily working routine. Until I finally decided to take residence in a small room above the bar, I walked the two miles between home

and the village, arriving at the bar at three o'clock sharp for opening at four o'clock.

By the time I saw the last customer off the premises and I had
completed my tidying-up, the clock chimed the wee hours. By the
time I arrived home, the dawn star was high in the sky.

As word spread in the village and the general locality of my
replacing Bessie, the bar saw a nightly increase of new custom as
drinking men deserted their usual haunts about the village and
came to the bar to compare hostelries and observe this new bar
manager. Their presence in the bar caused much annoyance to
the twelve apostles, who considered these newcomers and non-
regulars to be a serious invasion on their private territory.

There were mutterings and asides, all loud enough for me to
hear.

"Humph! Can't have a drink in comfort these days."

"She'll be running *céilís* or whist drives next!"

"Bessie would never have allowed this."

Until things went back to normal a month or so later, the
apostles nightly grew more and more grumpy and much put-
upon, with promises and threats of taking their custom to qui-
eter corners in other premises in the village.

"When you find the bar that will have ye and put up with ye,"
I said, as if I cared not a jot whither they stayed or departed. "I
hope ye'll be happy there."

I said no more and thought of Bessie's sound advice to keep
my deepest thoughts to myself. The men continued to grumble
and complain under their breath, but they stayed put. As the
days passed, they continued to drink their pints of porter and
glasses of whiskey or wine, and take their snuff or puff at their
pipes while discussing everything from potatoes to *poitín* to
Plato.

I realised that I was still being assessed at my apprenticeship
and that my actions and general behaviour over the next few

weeks would determine my future success or failure as a public housekeeper.

As I said, I had learned many things at the end of my first week.

At the end of my first month, I had learned yet more: three things above all else. The first was that the hours were long, sometimes busy, sometimes empty and mostly tedious. The second was that Bessie was her own best customer – now living almost entirely on brandy punches, which I mixed and delivered to her bedside or armchair. The third, and most surprising fact I learned was that, far from being the thriving business Bessie had initially described, the pub was deeply in debt to its main supplier, H. Sharman Crawford, Wine & Whiskey Shipper, of 69 Abbey Street in distant Dublin city. The last neatly typed letter from the company head office threatened the closure of the account if immediate or genuine efforts were not made to settle the outstanding sums owed.

As I considered these harsh facts, it did not seem to me then that I had made a good or wise decision. Nevertheless, my new position seemed as a challenge to me and I resolved there and then to allow myself, and the bar, a six-month trial run.

If, I resolved, after that period of time had passed, I still felt I had made a mistake, I and Bessie and the pub would go our separate ways.

CHAPTER EIGHTEEN

As THE DAYS went by, it became obvious to me that if I was to conduct the business truly to my satisfaction, I would have to put my stamp of authority on the day-to-day running of the bar. By the end of the first month, I had had my fill of dark, sideways looks in my direction from my patrons and of the grumpy, strained responses to even my warmest and most sincere attempts at engaging the men in polite conversation. Most of all, I grew both weary and angry with the continued under-the-breath but meant-to-be-overheard mutterings and whisperings of some of the regular customers about how things were different and so much better when Bessie ran the bar and how Bessie would, or would not, do this, that or the other. I was losing my patience with the situation. Something had to be done – and soon; otherwise I would never gain the respect that I felt I deserved.

It came to a head on one Saturday afternoon when, having served Bessie her dinner in her upstairs room, I entered the bar and saw one of the apostles – Barty Kelly – inside the counter, cheekily and boldly pulling and pouring himself a pint of porter.

I coughed loudly to let him know I was in the room. As I stood there, he looked me straight in the eye and casually continued to fill his pint glass while continuing to converse with his fellow apostles at the other side of the bar counter.

As I viewed this scene, a cold anger arose within me.

"Put down that glass," I said quietly and slowly. I stood my ground and glared at Barty, now frozen in mid-pint filling. I was aware of every eye in the bar turned on me.

"Put down that glass this moment and get back to your side of the bar. And never again let me find you . . . or ANY of you," I glared at the others at the bar, "on this side of the bar!"

Barty's face was an embarrassed grimace as he placed the half-full glass on the counter and moved to the other side of the bar.

I decided right there and then – especially now that I had the full attention of the company – that I had to take a stand to defend my position. It was, I knew, the ideal opportunity to establish some new laws. If I did not, I would never have any real control, or respect, in this place.

"Gentlemen!" Though my heart thumped wildly inside my breast, I solemnly addressed the gathering. "Can I have your attention?" I called out. A silence you could cut with a knife settled on the room.

"First off, I want to say to you that you are all most valued customers on these premises – each one of you. But I have to inform you that your old landlady, Bessie Moran, no longer runs this house. I do! She has hired me to do that job, and I intend to do it to the best of my abilities. And, I might add, I have her full support as manager of this establishment. As such, I must insist that a number of house rules be observed if you, or any other customer for that matter, wishes to continue to enjoy the hospitality of this establishment."

A hush descended on the bar, broken only by the ticking of

the wall clock. With all eyes on me, I could not allow the moment to slip by without further comment.

I now had their unwavering attention as I informed them that from this day forth, there were to be no drinks obtained by patrons other than those served by me or a person detailed by me to do so; there were to be no drinks served to a customer deemed to be inebriated beyond an acceptable level or belligerent or troublesome in any way; no drinks or tobacco given on tick to any customer who made no effort to clear his slate at the end of each month. There was to be no tolerance of the spillage of beer or liquors or spitting on the floor; no putting out of pipes, cigars or cigarettes on the marble bar top. There were to be no sheep, pigs, calves or other animals other than dogs accompanied by their owners brought into the bar on fair days. There was to be no drinking on the premises beyond the legal closing time of midnight and no feuding or fighting, no aggression or the abusing of any travelling man or shawlie tinker women who might wish to enter the bar and take a drink in the snug.

Finally, there was to be no taking the Lord's name in vain, no disparaging remarks at the expense of other God-fearing religions nor the use of foul or offensive language of any colour to be used in my presence.

Not that I was shocked by bad language. Indeed far from it. My uncles, Tomás and John, could swear in not one but three languages and had done so in my presence even when I was a young girl. But I was determined to run a bar into which a woman could come and sit in the snug without overhearing or being subject to the uncouth and profane language of rough countrymen outside the civilising influence of womenfolk.

I thanked those present for their attention and, still shaking inside, I picked up a bar towel and, adapting as cool a demeanour as I could, continued to busy myself with polishing glasses and the marble bar top.

To my amazement, I lost not a single customer, and from that day on, the twelve apostles, especially, were on their best behaviour – barring the odd acceptable argumentative or inebriated outburst. Also from that day on, they referred to me as "Miss Mariah".

Indeed, it was Barty Kelly who was usually the first to come to my aid whenever there was need for assistance to quiet a loud and boisterous drunk or help remove a rowdy or unruly customer from the premises. He also became the one in whom I could place my trust to keep order if ever I had to be away from the premises for whatever reason.

The result of all this was that the word soon went out that I ran the best-behaved public house in the village. And because of this, more than a few drinking men abandoned their usual pubs and became regular customers.

A bigger and more difficult stone to get around on the road to wherever my new life was to take me was the clearing of the large debt, run up during Bessie's management, owed to the wholesaler, H. Sharman Crawford, whose regular demands for payment had taken on a somewhat threatening tone.

Every Monday morning, Jack the Post brought another "demand invoice", and as much as I could manage from the weekly take, I forwarded some monies, however small, to offset the amount demanded and ensure continued deliveries. The company representative was a Mr Edward Mitchell, an educated, soft-spoken, well-turned-out gentleman in his fifties, never seen without his black Homburg hat and Crombie overcoat, who called to the bar on the first Tuesday of every month. I had been in my new position for just over a month when Mr Mitchell made his visit. I could tell he was more than surprised to encounter me behind the bar.

"I was expecting to see Mrs Moran," he quietly announced. When I explained the new arrangement, he warmly welcomed

154

me to the pub business. I couldn't help but notice that while taking my monthly order for bar supplies, he never once made mention of the outstanding debts owed by Bessie to his company back in distant Dublin.

On receipt of Mr Mitchell's order in the Dublin wholesalers, the consignment of bottles and barrels of ales, wines and whiskeys were duly shipped from Dublin Quay to Kilrush Quay. From there, they were transported by rail on the West Clare train to Corofin Railway Station, and from there, the goods were brought by cart directly to the door of the pub.

Johnny "Haul Away" Donlan was the official carter to the village, a job he had done in hail, rain and shine since the coming of the West Clare Railway – in which my Alexander had played his part – in 1892.

When he wasn't carting goods to and from the village, Haul Away was employed by the workhouse to carry the dead in false-bottomed coffins to their unmarked graves in the graveyard outside the village. His father, Pakie, had been similarly employed in the days when the Great Hunger saw to it that he was worked seven days of the week earning one penny for every corpse he carried in his cart to the graveyard.

They say that on one journey, carrying a recently deceased corpse from the workhouse to its final resting place, there was a sudden thumping sound and a muffled cry from within the coffin. Pakie halted the cart and pushed aside the coffin lid. The "corpse" inside struggled to sit up inside the coffin.

"I'm alive! I'm alive! I'm not dead! I'm alive!"

"Hush up in there and lie down in that coffin like a good man," said Haul Away Pakie, cool as you like and fearful that he was about to lose his penny-per-corpse pay for his current undertaking. "The workhouse doctor declared you to be dead, and his word is final and good enough for me. A corpse was delivered to me, and I'm taking that corpse to the graveyard up yonder, and once I've dispensed with it as I have all the others, I'm returning alone, and that's that, as far as I'm concerned!"

We never heard the final outcome of that story, but knowing Haul Away Senior, he was not going to let such a technicality divert him. I would say he probably collected his well-earned penny for work completed that day.

It's my firm belief that my drink wholesaler, Sharman Crawford, would have foreclosed my account had it not been for the kindness shown me by the company's representative, Mr Edward Mitchell. Between you and me, I do believe that Mr Mitchell had an eye for me. Though being the thorough gentleman that he was and as befitting our professional relationship, he never once expressed his true feelings directly to my face. Nevertheless, I could see the signs were there.

In any case and unknown to myself, as I learned later, Mr Mitchell had reassured his head office that Bessie Moran's public house was now under new management and assured them of my eagerness and full intentions to pay off all outstanding sums owed to the company. The initial response from the company was to reduce my orders by half. This was a situation I could not accept. If I was to clear all debts and hold, or even increase, my customers and my turnover, I had to conceive of a plan which would ensure I continued to receive full deliveries as ordered.

To this end, I devised a simple – though, if I may say so, an extremely effective – plan. Taking a scissors to two ten-pound notes, I cut them both in half. I then wrote to the company, including in my letter one half of each note, with the promise that if, and when, they fulfilled my order for a full delivery as ordered, the two matching note halves would, in good faith, be promptly forwarded.

I must admit I waited for the outcome with bated breath. Would my cheeky plan work? I fully realised that should the company refuse to supply me further, the future of the pub as a successful business looked bleak indeed. But to both my amazement and surprise, Haul Away's next delivery from the West Clare train the following week was exactly as I had dictated to Mr Mitchell, down to the last detail.

My plan had worked! By return, as promised, I posted the two remaining half-notes to the company to be rejoined to their matching halves to be redeemed for their full worth.

To their credit, the good people of Sharman Crawford seemed to be happy with, or at least to accept in good faith, our unusual little arrangement. From that day onward, this was how business was conducted between us for a period of eight or ten months, until I had fully paid off all outstanding debts. This news was happily received by Bessie, who admitted then that she had not exactly given me an entirely true picture of the state of her business when I took it on.

"To be honest, Mariah," Bessie laughed, "I was reluctant to reveal to you the full truth of our financial affairs. Indeed, I gave you no more than three months at best before you would be forced to close up shop. But I knew that if anybody could do it, you could. You've performed a small miracle, so you have!"

I was angry with Bessie for withholding this information, but I had to admit that, as she supposed, I would not have taken the position had I known the true state of her financial affairs.

Bessie then fetched two of her best cut-glass tumblers from her sideboard and, cracking open a bottle of her best French cognac, I joined with her in celebrating my small miracle.

CHAPTER NINETEEN

TIME PASSES, AND the six months I had given myself to make a decision to go or stay in my new employment passed quickly enough. In the precious few free hours I had to spend at home, I would go to sit quietly by the lightning tree and mull over my life and my future. One day I would decide it would be best for me to quit; on another that I should stay and give my best efforts to make a success of the business. I finally decided I could not resist the challenge being offered me. Though I didn't admit it to myself at that time, I also had found a certain growing satisfaction from being in such a position of responsibility. I decided then that I would stay till the tide of fortune directed me to follow some other path in life.

By then, I had settled into my work at Bessie's bar. I had, as I mentioned, moved into a spare room over the bar in Bessie's private rooms. Though it was my very first time living in a house other than my home, I was relatively content and comfortable in my new accommodation.

I soon established a daily routine. Once or twice a week, I walked the two miles home to see my mother, now advanced in years and plainly aged and feeble and more and more confined to her bed.

Generally I would arise early, and, after a breakfast of porridge and a mug of hot sweet tea, I would take the road out of the village on a brisk walk to breathe the air and clear from my head the cobwebs of the night before. Sometimes I walked the mile or so to the railway station to stand at the large green gates and marvel at the sight of the great steam engine train as it deposited its passengers and goods on the station platform.

If my timing was good, I might find a train arriving or about to depart from the station. I always stayed long enough to view with amazement the great machine as it pulled away from the station to puff and rumble down the tree-lined tracks on its run westward to Ennistymon, Kilrush and on to Kilkee in the far west.

I promised myself that one day soon I would step aboard that train and travel in style and comfort to Ennistymon to see the great waterfalls that flowed by the McNamaras' big house, or to Lahinch to visit the strand and look out on the Atlantic Ocean. And who knows, one day perhaps I might journey on this great railway to such distant destinations as Kilkee, or Kilrush at the end of the line.

Some mornings I directed myself the two miles in the opposite direction to view Lake Inchiquin. I was both glad and surprised that I was now able to stand and look out on the lake waters that had robbed me of my true love all those years before without being overcome with tears of grief. Initially, I felt that those waters still held some secret deep beneath the surface. A secret it was reluctant to impart to me.

But time is always a healer. Now, no matter how troubled or unsettled my mind, the gentle lapping of water at my feet and the swans gliding on the still or choppy waters always calmed me. One time I counted as many as sixty swans floating as peaceful, graceful and content as you could imagine.

Did you know that swans mate for life? When a swan loses its swan partner, the living swan separates from the flock to grieve and live out his remaining time alone and sad. We could surely learn a thing or two from them.

Returning from my daily walk, I would busy myself cooking a good dinner for Bessie and myself – the mutton or beef fresh from Power's butcher's shop and the vegetables fresh from Pat Keane's kitchen garden – which we would eat in her small dining room overlooking the village street.

After the meal, with a glass of brandy in her hand and a glass of stout in mine, Bessie would sometimes regale me with stories from her youth and her life running the bar after the loss of her husband.

"I was born in the parish of Rath in January of 1831," she told me. "The very day I was being christened in Rath church, the old magistrate, William Blood, a decent man by all accounts and not the worst of our overlords, was shot to death in cold blood on the road by some lawless ruffians from the Terry Alts. These were a secret society formed to oppose the landlords who had raised the rents that year because of a failed crop."

I had heard from my father dark tales of the mysterious Terry Alts and the activities they engaged in.

"The RIC Peelers rounded up eight of the gang who were involved in carrying out the murder, and after a speedy trial in the Ennis Assizes, all eight accused men were sentenced to be hanged."

Bessie's voice fell to a whisper.

"They hanged four of the wretches near Kilfenora, two inside the gate at McMahon's field in Rath and two outside the village here at the crossroads. The bodies of the poor men were left dangling from the gallows tree for several days – weeks even – as a grim warning to others who might follow in their footsteps and rebel against the law. Father often told us young ones that when he was a youth he would sometimes pass by that bloody spot at dusk and see the bodies of those poor hanged men dangle and sway in the wind. On the shoulder of one of the hanged men one evening – so he told us – sat a single busy scald-crow. Can you imagine that sight? It was one that haunted him all his life. When I was young, I used to run by that place in fear, especially at twilight, when I fancied I saw the hanged men at the end of the ropes. The Hanging Field – that's what they call that haunted spot and where to this day birds never sing."

Bessie ended her grim tale, crossed herself and tossed back her large brandy.

Now, in the full light of day, a cold shiver ran down my spine. I knew well that grove near the village, known to all as the Hanging Field. I knew, too, of that terrible event that had occurred near the crossroads, not five hundred steps from where we now sat.

My father spoke often of those troubled times of unrest and rebellion and of the activities of the "White Boys" and Terry Alts, those desperate men who dared challenge the law of the land. He told us, too, of the terrible cold-blooded murder-most-foul of William Blood and of the capture of his killers and the trial and executions that soon followed.

Whenever he told this story on dark winter nights, we children would run to our beds and pull the covers over our eyes, but in the darkness imagine those men swinging lifelessly from the gibbet in the Hanging Field.

I always made the sign of the cross whenever I passed that awful place, and I would pray a silent prayer for the souls of those poor wretches.

At 4 p.m. sharp, with fresh sawdust spread on the bar-room floor, glasses and tumblers cleaned and shelf stock replenished and the street outside washed and brushed clean, the window shutters came down, the main door was opened to the street and the bar was ready to welcome its first customer of the day.

Usually this was the parish priest's housekeeper, Molly Dolan, so punctual I could set the clock to her arrival. Molly's bird-like figure was generally the first to greet me the moment I unlocked and swung open the front door. The can would then be filled to the brim with porter, and she would carry it, along with a naggin of Power's whiskey, back to Father Murphy, her employer and parish priest to the three parishes.

If there were no other customers in the bar, and usually there were not at that hour of the afternoon, Molly would follow me into the bar. Always eager to chat and gossip, she would linger awhile and would slip into the snug and sit herself down in the corner to watch the thick, black liquid flow from the porter barrel into the tin can. She and I would then sit together in the snug to sup a glass of stout or brandy-wine and she would regale me with all the news and gossip from the village and from the three parishes.

By the time Molly departed with her employer's daily alcoholic requirements, the first of my regular twelve apostles – usually this would be Tommy Reilly – stepped into the pub to take his first drink of the day and lay claim to his usual fireside seat at the end of the bar-room. All who knew Tommy and his habits left this seat free, and woe betide a stranger who might wander in from the street and unknowingly sit in Tommy's chair.

When he was settled, he would light his pipe and watch the first of the many black pints of porter he would drink that day settle in his glass. Then he would take a long draught from the glass, lick his lips, wipe the froth from his moustache and proclaim, "Ahh! There's eating and drinking in a good pint." Then he would puff contentedly on his clay pipe while perusing the latest edition of *The Clareman*.

"*The Clareman* says," he would declare to all and to nobody in particular, "Pope Leo the 11th has passed to his heavenly reward.

162

They're bound to put an Irishman in his place. Haven't we earned that at the very least? I just can't understand why an Italian always has to be elected Pope. The whole of Europe would still be an uncivilised pagan godless place if it wasn't for our Irish saints and scholars."

A lively debate usually followed to discuss that possibility and to name some possible candidates, usually Claremen, for the job of pontiff.

"*The Clareman* says the great Irish explorer Mr Ernest Shackleton is on his way to find the South Pole with another Irishman at his right-hand side. A Mr Tom Crean from Co. Kerry, no less! And who was it put that pole in that wilderness in the first place is what I'd like to know?

"*The Clareman* says that two brothers called Wright have gone aloft in a heavier-than-air machine in a place called Kitty Hawk in North Carolina. I could maybe do the same if I drove my horse and cart off the Cliffs of Moher.

"*The Clareman* says in this year of 1904, there are now over sixty motorised machines and sixty licensed drivers on the streets and roads of our country. These machines run on some sort of a special liquid fuel and have the pulling power of twenty horses, so it is reported. We will see such a contraption on the street here before the year is out. The days of the bicycle, tandem and the like are gone. Mark my words!"

It was a few years before Tommy's prediction came to be, at least as far as the motorcar was concerned. And when a motorised vehicle finally did appear on the street, it caused quite some commotion I can tell you! It near scared every animal – not to mention a few elderly people within earshot – half to death, what with its huffing and chugging and rattling and rolling its way through the town. Jackie Lane's horse, a high-spirited and jittery three-year-old mare, was tethered to a pole outside Jackie's favourite watering hole at the other end of the village when the smoke-belching contraption came rattling up the street. The nervous mare panicked and, her tail high in the air, took off down the street ahead of the motor, dragging the uprooted tethering pole behind her. The horse was found safe but in a terrified state, entangled and trapped in a hedgerow, a halt brought to her gallop by the trailing pole snagging in the bushes.

Later, her owner was seen back in the pub swearing he would bring down the full rigour of the law on the driver and operator of this dangerous new mode of transportation.

However, on learning that the driver of the horse-scaring carriage was Captain Henry Butler, the Colonel's youngest son, home from London, who had purchased this motorcar, there was no further pressing of any charges. Captain Butler had driven his motor – a Model T they called it, and it was the first motorcar seen in the area – into town alongside a friend who sat astride a motorised bicycle.

"Look at the horse with her foal," called out some wag as the pair rattled and thundered through the village.

In any case, it wasn't too long before the horses, not to mention the dogs, cats and all the other inhabitants of the village street, learned to ignore these noisy new contraptions which were to be seen more and more on the village street as time passed.

A year later, sometime in the summer of 1904, *The Clareman* changed its title to the *Clare Champion*, and many decades later, apart from several months out of print during the troubled times of 1918, the paper is still going strong and is still with us. Tommy was disgusted with these changes. For several months following the newspaper's change of name, he remained unsettled and suspicious, refusing to buy or read the newly named *Clare Champion*, while swearing the news printed in the new paper was probably "imported news" and less important, and less believable, than that printed in his beloved *Clareman*.

"Sure it's just the paper title that has changed, Tommy," the other apostles argued. "The content won't change. You'll still have your same paper with a different name, that's all!"

But Tommy wasn't having any of this, swearing he would change allegiance to another paper for this, as he saw it, betrayal, which he took as a personal affront to his allegiance over the years to the old paper.

Other than browsing the odd national or local news item when not too busy at my work, I felt I didn't need to read any news from the printed page. Between overhearing the general and more-than-lively conversations at the bar, the gossip from the street, Molly's local news and Tommy's weekly pronouncements on county, national and international news from his newspapers, I was kept well up-to-date and regarded myself to be better informed than the royal advisor to the King of England.

Aside from the usual flurry of activity surrounding Sunday morning mass, funerals, cattle or horse-fair days, weddings and the odd christening, the hours between four and seven o'clock were usually quiet hours in the village.

This peace and quiet might be broken only by sounds which would echo along the street valley of houses. I can still hear those sounds: a dog barking; a door slamming shut in a sudden gust; that same winter wind taking an empty milk can or zinc bucket on a rattling wild run down the empty street; sparrows in spring-time making a racket in the tree across the street outside Murphy's; voices raised in laughter, in argument or sometimes anger; and sometimes the loud cawing of crows at twilight as they returned to their nesting trees about the church and the priest's house.

Sometimes a worse-for-wear farmer on a rare visit to the main street or maybe a vagabond tinker, ejected from one of the other pubs in the village, would amble into the bar and, often with

165

Barty's help, had to be removed from the premises following an unnecessary display of rowdiness. But in my time, I have to say, few gave any real trouble, and if they did, there was always Barty or one of the apostles at hand to help out and assist me in dealing with the situation.

Sometimes a ragged starving beggar, a travelling man of the road evicted from his home and land, a deserted wife or a mendicant widow – and there were many in the village – would come to my door to beg for alms or food.

I remember one bitterly cold winter's day I was busy lighting the bar lanterns and preparing to open for business when I heard a song being sung out in the street. I stopped work and listened to the song.

> 'Twas down by the Glenside
> I met an old woman
> A'pluck' young nettles,
> She ne'er saw me comin'
> And I listened awhile
> To the song she was hummin'
> "Glory-o! Glory-o! to the Bold Fenian men".

I went to the door and peered outside. It was snowing softly and the village street was covered over in a feather-white blanket of soft snowflakes. The only living soul to be seen was an old tinker woman, a shawlie, Mary Sherlock. Sitting under the tree across the street from Bessie's pub, Mary sat singing her quiet song as if to some unseen listener while the falling snow gathered about her shoeless feet and lay as a white stole on the ragged shawl about her shoulders. For whatever reason, Mary had long ago deserted her tinker clan, and now she travelled the roads alone.

Around Hallowe'en she would stop her ramblings to take up winter residence in a little abandoned *tigín* at the edge of the village. Everybody all about knew her well and watched out that she did not go hungry. Each and every day during her settled period,

Mary would sit, regardless of the weather, under a tree across the street from Bessie's pub, where she collected the odd coin dropped in her tin can.

Through the falling snow, I beckoned her over and invited her to come inside and shelter from the sudden heavy snowfall. She willingly accepted, and I treated her to a hot punch and a bowl of soup.

"God reward you, girl," she spoke to me in Irish, shaking the snow off her shawl and looking at me for a long while.

"I know you. Aren't you from the crossroads up the road?"

I nodded as I prepared her whiskey punch.

"I remember you as a *cailín óg*. Your family were always good to Old Mary, and Old Mary never forgets a kindness. So let me tell you your future. For as long as you live at that crossroads, you will live the life of a spinster. Women born near a crossroads, and who remain there, stay single all their lives."

I made no response as I handed her the hot punch.

"Ah," she said, giving me a toothless smile. "Is there a better soup to warm cold blood and bones on a day such as this?"

I could only agree and filled one for myself.

From that day onward, and all through the winter months till she took up her summer travelling, Mary would slip into the snug at nightfall and I would treat her to a bowl of hot soup and a wedge of soda bread. When she had a few pence in her tin, she would buy a mug of porter or a glass of mulled wine and tell me stories of her hardships and travels and her life on the highways and byways of the county.

From Mary, mother to fifteen living "childer", as she said herself, I learned a lot about real life and both the wisdom and wit of those who lived their lives on the roads of Ireland. From her, too, I learned of cures and remedies unknown to me or to Brian, and I recall and use them to this day.

Mary died, worn from her years of hard travelling, near Bally-vaughan not many years later. They say that as her end approached she called for a priest, and when she began to make her final confession, she spoke to him in Gaelic. Not having a good grip of the language, the priest politely asked that she speak only English.

From her deathbed, Mary replied angrily, "Does your Reverence think that I will speak my last words on this earth to Almighty God in the language of the Sassenachs?"

About six months later, Molly Dolan, a big smile on her face, called to the bar and handed me a package wrapped in an old ragged shawl.

"This is for you, Mariah," she said. "It was delivered today to the parochial house, by Father Mooney from Ballyvaughan. It was Mary Sherlock's dying wish that you get all she owned in this world."

I could see that Molly was eager – as I was myself – to discover the contents of the little bundle, and as she sat on in the snug supping a glass of porter, I unwrapped the mysterious package. There, within the tattered rags, lay a gold and silver fob-watch and chain and a number of tattered, yellowed pages on which were scribbled some old cures and remedies and many of the old ballads she had sung so often under the tree across the street.

So it was I got the name for never turning a soul in need from my door, and I never sent any away empty-handed. Except on a Monday. It was considered good luck to cut your toenails on Monday, but bad luck to give to beggars, for you would go in want all week.

"There but for fortune," I would say to myself. "There but for fortune!"

CHAPTER TWENTY

THURSDAY THE SEVENTEENTH of September 1908 was a day that will be remembered not only by myself but also by everybody in the locality for many a long day to come. This was the day an elephant – a real live elephant – walked down the village street, strolling in from one end of town and going out the other as would a cow, horse, pony, mule or donkey.

It all started a week earlier with Tommy Reilly's reading from the *Clare Champion* newspaper. "The Champion says that Duffy's Circus is on the road touring the country and is due in the county next week."

For once, Tommy's reading got the undivided attention of all at the bar. Realising he had an audience, he cleared his throat and, with great gusto, took centre stage and continued reading from the newspaper advertisement.

> *The Great Duffy-McLean Monster Circus!*
> *The Greatest Touring Circus in the Country!*
> *Often imitated! Never equalled!*
> *In your town! One night only!*
> *Seeing is believing!*

African Lions! Bengal Tigers! Bare-back riders!
Jugglers! High-wire Trapeze Artists! Clowns!
And for the first time ever
A full-grown, real-live Indian elephant!
Not to be missed!

Printed underneath was a listing of the towns and villages the circus intended to visit on its tour about the county.

"And it arrives here in the village Thursday, September seventeenth. By the hokey, that's next Thursday," added Tommy.

Suddenly the bar was as alive as a hive of excited bees with everybody talking at once.

"Tommy, that's the best news you've ever read from that newspaper of yours."

"I've never seen an elephant."

"What's a Bengal tiger?"

"My Uncle Tomás saw several in India when he soldiered there," I said, though nobody seemed to listen and everybody talked at once.

"Do you remember a few years back? When that tiger almost pounced on his trainer?"

"I thought he was done for. My heart was in my throat!"

"I'd say that was all part of the act."

"I couldn't bear to watch those high-wire walkers. They make me dizzy with their acrobatics."

"Those clowns and their carry-on are as good as a tonic."

And so the conversation went for the best part of the evening as the apostles discussed, compared and argued on the different circuses to visit the village over the years.

One thing all in the bar were agreed on: the circus was coming! And what a day, and night, to look forward to.

Whatever people felt about other events throughout the year – Christmas Day, Easter Sunday or the spring and winter cattle and horse fairs – there was absolutely no disagreement about the one day that everybody, from nine to ninety, looked forward to: the day the circus came to town!

Everybody, myself included, looked forward to the welcome sight of James Duffy's horse-drawn wagons, painted and decorated in the gayest of colours – blood reds, sky blues, pinks and greens and edged in gold – parading down the street with a full band and with flags and banners weaving their way to set up their canvas tent in Power's field. There they would park their wagons and, hail, rain or shine, immediately set to work raising the huge tent on tall poles and rig it with all manner of coloured flags and banners and the rest of the circus paraphernalia.

By late afternoon, the circus work gang would have completed its labours. Now all that remained was to await the arrival of the throngs from every corner of the three parishes to witness such extraordinary sights and sounds and such magic as they would not experience till the circus returned the following year.

For the rest of the week, the main topic of conversation in the bar was of James Duffy and his travelling circus show. For over thirty years, since the early 1870s, the troupe had travelled to every city, village, town and country crossroads the length and breadth of the land to put on a show. In those days, they were nothing less than an entire travelling village with their own butchers and bakers, tailors and dressmakers, and even smithies to mend equipment and tackling and look after the horses.

Father, who in those early days was often called in to administer a potion or salve to various injured animals, said that at one time they had as many as 250 horses to pull the wagons and perform in the circus ring.

"Some of the finest horse flesh I have ever laid eyes on!" he would say in awe and admiration. "From Arab and Russian breeds to Connemara ponies. You would not see the likes at the fair of Ballinasloe or Spancilhill."

When the circus entourage finally arrived in the village on that bright September day on their once-a-year visit, they were truly a sight to behold.

"They're coming! They're coming! The circus is coming!" I heard somebody shout from the street.

Even before I could spy a single wagon, I could hear the blare and rumble of trumpet and drum, the rattle and roll of wagon wheels, the creak of leather and jingle of harness and the clop of hoof on the gravel street from the south end of the village.

I could hardly believe my eyes. There, leading the parade of coloured wagons was as huge a beast as I had ever laid eyes on. So it was true! This year they did have a real living elephant on show.

There he was, in all his massive glory. Gigantic of body, legs, ears and trunk and with a jewelled harness on his massive head and a brown-skinned, turbaned lad perched on his neck, he came lumbering down the street toward us like several huge moving haystacks.

I could hear the gasps of excitement from the people now pouring out of their doorways on to the pavement to witness this extraordinary sight.

Immediately behind this mountain of brown flesh came James Duffy in his ringmaster's black top hat and crimson-red coat-tailed jacket, white gloves, white riding jodhpurs and knee-length, well-polished black leather boots, cracking his bullwhip left and right and shouting in his bellowing ringmaster's voice.

Behind him came the circus parade of the circus brass band of blue-coated buglers and drummers, followed by the laughing, flag-waving performers: the satin-suited jugglers and acrobats, the red-nosed, gaily suited clowns and harlequins. Behind them came the brightly painted horse-drawn wagons and animal cages.

The ringmaster snapped his bullwhip and called out his circus street cry.

Oh Yeh! Oh Yeh! We're back in town!
The Greatest Show in all the land!
With animals both wild and tame,
and an Indian El—ee—phant!

A huge roar went up from the crowds, which now thronged the pavements on both sides of the street. At the sound, the great elephant raised his massive head and trunk and roared such a roar that fairly silenced the onlookers, scared the wee ones almost to death and rattled every window and door up and down the street.

The regular street dogs and cats scampered for safe cover, and more than a few people panicked and grabbed their children and pulled them back to safety behind closed doors.

"Don't be afeared, good people!" cried the ringmaster. "This magnificent beast you see before you – all the way from the jungles of distant India – is as gentle as any lamb of the fields."

From his pocket he drew and offered to the beast a large bread-bun, which was taken on the tip of his swishing trunk as gently as a baby might reach for a rattle.

"And he has a taste for a drop of porter," the ringmaster roared, calling out to Paddy Brohan, standing at the door of his public house. Paddy laughed and went inside and in a moment returned with a bucket filled to the brim with the leftover porter slops from last night's drinking. He marched out and placed the full bucket in front of the huge animal.

The elephant came to a lumbering halt, and, before you could say Jack Robinson, the animal had dipped his trunk inside the pail and had sucked every last drop of the black porter from that bucket.

A great laugh erupted from the onlookers.

"I bet you wish he was a regular customer, Paddy!" A wag called out from the onlookers.

Soon the other pub owners along both sides of the street –

including myself – had gone inside their premises to fetch out the porter slop buckets and place them by the side of the street to await the attention of this great, waddling, porter-loving mammoth. As the parade slowly proceeded up the street, the thirsty elephant greedily and speedily sucked up the contents of each and every bucket placed in his pathway.

He finally arrived at my bucket and was about to slake his enormous thirst when he spied a crate of vegetables sitting outside Biddy Flanagan's grocery shop next door. His huge body turned, and in the blinking of an eye and with a single whisk of that great trunk, he snatched up a large bunch of carrots, which instantly disappeared within his cave of a mouth to follow the gallons of porter already ingested.

Biddy Flanagan was as sour-humoured, peevish and argumentative an old harridan as you could meet, and unfriendly with almost everybody in the street. With a great shriek, she grabbed up a sweeping brush and commenced to beat and whack the poor beast about his flapping ears.

Well, the elephant, being bigger than Biddy, wasn't having any of this. As cool as a breeze, he dropped his trunk to suck up the contents of my slop-pail – a gallon and a half at least – and turning his trunk in Biddy's direction, he proceeded, with a great "whoosh", to shoot the entire contents of the bucket all over the bad-tempered old dame. The porter-soaked Biddy gave another great shriek and rushed forward with the broom to place a few wildly aimed whacks on the elephant's rump.

What followed was as good as the actual circus performance in the big tent. The elephant snorted in disgust, and with another swish of his tail, he curled his trunk around the woman's waist and lifted her high in the air before dropping her flat on her back on her stall of vegetables outside her shop.

The outburst of applause and laughter the beast received was as great as he could ever hope to win for his evening tent performance. Then, with a great snorting bleat, he lumbered off on his boozy way down the street, eating and drinking all that was offered to his trunk.

With the offerings of eight pubs consumed, the elephant now had only four more buckets to visit, and he seemed determined not to miss a single one.

In the meantime, the ringmaster had to use all his powers of command to stop the shouting and laughter and commotion among not only the onlookers but from his own troupe of clowns and jugglers and trapeze artists. The poor man also had to use all his powers of diplomacy to calm the rattled but furious and beer-soaked woman.

While the obvious star of his show rumbled ahead, the ring-master offered profuse apologies to Biddy on behalf of the entire circus. He especially offered apologies on behalf of the poor old elephant, who was now half-drunk and leaning sleepily against the post office wall, while his driver tried to get him back on all feet and gee him into action.

Biddy was having none of the ringmaster's apologies. Threat-ening legal action, she turned on her heel and disappeared indoors and was not seen outside for the best part of a week.

The circus and the offending animal were, by that time, long gone.

As usual, the big tent – smelling of creosoted timber, sawdust, crushed grass and animal dung and lit by oil lanterns and several blazing barrels – was filled to capacity with men, women and children who had come from all corners of the three parishes. It was as happy and carefree a gathering you could see from one end of the land to the other.

I had gone there with a feeble but determined Bessie by my side.

"I wouldn't miss seeing Duffy's Circus for all the tea in China," she said as we climbed the wooden plank stairway to take our seats high up the tiered seating with a full, clear view of the ring. Once my eyes had adjusted to the smoky light, I gazed all about me; on the wooden seating were many people whom I had not seen since the circus had visited the village the previous year.

Much of that night's individual performances are beyond recall, but I do remember that the performers were in great form. Moustachioed men in fantastical sequined suits and capes walked on stilts and on the high-wire or flew like birds to defy gravity and had us all gasp with fear as they dived and swooped and glided high above our heads. A bronze-skinned magician in a jewelled silk turban pulled a white rabbit from his silk top hat and a pair of white doves from inside his sleeve. Then, to gasps of amazement from all, he sawed his woman assistant in half, though she appeared in full figure and in perfect health a few moments later. With another wave of his silver wand, the magician then caused one of the poor clowns to disappear in a puff of magic smoke.

As the show progressed, each act seemed to be even more amazing than the one gone before. Our eyes stuck out on stalks. Tumblers tumbled and jugglers juggled with hoops and hammers and balls, boxes of all sizes and torches of fire. To the gasps of us all, the knife and hatchet throwers missed injuring their assistants lashed to great spinning wheels, and the clowns' antics were funnier than ever as they went running and tumbling and falling over each other and throwing fake buckets of water out into the audience.

But at the heel of the evening, everybody was in agreement. It was the great Indian elephant – sober enough now but still sleepy-eyed from what I could see – who was the star attraction and, to great outbursts of applause and cheering, he was marched about the ring till both man and beast must have grown dizzy.

The ringmaster stood in the centre of the ring, cracked his bullwhip to get our full attention and loudly called out: "Can I have a volunteer from the audience to ride on the back of this great Indian elephant? Step up now! Don't be shy! It will be a once-in-a-lifetime experience and something you will tell your grandchildren in the years to come. Step up now!"

Everybody looked to their neighbours, yet not one in the audience was willing to answer his call. Finally, to a great round of applause, it was none other than Biddy Flanagan's son, a gawkish, dour lad of seventeen, who came forward – some say he was pushed – and was promptly scooped up on the elephant's trunk and placed as easy and as gently as could be on the animal's broad back.

The brass instruments blared an ear-splitting fanfare, the drums beat loudly, the ringmaster's whip cracked and snapped louder than before, and we all roared and clapped as the elephant raised his two front legs to stand on his back legs and push a huge rubber ball all around the ring with the terrified lad hanging on to the beast's neck for dear life.

The roar from the crowd was so loud that old Mrs Cleary, who was too bed-ridden and too frail to attend on the night, said she clearly heard the tumult at the other side of the village.

Too soon the performance came to a close, and Bessie and I left the tent and stepped out into the still-warm September night air feeling as giddy and light-hearted as a couple of young girls.

I had not been so happy in a long while. Nor had I seen, all about me, so many people so happy and carefree as on that September night when the circus and the great Indian elephant came to town.

Early next day, with a heavy September mist lying thick on the land, I set out on my regular walk. I decided to go by Power's field in the hope I might catch a last glimpse of the elephant. But to my amazement Power's field was utterly deserted, its gate closed. My spirits fell as I watched the mist settle over the circus field, which now looked abandoned and forlorn, empty of performers, animals, cages and the great Indian elephant.

Duffy & McLean's Monster Circus – with all its tent canvas, poles, ropes, animals and animal cages, coloured hoop wagons and people – had packed before dawn and moved on to weave its magic in another village somewhere away to the west.

The following day, a ripple of news spread through the village.

"Young Billy Flanagan had disappeared from home."

"Gone he is. Run off with the circus."

"Biddy says he's been kidnapped."

So it was reported. In truth, young Billy Flanagan had vanished as if into thin air.

A few years later, we heard news he was on the road with a big circus touring in England.

His job? He was looking after the circus animals and in particular learning to be a bareback rider and to train the mighty Indian elephants.

CHAPTER TWENTY-ONE

SEVEN YEARS! I could hardly believe I had stood and served the bar and managed all business affairs for Bessie Moran's public house for seven years! All that was to change the week that my mother Mary Ellen died.

This was in early March of 1909. She had reached her ninety-fifth birthday – my age now – when she let go of life to go to her well-earned rest.

In the hard winter months before her last days, she had taken to her bed where she daily prayed for God to release her from life. Her prayer was always the same one: to take her from this world and let her join Michael and all those souls who had gone before her in the heaven she believed awaited her.

To us she complained of how unfair it was that her spirit was ready and willing to give up the ghost, but her body was not.

"Your father had bottles and potions and pastes and cures for every known ailment," she complained. "He cured from Loophead to Lisdoonvarna, but he never had a bottle to cure life, now, did he? Or did he have a potion to cure himself at the end? Oh, Michael, why did you go before me? Now it's my time to die. I'm fully prepared to face my Maker, yet here I am. I don't know why God doesn't heed or hear my prayer to take me."

"Hush that talk, Mother," we would tell her. "You'll make the hundred. Weren't all your side of the family long livers?"

But we could see right well that her light of life was dimming and her time was nigh.

When I would visit her in those final weeks, she seemed to be slipping further and further into a distant place that gave her suffering some ease and a place from which, we knew, she would not return to us.

Once she thought Brian to be Frank in distant Australia and me to be her mother come to tuck her into bed for the night.

One night, while the candles flickered around her bed, she thought me to be her sister Julia and, as excited as a sixteen-year-old girl, talked of going to a house dance where she might once again meet a man named Michael from the south Burren whom she was sweet on.

"Julia," Mary Ellen whispered to me, "don't breathe a word of this to Father or Mother. It's our secret. Promise me!"

"I promise," I whispered, pressing her hand in mine. "It's our secret."

Once, as I sat with her in the small hours and in the hushed silence of my vigil, in a voice, tiny and whispered, that seemed to come from some distant place, she recited a half-remembered poem.

> *Up the airy mountain,*
> *Down the rushy glen,*
> *We daren't go a-hunting*
> *For fear of little men.*
> *Wee folk, good folk,*
> *Trooping all together;*
> *Green jacket, red cap,*
> *And a white owl's feather.*

Another time, coming out of a deep sleep and in great excitement, her face shining with happiness, she called out for me to comb and brush her hair and prepare her best dress for her to wear at the St Patrick's Day soirée at Butlers' big house.

"I want to wear my finest and look my best! There will be high style there, and I have to look as well as any lady there," she said, and her eyes glowed like those of a child on Christmas Eve. Her excitement brought me back to that night nigh on thirty years before, when she and I dolled ourselves up in this very room for the Butlers' soirée.

So it was with heavy heart that Brian and Robin and I watched her slip away from us to lose herself inside her fancies, imaginings, dreams and memories. It was a lonesome time, for each of us knew it was time to prepare to take our leave of this warrior of a woman, who had lived through famine and flood and who had withstood every hardship that life had flung at her.

The bar had closed late that night following a particularly rowdy evening of drunkenness, argument and bad behaviour among my customers. Earlier that day, the "Black" Ruhane, the undisputed king of the faction fighters, had been laid to his well-earned rest in Kilvidaan graveyard outside the village. As a parting gesture, he had willed that two gallons of whiskey and two gallons of poitín be put up in Bessie's bar for his old comrades-in-arms to drink to his memory.

Before the final sod was laid on his grave, the bar was filled with his mourning relations, friends and neighbours, not to mention every drunk and tinker from the three parishes, all gathered to celebrate his fighting life.

And celebrate they did. The drinking continued steadily all through the afternoon and into the night. It was well past midnight before I managed to prise the final drinker – one of my regular apostles – from his bar stool and get him out the door and on to the village street. As I pushed the worse-for-ware toper, with several bottles of stout in his coat pocket, towards the door, he swore that the Black Ruhane himself had been among the mourners and they had shared several glasses together.

After the excesses of the day and the effort of cleaning and tidying up after the Black Ruhane's funeral celebration, I was utterly drained and exhausted and very glad to see my bed that night, I can tell you.

However, I was asleep but a short while when a vivid dream came into my head. In the dream my mother, again young and in her prime, came and stood at my bedside at the edge of my sleep, and I heard her clearly say, "Mariah, it's time. Walk with me one last time to the well. You must carry home the water, but I will stay and rest there for a while. Come! It's time!"

I came awake to the sound of a gentle rapping, flapping sound. Outside, the moonlight spread her soft pink glow over the night. There was that tapping sound again. When I peered out the window, I saw a small dark night bird perched on the sill and pecking at the frosted glass. I was now fully awake and, with my mother's voice still ringing clear and loud in my head, I quickly arose and lit the candle at my bedside.

I knew what I had to do.

As quietly and as quickly as I could, I dressed, pulled on my strong boots, wrapped my shawl about my shoulders and, hoping not to disturb Bessie, tiptoed downstairs to let myself out on to the street that glinted and sparkled under the moonlight like a million diamonds in the hard March frost. It was not yet five of the clock, and the night was still and silent and bitterly cold, with the setting moon hanging like a pink lantern in the western sky. I wrapped my shawl over my head and shoulders and set out to walk the two miles home.

"Dear God," I prayed as I walked, "just let me get there in time to say goodbye."

A mile out of the village I passed the shores of Lake Inchiquin to my left and stood for a moment to rest and breathe in the ghostly beauty of the lake at night. From across the lake, I could see the ruined Inchiquin Castle, its windows alight with pale blue lights. Corpse lights, the old people called the flickerings that would disappear as soon as you might approach the haunted castle. Out on the lake stood the two islands: the Woody, overgrown with a thick carpet of trees, and its sister island the Slatey, covered in flagstone and barren of any growth.

A wispy, soft mist coloured pink and woolpack white lay low on the moonlit waters with the softness of a flight of angels at their rest. In the tall reeds by the lakeside, I spotted three sleeping swans, their heads tucked beneath their wings and gently bobbing in the icy, crusted water. For a moment, as I stood there in the silent, frosty moonlight, I thought I looked upon the Swan Woman and her cygnets, still hidden from her long-dead husband, the Lord Conor O'Quin.

Across the lake, a nightbird called, and its lonesome cry sang out across the waters to lap on the far shore, then roll back along the shining surface water to echo again beneath my feet.

I shivered, pulled my shawl about me and walked on. There was not a house showing light at this hour, but there were as many stars twinkling on the frosted road under my feet as there were in the sky above my head. Leafless trees by the roadside stood like skeletons with arms stretched to the starry sky.

A lone fox, with frost gleaming on her bushy tail, trotted across the road ahead of me, while above, the silver moon sailed along to keep this night-hunter and myself company and light our journeys home.

As I came close to the house, I stopped by the bridge to see a yellow light flicker in the window of my mother's bedroom. She was still with us! I knew it.

I looked skyward. Above the house to the north hung a carpet of dark cloud, the colour of tea leaves at the edges and as black as night at its centre.

A shiver not caused by the bitter cold ran down my spine, and I hurried my steps to the front door and knocked gently. It was Robin, his tired face haggard, pale and sad, who opened the door to me, and as I stepped into the kitchen he just looked at me and slowly shook his head.

"Am I too late?" I whispered.

"No, Mariah, you're not late. She's still with us, but she hasn't got much time," he answered softly.

With my heart in my mouth, I followed him on tiptoe into the bedroom. The oil lamp cast a ghostly glow, and two yellow candles stood at each side of the bed head. The same kind of wax candles had stood at the bed head when my father and grandmother had died in that same bed.

Brian sat at Mary Ellen's side, holding her tiny, bloodless hand in his. He looked at me, and even in the soft lamplight I could see a tear glisten in his eye as he shook his head. I looked down at Mary Ellen's face. Suddenly all my fears and worries left me like a flock of small birds rising from a wood, and in that moment I was filled with a great sense of light-headed peacefulness.

Mary Ellen slowly opened her eyes, and her face was as peaceful and serene as ever I had seen it.

"Mariah, is that you? Are you all here?" she whispered and smiled and raised her head off the pillow.

"Yes, Mother," I said. "I'm here. We're all with you."

"Frank, too?"

There was a moment's silence. Brian looked at me and I nodded in his direction.

"Yes, Mother, I'm here too. We're all here," Brian said, his voice trembling, and I could hear he was close to tears.

"I knew you would come back, Frank. You've been gone too

long. Now you're all here and I can start my journey. I am ready and I'm not afraid. I've made my peace with my Maker."

With those words she lay back, sighed once and closed her eyes to the world. A candle flickered in the still room, we hardly dared take a breath, and time itself seemed to stand still. In that sacred moment, I realised that she had left us.

After a long while, Brian whispered, "She's passed over. She's at peace." He reached out and touched her cheek.

Together we stood around the bed and, holding hands, we cried out our grief and recited a prayer for her soul, which we knew had gone over to a better place.

There were a great many things now to be done. I lit a taper and from it lit both candles by her bed head. Robin wiped his eyes of tears and placed two pennies on her closed eyes to ward off any bad spirits that might enter. Brian opened the bedroom window to let her soul go free. A March night wind whipped into the room and one candle blew out. The other flickered but stayed alight.

When our prayers for her departing soul were spoken, I moved about the house covering every statue, mirror and picture with the black drapes of death. Finally, I stopped the clock to show the hands sit and point the time of her death.

I went out by the hedge and picked a single daffodil and, it being early March, the season of the alder, a sprig of early blossoming alder from the tree behind the forge barn, and placed them in her hands. How Mary Ellen loved that ancient alder tree. She would tell us of how the tree was beloved by water spirits and about the white fairy horse that would rest beneath its boughs and how St Brigid blessed the alder to have it bear two-thirds apples and one-third sweet sloes. Each autumn, she would pick its fruit of dark berries from which she would make a dark dye.

Brian, Robin and I then gathered in the room about her body

185

to pray for her soul and also to cry and to laugh and talk about her long life and times till the dawn crept slowly over the land.

We well knew that these few precious moments with her were to be the only private time we would have till the wake and the funeral was over two days hence.

"We have a wake to arrange," Brian said.

Indeed there was much to be done, though we knew well what was required of us, the living, to do for the dead. We all had been through this when Grandma Maudie died and when our father, Michael, had died back in '98. Robin set off to tell the neighbours and to inform Father Murphy of her passing and arrange her funeral mass. Brian went off to arrange the digging of the grave with the men who usually carried out this task and then on to the house of Oscar Mór Carey, the carpenter, to ask him to prepare her coffin.

Brian learned from Oscar that Mary Ellen had long ago called him to the house and placed an order with him for her coffin. He had taken all measurements, as would be expected of a man of his profession, and had chosen and cut the wood, and so he was prepared for this day, with her coffin already made.

"She'll be as snug in that as she will in her own bed." Oscar was as proud as punch as he and Brian looked over his fine work of carpentry.

With Brian and Robin away, I immediately set about cleaning and dusting and tidying and preparing the house for the flurry of activity I knew was to follow. There was much to be done. There were breads and cakes to be baked, bacons and hams to be cooked and gallons of tea to be made ready to be served piping hot to each and every caller to this corpse-house throughout the day and all through the night to come.

In the misty morning light, I walked to the old pathway to the well to fetch a bucket of spring water. As I dropped the bucket into the water, I saw deep in the water the face I had seen as a child all those years before when Mary Ellen had told me of the

Woman of the Well. At first the image of the face I saw there was clouded and unclear to my wet eyes, but suddenly I realised that the face that looked back at me from deep in the well was that of my mother, and she was smiling up at me. I remembered then the words she had spoken to me in my dream earlier.

I stirred the water with my finger, and as Mary Ellen's face dissolved at my touch, the face I now saw was my own, and my tears splashed down on the water's surface.

Then, from deep in the well – or was it from high above my head? – I heard a distant keening, sobbing, crying. I knew this cry. I had heard it as a child, and I had last heard it the night Father passed over.

It was the voice of the ancient Woman of the Well.

It was the mourning of ancestors.

It was the lament of the *bean sí* who cried now for Mary Ellen and for me and for you and for decent country folk who are visited by Death.

There, by the well, I listened again to her lonesome crying as I would to a song of prayer or a hymn to life.

I crossed myself, then made the sign of the cross with my finger over the contents of my bucket and walked back to the house.

When I returned from the well, our good neighbours Mary Hynes and Kate Reilly were already in the house and busy laying out Mary Ellen's corpse. I was glad they had taken on this task, and I busied myself cleaning and tidying the house and preparing for the many callers who would soon cross the threshold to wake the remains of the eldest woman in the three parishes.

The rest of the day passed in a flurry of activity in the company of relations, good neighbours, friends and other visitors calling to sympathise with the three of us. Most had known Mary Ellen all of their lives.

Many stayed for much of the day to sit by her corpse and recall their own memories of Mary Ellen and to retell their stories – a litany of her life – and to contemplate on their own lives and mortality while sipping tea, sherry, spiced port or something stronger. Even Bessie, as feeble and weak as she was, who had learned of the news from Robin, made the journey from the village in a hired pony and trap to pay her last respects.

"You need not have come, Bessie," I said, welcoming her to the house. "It's a bitter day. You could catch your death."

"Oh hush, girl. I had to come to say my goodbyes. Blood is blood," was her only response. On her insistence, Robin tackled the pony and cart and returned to the pub to fetch back a barrel of porter, a cask of whiskey, a supply of *dúidíní* (white clay pipes), tobacco for the men, and bottles of port, sherry, wine and a supply of loose snuff for the women.

Later, when I came to settle the bill, she waved a hand in front of her face.

"No, no. All settled, Mariah. Not a penny owed. We gave her a good send-off. It was as good a wake as I've been at for years . . . and probably the last, until my own. And I won't be there to enjoy that." Bessie was a big-hearted soul, and I loved her dearly.

By nightfall, the house was full with people from the three parishes, and Mary Ellen's wake was well under way.

So it was all through the long night we kept watch over Mary Ellen with prayer, stories and even the odd song or recitation till we said our last goodbyes. We laid her in her plain coffin and shouldered her to the church with the sad funeral bell tolling in our ears. From there we took her to her resting place by the old graveyard wall not a hundred paces from her own house to join her husband Michael; and where I, too, in my own time, will lie till Gabriel's final trumpet calls us all to account.

After we had laid Mary Ellen to rest, the men repaired to Bessie's and other public houses in the village to wash the sour taste of the grave from dry palates.

I walked home and sat alone by the dying fire.

There is no sadness so bleak and deep as that sadness that both fills and bleeds the heart and soul when, having laid your mother in her grave, you walk from the graveside to return to the house where her spirit still lives. That is as lonesome a moment as you can have in your life and fills you with an emptiness you know in your heart will never, ever again be filled. But life flows on, and we can but flow with it while yet we live.

Though Bessie suggested that I not return to the pub and that I remain at home with Brian and Robin in our time of sorrow and grieving, I went back to work in the bar the following day. By now, however, I had decided that it was time to take my leave of this work, and so the following Monday morning I sat with Bessie in her upstairs room and told her of my decision.

She accepted all this in good grace.

"Though I would have it otherwise, I knew that this day would surely come, Mariah," she said. "You will be missed. I will miss you . . . as will the twelve apostles."

She still referred to her regulars as such, though Andy Furlong, the eldest of the twelve, had died two years before.

"And who will I get to replace you, Mariah? For if I cannot, I will close my doors. I am too old and tired to manage on my own."

I thought on this for a moment. "There is one I think I could recommend."

"And who might that be?" said she.

"Barty Kelly," I replied. "He has a mind and a liking, I think, to be at the business side of the bar counter. He's tough, but he's honest and he knows his ground. You could do worse."

She laughed at that and nodded her head. "Well, you could be right. He surely has served his time outside the bar counter."

Bessie took my advice, and indeed Barty was to become the bar manager until Bessie died a few years later. Later I heard that on the very day he took over the premises, he took the pledge to quit the drink. From that day on, he kept a good reputable house, and so the business continued to flourish and thrive.

A week or so following my informing Bessie of my new plans and when all arrangements had been made, I raised a glass of brandy in the bar while making my farewells to Bessie, to the apostles and to my workplace of these seven years.

Holding back a tear, I stepped out the door to join Robin, who had come to the village with the pony and trap to help move me and my few belongings back home.

I made it my business to drop in on Bessie each and every time I visited the village, sometimes for advice, but mostly for lively conversation and to hear the local gossip and raise a glass or two together. I valued her friendship, her honesty and her many kindnesses to me in the seven years I had worked in her premises. I valued her observations of life and wise advice given whenever I sought it, and I grieved for her as I had for my own mother when she died about five or so years later.

Did I regret my time in Bessie Moran's public house? I did not regret a single day of it! I had taken the job and had worked at it all the years to the best of my abilities. I also knew I brought with me many gifts from that place: a wealth of acquired business knowledge and the memories of countless days and nights of lively conversation with both regular and stranger; of the spinning and the telling of happy tales, sad tales, tragic tales, tall tales and stories great and small; and not to mention more than a fair share of madness and mayhem.

Most of all I took with me from that place a keen and invaluable insight into the human spirit and the human heart with all its frailties and its weaknesses, its strengths and its courage. This was the gift I came to treasure most, perhaps above all others, and which I put to good use in the years and decades that followed.

CHAPTER TWENTY-TWO

I T WOULD BE easy for me to sit here and tell you that, in the
years following Mary Ellen's death and my return home to
live with my two bachelor brothers, I had a plan, that I had
in mind a scheme to follow or a goal to achieve. In truth I did
not. I may have convinced myself that I was embarking on a new
path, a definite road with an end in sight, but – I know now – that
was not the case. What I did in reality was to step back into the
river of life and let it take me where it pleased. And it took me
back to the home and the house in which I was born and raised.

As the days and weeks passed following my return home, I
found I had slipped quietly into the gentle rhythm of work and
life I had known before my leaving the house seven years earlier.
While Brian and Robin worked the land, I kept house and hearth
and tended the kitchen gardens and foddered and fed the farmyard animals and fowl, as had Mary Ellen up to her final weeks on
earth. Robin, always quiet and retiring, was happy working alone
in the fields and gardens or tending to his horses. I can see him
still, leading one of his horses out to work the fields, his pipe
alight and not a care in the world on his shoulders.

Brian, the more outgoing and sociable of the two, preferred being out and about among people or working in the forge, where he was never short of conversation or company. Brian was also the one who traded and sold cattle at the fairs, and sometimes if there was a lull in the work on the farm, he hired himself out for seasonal work at Colonel Butler's big house.

But whatever the work, whatever the season, there were few idle hours to be enjoyed, and the house was still open to all who might come for the cure.

I suppose it's true to say that in the years following Mary Ellen's death, it seemed that more and more people from further and further afield sought us out to heal the many ailments from which they suffered.

In the seven years I had worked at Bessie's pub, I can say I had earned a reputation as a healer with a gift – or "power" – equal to that of my father Michael. Or indeed, to that of Brian, whose fame as a healer in these years had spread far beyond the three parishes.

No day, it seemed, went by without someone, a local or sometimes a complete stranger, knocking at our door.

"Is the man with the charm within?" they would enquire. Sometimes they would ask, "Is the healer within?"

We would go and fetch Brian, who might be at work in the fields or the forge, and right away he would leave whatever he was engaged in and return to the house, there to take the visitor into the parlour or into his forge to talk in private and dispense his remedies.

As his fame grew, so too did the volume of visitors, which, in turn, took up a great deal of his time. Much to Robin's irritation, Brian's work in the fields was often neglected because of this.

Robin must have had private words with him, because soon after my return home, Brian came to me with a proposal.

"I've come to believe that there are some who are too shy to

ask for my help with their ailments. So, Mariah, this is what I pro-
pose we do. I will deal with all the men and you will look after
the woman visitors, who may be more comfortable with that
arrangement."

He was shy to say it outright, but he was aware that many
women callers were embarrassed and uncomfortable to have to
discuss or divulge their private ailments with a man, even though
he had the power to cure them of their sufferings. I could not
disagree with that and I went along with his suggestion.

It was true that these days much of my time was spent in the
company of the many woman callers to the house. This was not
just to ease their pains and ills, which Brian could have done, but
to offer woman-to-woman advice and to lend, without judgement, no less than a listening ear and an understanding and
compassionate heart.

Brian's suggestion was a wise and sound one. Very soon our
callers would specifically ask for either Brian or me, and soon a
division of labours and a suitable working routine was established
between us.

The light was dying when the figure of a frightened-looking
young girl, pale and breathless, appeared at my door. I recognised her as Maeve, the youngest daughter of James O'Brien, a
herdsman and farmer who lived about ten miles to the north.

"Come in, child," I said. There was a wild look of terror on
her face, and I could see that the fever was upon her.

"What ails you, child?" I asked, handing her a glass of water.

"You have to come right away. My father has the beggar's
curse on him and will not live out the night." Her tears began to
fall.

"Shsssh. Hush now," I said, handing the poor, trembling girl
a mug of hot tea. "Sit and tell me all that has happened in your
home."

It was always the custom to give a night's lodgings to all travellers or beggars who might ask for it. Not to do so might earn the person who refused that shelter "the beggar's curse", which would bring all kinds of bad luck into the house. A woman with child would never refuse shelter in the belief that if she did not take a beggar in, she would miscarry and lose her child.

But what the poor people did not realise was that the real curse that might come upon them was often the disease brought into the house by the traveller or beggar.

On a night of bitter frost, such a beggar woman had called to the home of James O'Brien. Not knowing that she was infected with the fever, he opened his house to the misfortunate woman and took her in from the night to eat at their table and sleep under their thatch. The following day, his wife took sick, and soon his three children fell sick and feverish and had to take to their beds. James right away went to fetch the priest and the doctor, who gave them as much relief as he could.

When James himself fell sick the following day, fearing for his life and the life of his family, he roused one of his daughters from her sickbed to travel the miles to ask for my help.

His sister, so he told me later, had come to consult with me in the snug of Bessie's pub the previous year. Soon in the full of her health, she had claimed to all her family and neighbours that I had cured her of a nagging, long-suffered liver complaint, from which she had had no relief from any medicine.

Right away I tackled Paudie to the trap and went directly with the child to the side of James O'Brien. I arrived at the house in the dark of night to find the situation to be as was told me by the girl. I soon confirmed that the children were not gravely ill, but I saw that their father was indeed sickly to death and in need of my urgent attention. I knew immediately what I had to do.

Right away I closed all doors and windows and built and piled high the fires till the heat in the room was almost uncomfortable to bear. I then concocted and applied a hot mustard poultice to James' head and chest.

Finally, from the blue bottle I administered a healing potion, which I had not long since mixed, to the sick man and also to his wife and to each of his children. Lastly I touched each one three times on the forehead with the small silver hammer I now kept about my person at all times. Stoking up the fires, I settled down to keep watch by their bedsides all through that night and finally to see the fever break the following morning.

James O'Brien later claimed that I, and I alone, had saved his life and the lives of his entire family.

CHAPTER TWENTY-THREE

S O MANY HAVE asked, what is this cure? What is the charm? And where does it come from?

For me, it is an unexplainable spirit or force which springs from a well deep within and which bubbles up to fill the body and the mind. It is a deep knowing, a pure wisdom that does not come from learning or listening alone.

It is a fine-tuning of the senses, a quickening of the pulse, a flowing of the blood, a heat in head and the hands, a sureness of the eye, a sharpness of the ear. It is the dreaming of an old dream hidden deep within, understood only to the dreamer and only part remembered in the cold light of day.

It is a quiet voice from some unknown and unknowable place deep within that speaks a truth that does not come from human tongue nor can be seen by human eye.

There are days when I hear that voice; there are days when I cannot. It is not for me to question why, for I cannot bid it to my will. All I can say is that when it speaks I am open to its message. I am then fully alive, and I feel a surge of a strange power from within me. When I do not hear – when the voice is silent and does not speak – I am empty and I am barren.

It came, too, from our knowledge of the earth all around us. It came from the simple plant, from the shy, hidden herb, from the bark of the tree, from the essence of blossom and petal and from the pure water, which gives us all life.

But as I mentioned, this healing gift – this charm as they call it – did not come to our family without a price.

For Brian especially it was sometimes more a curse than a blessing.

It was while at the November cattle fair of Kilfenora that his mettle was tested. The trouble started in a pub with two men engaged in a political discussion, each one standing firm behind his opposing political wall. A quantity of drink had been taken, and before long, strong words and insults were exchanged. Tempers flared, blows were struck, and the two men were invited by the publican to take their argument out to the street.

There, among the throng of cattle and herdsmen, the argument became fierce. Steel was drawn, a blade plunged deep, red blood began to flow, and a man's life ebbed slowly from his body.

Someone who knew Brian stood with his cattle at the other end of the village; he ran and summoned him to attend to the injured man. Brian came directly to the scene, instantly took stock of the situation and in a short time had stemmed the flow of blood from a severe neck wound.

"You did well, Brian. You stopped the blood flow. But you're lucky that the man wasn't too badly wounded," said a bystander.

Brian stood, looked the speaker directly in the eye and said, a little too boastfully perhaps, "Lucky, you say? You think me lucky, do you? Well, let me tell you, lucky has nothing to do with it! I'd stop this man's blood if it was flowing from his heart. I could bring this man back from death's door . . . even from death itself."

As he continued to administer to the wounded man on the ground, Father Tobin, a recently appointed priest to the locality and a witness to the action, pushed forward through the crowd gathered around, raised his blackthorn stick and called loudly, "In the name of God, you go too far, sir! Do you claim to do miracles? No ordinary man can do as you claim. Either you are a lost soul in league with Satan or you are a common fraud, a trickster and a rogue! You should get on your knees in this place and ask God's forgiveness for claiming a power that only He dispenses."

The crowd drew back like an ocean from the shore.

Brian stood and, as cool as a breeze, looked the priest straight in the eye.

"Well now, Father," Brian said. "You are a man of God, with special powers, powers dispensed directly from Him, are you not? Do you see those blackbirds on that tree yonder?"

All eyes turned and followed his pointing finger.

"If I care to, with a simple wave of my hand, I can summon them to come and land on this right arm of mine. With all your powers, Father, can you do the same?"

The priest turned deathly pale, stared at Brian in silence before turning on his heel and, without uttering another word, walked quickly away from the scene. A large group of onlookers had now gathered about Brian and the wounded man.

Everyone started talking at once.

"Did you mean what you said?" enquired a man standing close by. "Could you really do as you said?"

Brian laughed loudly at this. "Don't be daft, man! Of course not. I have it in my gift to cure most any form of human sickness. I can give relief to liver and kidney complaints, back and chest pains. I can heal skin sores, bruises, rashes, ulcers and sprains. I can cure coughs, back pain, headache, toothache and fits. I can stop a serious blood flow, as I have here with this poor devil. I have knowledge to heal a broken body or spirit and to give ease to the suffering. But I am not the druid, wizard, magician, fraud or the common three-card trickster this priest wants to believe me to be. Where is his real faith? He should trust only what he sees with his two eyes and not what he fears he might see in his imagination."

That was what happened at that November cattle fair in the village of Kilfenora, and that is exactly as Brian related it to us on his return later that evening.

Brian soon forgot all about this incident.

Father Tobin, however, did not.

CHAPTER TWENTY-FOUR

NONE OF us, especially Brian, was prepared for what was about to unfold. How could we know that the result of our activities – the healing and curing of the sick of body and soul – could bring about or be the cause of such pain and suffering for our family?

It happened like this.

Father Murphy, a simple, good, decent man who cared for the welfare of all his flock, was at that time our local parish priest. Soon after Mary Ellen's death, when I had moved back home, Father Murphy was joined by Father Tobin, a young priest from across the Shannon, to help out in the three parishes. You could see from day one that this new priest was cut from different cloth from that of the kindly old Father Murphy.

Where Father Murphy was easy going, understanding, compassionate and forgiving and had a way with the ordinary man or woman, Father Tobin's attitude – not to mention his sermons– was severe, proud and haughty. His general surly demeanour won him few supporters and fewer friends as he moved among his new parishioners.

He had not been too long in the parish before he heard of our family, of the cure we possessed and the reputation we had for healing the sick who came to our door. While he never visited the house or, for that matter, spoke directly with any one of us, it very soon became clear from his weekly sermons what this priest's thoughts and feelings were regarding our various healing activities.

There was not a single Sunday that he would not denounce from the altar those among us who, in his words, "were slipping back to the old religion" and "going back to godless paganism", as he put it. There was not a single Sunday when he did not make pointed mention about those among us who knowingly turned our hearts and our souls from the grace of God.

Worse still, he loudly proclaimed one Sunday, there were "certain individuals" – and at this he paused and glared long and hard in Brian's direction – who were putting their souls in mortal danger by engaging in dangerous, non-Christian activities. These he listed as the casting of "spells and incantations" and the healing of dumb animals and Christian beings through the administration of unholy mixtures, potions and other magical concoctions.

Such behaviour, so the priest pronounced, was nothing short of heretical and could find favour only with Satan and the powers of darkness. This, so he informed the congregation, was what he had witnessed since his coming to this place.

"A flock going astray!" he said. "A flock in need of a Good Shepherd to guide them back to the paths of righteousness and away from the influence of heretical thought and actions. I know who these heretics are among you! And so do you!"

Standing on that altar, he looked and spoke like a man possessed.

"As an ordained priest and as shepherd of this flock, I tell you now, it is my intention to root out those among you who would put their souls in peril and embrace these powers of darkness."

I can tell you it was a silent, sober congregation who left the church that day. Though no one person uttered a word to us, everybody attending mass that Sunday morning knew at whom it was Father Tobin's remarks were aimed.

At this stage, Father Tobin and Brian had never actually met face to face. However, the priest's sermon on the Sunday following his confrontation with Brian at the Kilfenora fair was direct and to the point.

"There is a man of this parish. . ." Father Tobin's voice could barely conceal his rising anger. ". . . who sits here among us today. A man who sits here in this house of God as he does every Sunday. A man who calls himself a Christian! A man who calls himself a Catholic! Yet this man, by his own actions, mocks and laughs in the very face of the good Lord who laid down His life for this man and for all here!"

Father Tobin's face was red as a turkey cock, and he fairly spat out his words. You could have heard a pin drop in the church as the congregation held its breath.

He continued his tirade and his words echoed around the church.

"This man – not to mention others of his family – dares to place himself outside the embrace of Holy Mother Church and her saints. This man dares to call down healing power through magic spells, unholy litanies and dark incantations! This man dares to dispense a special grace – that of true healing – which only Jesus or his Holy Mother – and NOT MAN! – can dispense."

Here he paused and his words fell to almost a whisper.

"I tell you today that this man is in league with the devil and places the salvation of his very soul in mortal danger. This man, unless he renounces all his attachments to the practice of the Black Arts, unless he repents, begs for God's forgiveness and comes back to the fold this very day, is on the road to hell!"

At this, Brian arose from his pew, moved out to the aisle,

turned his back on the priest and walked out of the church. I felt the entire congregation stop breathing. Even Father Tobin fell silent and turned back to face the altar to continue the saying of the mass.

Mass over, Robin and I walked home together in silence and in dread to find Brian seated by the fire, his face a deathly pale and a glass of *poitín* in his trembling hand.

"Did you hear all that?" I had never seen Brian so distraught and overcome with emotion. "Is this priest in full command of his senses? How can I be in danger of losing my soul? How can that priest say that I – you too, Mariah! – get power to heal and cure from Satan and not through the goodness of God? Our potions and herbs come from God's good earth and are available to all who would seek them. How can this be bad? Do we not make the sign of the cross over each and every one who comes to us for help? How can all this good that we do for those who suffer be evil?"

I had never seen Brian so visibly upset. He was silent for a long while, and then he spoke words that I hear in my head to this day: "I will not return to mass nor set foot again in that church while this priest remains in the parish."

Knowing Brian to be as determined as a man could be, I knew he meant what he said.

Robin and I could only agree with him that the priest's attacks were unfounded and unfair. However, we both pleaded with him, for his and all our sakes, not to take such a drastic course of action, for it would lead only to greater trouble with the priest and the Church.

I counselled – indeed, begged – Brian not to take this route and instead to meet privately with Father Tobin to discuss their differences of opinion.

"Talk to him, Brian!" I pleaded. "Talk to him and show him you are not what he accuses you of being. None of us is."

I urged him that if he could not convince Father Tobin, then he should go to our parish priest, Father Murphy. He, I knew in my heart, would be both understanding and forgiving. After a while pondering on this, Brian promised he would go first to see Father Murphy and he would do it the following day.

True to his promise he did go to the parochial house to talk with Father Murphy, only to find that the priest had, that very day, been taken into a nursing home suffering from severe pneumonia. Taking Father Murphy's place as parish priest till his return to full health, so the housekeeper informed Brian, was none other than Father Tobin.

Brian returned home that evening in very low spirits, and in the days that followed he refused to see any callers and kept very much to himself.

Sunday came, and as he had threatened, Brian did not attend mass that morning; nor did he attend the church on the Sundays that followed. Brian's absence was well noted by the congregation, and especially noted of course by Father Tobin, who continued to denounce Brian from the altar each and every time he stood to make his sermon.

The priest's continuing attacks, coupled with Brian's continuing absence from church, resulted in the turning away of many old friends and neighbours from the family. Our regular night-callers stopped their *cuairds* to the house. I would hail local woman friends or acquaintances on the road, only to see them draw their shawls about their heads and turn their eyes away from me, in fear, so I learned later, that I might put the evil eye on the poor deluded souls. Many reacted in the fear and dread that any social contact with Brian, Robin or myself would result in the bringing down on them of the wrath of this priest. Some truly began to believe the priest's accusations that Brian was indeed in league with the devil. What other explanations could there be for his unusual, and inexplicable, powers?

It was a hard and bitter time for us, and for Brian especially, I can tell you!

But worse was yet to come.

Some months later, on an overcast January day of cloud and sleety rain, we had a visit from Thread-the-Needle John, the hawker. Every three or four months, Thread-the-Needle John – some say he was a wandering Jew, some say he was an Indian or Pakistani, and others say Armenian – would arrive with his ass and cart to sell us the little items, nick-nacks and the like, we could not get in the village shops.

I remember, as children, we would rush to greet him with whoops of joy and delight when his cart was sighted on the road approaching the house. He would tether his donkey to the forge door, unload his battered old leather cases, and there on the kitchen table would lay his treasure trove before our bulging eyes to tempt us to buy, which usually we did.

One leather case held hardware: spoons, forks, knives and scissors, thimbles and sewing needles, shirt and coat buttons, collar studs, nails and tacks, spectacles, hand mirrors, combs, candles and candle sconces, pens, ink, notebooks and writing paper, perfumes, soaps, spices of every scent, colour and taste.

The other leather case was packed with hard and soft fabrics: tweeds, velvets, shawls, coloured hair ribbons, woven waistcoats, stockings and shoelaces. There were sandalwood vanity boxes, rings, bangles, brooches and necklaces, and even coloured balloons, Christmas crepe decorations and other gimcracks that Santa Claus himself might bring the wee ones on Christmas Eve.

For countrywomen who lived in isolated places and rarely saw the inside of a shop from one end of the year to the next, there always were so many luxuries in Thread-the-Needle's treasure chests to lure and tempt them. He rarely, if ever, departed our house without some item of fabric, jewellery or fanciful bauble and money changing hands.

On this particular day, he had completed his business transactions and was about to continue on his way when he turned to me and said, "Oh, I nearly forgot. I met the postman on the road yonder. He gave me this letter to give to you."

The envelope was addressed to Brian, and it lay on the kitchen table till Brian returned home that evening.

"I saw Martin the Post on the road earlier. Did he call?" he asked.

"Thread-the-Needle was our postman today. There's a letter for you, Brian," I said as I lit the oil lamp and placed it on the table so as to illuminate his reading of it. I watched as he picked up the letter from the table; slowly unsealing the envelope, he sat down to read the single-page letter. In the pale glow of the lamp, I could see he had turned white as a ghost.

The letter was from Father Tobin, and its contents spelled out a dark sentence for Brian and indeed for the whole family.

Father Tobin's letter, written in small, sharp lettering, stated that he was writing as acting parish priest and also for and on behalf of His Grace the bishop. It went on to point out that many warnings had been issued from the altar to the family, and especially to Brian, to cast aside the works and pomps of the devil; as these had been ignored, now at last had come a day of judgement.

Brian had been singled out of all of us and – so the letter continued – because he had strayed from the path of righteousness, he was to suffer the most severe penance that could be meted out by the Church. He was, from that day on, to be refused entry into the house of the Lord. From this day onward, he was to be refused the sacraments and forgiveness for his sins. He was to be denied the grace of God till it pleased the Church that he had purged himself of his most grievous sin and abandoned all heretical thoughts, deeds and actions and returned to embrace fully the One True, Holy Roman Catholic and Apostolic Church.

That was the general gist of the terrible letter.

Excommunication!

My blood ran cold. I had never thought I would read such a sentence in my life. And to think it was now being issued to my own brother!

Under the light of the oil lamp, I read and reread the letter. Still the words rang steely cold like funeral bells tolling some terrible end.

So here, at last, was the day of reckoning. We well knew that there were many – especially this priest – who had difficulty with much of the healing and many of the cures we had brought about over the years. We knew, too, that there might be a price to be paid. Father always said that one day we might have to pay for possession of this gift of healing. To be admonished from the pulpit was one thing. However, to suffer such banishment from the Church and separation from the congregation was the ultimate sanction on a soul.

"This cannot be right or just," Robin said after I again read the letter aloud. "Is this the reward earned for bringing ease to the sufferings of the poor people who crave it?"

"What are we to do?" I asked Brian.

"Do?" he whispered the words. "What you will do – what we will do – is carry on as we did before. I will not refuse any poor soul who comes and asks for my help. I know in my heart of hearts I do not commit any sin, little or great, when I bring relief from sickness and suffering to those who ask it of me. I believe that it's no sin to make use of the gift of healing, which surely is a gift for good and not evil. I know in my heart that all power for good comes only from the Lord, who is good and great and merciful. It is with Him I will make peace, not with a cleric who would judge me wrongly."

With these words, Brian crossed himself.

For a long time that night we three sat in silence, each with our own thoughts, emotions and prayers.

Brian did just as he resolved he would do. While it fairly broke my heart to witness what he was going through, I have to give him credit for the strength and courage of his resolve. From that day on, as he had promised, he did not set foot inside the church for as long as Father Tobin remained as priest to the parish, though he well knew what lay ahead of him. Few got on the wrong side of the priests without paying a terrible price. Those who did fall foul of the clergy had little option but to flee the land to England or cross the Atlantic to the Americas.

"These priests lead us around like blind sheep. They wield too much power," Brian had often remarked. "Remember Father saying how they destroyed Parnell back in the '90s when they brought him down with slander and lies so they could put their puppet into parliament? Well, in my opinion, this priest is cut from the same cloth as those plotters."

Brian also now well knew that he had to look at his future and consider the options open to him. Should he remove himself to safer ground, or stay here in this place and face the consequences of his actions?

"Would you consider America?" Robin asked him one night. "They say the clergy don't have as much say or sway over the people there."

"America?" Brian shook his head. "No! I've made up my mind. To run will be to admit my guilt and as good as an admission that the gift is tainted in some way. Or worse, a gift from Satan and not from God. No, I'll stand my ground. I was born here, and I'll die here. Neither Cromwell's armies nor the Great Hunger could shift our forefathers from this place. The priests won't shift me. I will stay, and to hell with the consequences!"

But the whole affair was to take its toll. To be cast out and barred from the house of God was a terrible weight for any good-living person to carry and endure from day to day. This was especially true at Easter and Christmas or the funerals of friends and neighbours.

He resigned himself to his banishment from weekly mass attendance. A social banishment was also in force. In the days that followed, Brian's heart nearly broke to witness his oldest companions and neighbours turn their eyes from him when he approached them on the road or in the field or in the village street. Only Tom Cullinan, Tim Grady and a few others – good, true and especially brave friends to the family – remained staunch to the end. Tom especially never stopped visiting the house on *cuaird* or to offer help with work in the meadow, garden and bog.

Still, it was not an easy time. Those who had fallen sick or were in need of the cure were fearful to call to the house in broad daylight. Now they would come under the cover of dark night to consult with Brian or with me in the outhouse, forge or barn by the light of a candle or lantern.

In the meantime, life went on, and Robin and I regularly attended mass and tried to be as good Christians as we could. Though we were always aware of being viewed as suspect and guilty of the charges laid at our feet, at least it was some small consolation to all that Father Tobin had now ceased his tirade of accusations against us personally.

Though poor Brian found light and spiritual solace and comfort in his own way, we could see that this cross he had to carry was beginning to show on his features and on his spirit. His quick smile and good humour had dimmed and were now replaced by a grave and despairing air, which he carried as he would a great weight. We noticed the lines of care about his eyes and the streaks of grey now running through his hair.

It sorely grieved both Robin and me to see our brother in this troubled condition, and it broke our hearts to witness his terrible sufferings of body and spirit. Our pain was in that there was nothing we could do to ease his pain, nothing we could say that would bring solace to his heavy heart and troubled soul. We could only be there to offer our silent support and pray for an early end to this sorry affair.

What of Father Tobin? Even when Father Murphy eventually returned from the sanatorium to take up again his post of parish priest, he continued to work alongside his superior as priest to the three parishes. But a leopard does not change his spots, so it is said, and Father Tobin never did win the love, the respect or the regard of his parishioners, only their grudging tolerance, fear and distrust.

Five years or so later, he contracted consumption after a visitation to a house that carried the disease and soon after fell sick. He spent his last unhappy days in a sanatorium in Limerick city. It was told later that as his sickness progressed and he realised the seriousness of his situation, he pleaded that his carers send for Brian the Healer, the only man who might cure his terrible condition, to attend him in his hour of need.

It was Easter Week, a few days after the Easter Sunday of 1916, when Brian came home with a spring in his step to relate the news that was on everybody's lips. There had been an uprising of the rebels in the General Post Office in Dublin city.

"A great rising of poets and peasants alike, so they say. There are many dead, but the talk is of freedom at last for Ireland!"

"A rising, you say? We've risen before," Robin said sourly. "Where did it get us?"

"There was a Clareman, Peadar Clancy, involved with the rebels at the GPO. There is great talk of a general rising, and I hear in the village that Bertie Hunt is rounding up as many local men from the three parishes as want to join the Volunteers to fight the foe. He's fair determined, so they say, that this great rebellion should spread to all parts of Ireland, and all parts of Clare."

"War, fighting and rebellion: do ye men ever get enough if it?" I said.

"The tide may be changing. This one could sweep the country." Brian ignored my comment and added, as casual as you like, "Oh, by the way, I hear other news in the village. . . of Father Tobin. He died last week of the consumption in a Limerick hospital."

"God rest his soul," I crossed myself.

Brian crossed himself, too.

CHAPTER TWENTY-FIVE

BRIAN WAS WORKING with his beehives in the high meadow behind the graveyard on that Palm Sunday morning when Father Murphy drove into our yard in his pony and trap. Easter that year fell in late April, and Palm Sunday fell sunny, warm and bright.

Brian had been looking after these hives for over ten years, ever since a lone swarm had arrived one Midsummer's Day and lodged in a corner of the cowbarn. Brian built a makeshift hive from old timber butter boxes to capture and house the visiting swarm.

On a good year he would extract up to fifty or sixty pounds of honey from each hive, and Mary Ellen and I would be hard pressed to find jars and receptacles to store the fruits of the bees' labours.

In the deep of winter, when there was no sugar or sweetener to be had, we were glad of our store of honey and used it on meats and hams, in cakes, buns and scones and in herb drinks and on our morning porridge. One year, when good poitín was hard to come by, Father made a few gallons of mead, a honey drink that Fionn Mac Cumhaill – so he told us youngsters – and his Fianna warriors supped at their great feasts at royal Tara.

"This will get us through the Christmas," Father said as he sealed the mead jars. And so it did!

Whenever the common colds or virulent flu visited the house, Mary Ellen mixed hot whiskeys or a poitín punch and always added cloves and honey. A sore throat would be soon banished by mixing a half a cup of honey and vinegar and taking a few spoonfuls daily. Honey applied to any kind of skin disease or blemish never fails to cure. When Father went on his healing trips, he would sometimes use honey as a balm or poultice for sores and wounds, and it was exceptionally good for burns and ulcers.

"This warm sunshine will get the bees stirring after their long winter sleep," Brian had said as Robin and I prepared to go to mass that Palm Sunday morning. "It's time I paid them a visit."

I was placing the palm frond I had received at mass over the door lentil, as was the Palm Sunday custom, when I saw Father Murphy, who had said the mass that morning, pull into the yard and tether his pony and trap to the barn door. The last time he had been in this house had been to attend the corpse of Mary Ellen, and now I could only wonder at the purpose of this visit.

"Good morrow to you, Mariah," he saluted me, raising his black hat as he stepped down from the trap. "The blessings of this glorious day be upon you."

"And on you, too, Father," I answered him. "Will you come in for tea? Or something stronger maybe?" From my time at Bessie Moran's pub, I well recalled his fondness for a dram or two in the morning to stir the blood and soften the edge of the day ahead of him.

"Another time, Mariah. It's Brian I have come to see this morning. Is he about the house?"

I directed him up the pathway to the high meadow where, I told him, he would find Brian caring for his beehives.

"But be careful, Father," I warned him. "Those bees have no care whither or not you are a man of the cloth. Their sting lands just as venomous and painful on all skins, regardless of colour, creed or station in life."

"Ah yes," says he with a gleam in his eye, "honeybees. We kept a hive or two in the first parish I served in. I learned something of their nature whilst there. God's most perfect of creatures. Such skilled and tireless workers. Maybe the only true form of democracy we can yet observe on this earth."

An interesting viewpoint, I thought. I had never looked at working bees in that way.

"Did you know they were as much valued in the time of the pharaohs and in Jesus' day as they are today? Moses and his followers lived on honey on their flight out of Egypt into the Promised Land. The honeybee is sacred. Brian is right to study them. I suspect we could learn a thing or two from bees if only we had the time, inclination and patience to do so."

"And a hardened, leather skin for the job," says I.

"Just so, Mariah. I will stay at a safe distance, I assure you." With that the priest gave a chuckle and headed up the path towards the meadow to seek out Brian at work with his beloved bees.

An hour or more passed. Robin and I, who had fasted in order to take communion at mass that Palm Sunday morning, had finished our late breakfast when Father Murphy came down the path from the high meadow and into the yard. Once again, I invited him to step inside for tea or a drop of liquor, and once again he refused.

"Thank you, Mariah, but I'm late as it is. I'm sure you remember my housekeeper, Molly? She will kill me if I'm not back for dinner at the appointed hour, and that hour draws dangerously close. I was spared the bees' attention, and for that I gave them my blessings and prayers for a rich harvest Perhaps you will remember me when you draw the honey?"

"We will that, Father."

With that he unhitched his pony, mounted the trap and headed off down the road towards the village.

When Brian finally did return from the high meadow, I had to bite my tongue in my great desire to hear the true purpose of Father Murphy's visitation and what he had had to say. Brian just sat by the hearth with a mug of tea in his hands, and for a long while he was silent, obviously reluctant to talk and very much wrapped up in his own thoughts. It was after supper that evening when Brian finally got the urge to talk and tell us the gist of their conversation together.

"Father Murphy says I am welcome back into arms of Mother Church. I will no longer be regarded as a stranger to the flock – as he said – and will be welcome to return as soon as I make my confession. That can be this coming week if that is what I desire, so Father Murphy said."

Robin and I could hardly contain our happiness at this news. We could see he was deeply moved by this, and we remained silent and let him speak on.

"Father Murphy said he never wished nor wanted, not for a single day, this state of affairs to have come about. An excommunication in his parish! A terrible thing it was, so Father Murphy said, to be parish priest and preside over such a dark event. It seems that from the day Father Tobin arrived in the parish, his talk was about pagan practices among the people, the idolising of false pagan gods and goddesses."

Because this was a young priest, full of passion and zeal, Father Murphy had decided to let the man have his say, thinking all this would blow over in time, especially when the new priest grew to know his parishioners and in particular got to know our family and what we do.

But it was not to be. From day one, Father Tobin had given

him not a moment's peace till he was allowed to present his case in writing to the bishop. Before too long, His Grace had agreed that given the facts as presented to him by Father Tobin, Brian should be banned from the taking of the sacraments and any further attending of church, unless he fully recanted his grievous sin.

Things, so Father Murphy said, had got out of his control; and at that time, he himself was too weak and ill and did not have the strength to debate or argue with the fire and passion that drove Father Tobin to have Brian removed from the Church as an example to others.

Now that Father Tobin had gone to his reward, it was Father Murphy's intention to continue to be parish priest to the three parishes. There being one abandoned soul outside the embrace of Mother Church was more than he could bear, so Father Murphy said. His greatest wish was to bring about an end to this terrible state of affairs. The whole, awful business, so he admitted to Brian, had weighed heavy on his conscience and on his soul and so, he added, to his peace of mind and his general well-being.

"He could not let the situation continue, and it was with this in mind that he visited me today," Brian said.

"Now that Father Tobin is dead and with, as Father Murphy said himself, 'the shadow of death drawing ever closer', he has consulted with the bishop. It was agreed that, as things should never have been allowed to go as far as they did, I should be allowed back to the fold."

"Did Father Murphy say anything about the cures or the giving up of them?" Robin asked.

"He gave me his blessing to continue, just as long as I do my work in the name of the Good Lord. After all, he said, 'Wasn't Jesus himself a healer of men?' Father Murphy is a good, decent, Christian man."

By the time Brian had finished speaking, there were tears rolling down my cheeks.

"Thank God, Brian," I said. "Your trials are over you."

I looked at Brian and there were tears also flowing from his eyes.

Twilight had fallen, and in this half-light we three sat then in a silence that was almost sacred. The air was sweet and lighter all about us. I could hear the wings of a small bird beat at the windowpane and the sad song of a nightingale somewhere in the high, clear, night air.

CHAPTER TWENTY-SIX

THEY SAY THAT happiness often comes in a door you did not know you had left open. Though there was political trouble and strife brewing throughout the land, the year that followed Brian's acceptance back into the Church was one of great peace and contentment for our house and home. I had come back home following my seven years working at Bessie's pub with a mind to stay only for a short time while I decided what path my life was to take from there. Seven years had passed since then, and I sometimes realised to my dismay that I had not yet decided on a course of action. For a time I had a notion I would apply to join the Clare Red Cross Nursing Volunteers who were at that time active in the Great War, which had taken so many of our finest lads.

I had seen the recruiters in the town and thought to maybe present myself and "do my bit". But after a chance meeting with Dr McNamara in the village, I learned from him that I had neither the professional qualifications nor indeed the youth on my side to ensure acceptance into the ranks of that brave corps.

I realised then that I had been foolish to believe that my

particular gifts as a healer might not be a requirement on the front lines in this terrible war.

"Though from what I know and hear of you and your brother," says he, "you are doing as much work as healers to the sick hereabouts as I am myself."

I blushed at this, but I knew his words carried more than a grain of truth. Perhaps Dr McNamara was right. In any case, I soon came to realise I had no desire to sally forth into the world and that I was exactly where I wanted to be. I now fully accepted that my needs were few and simple and that peace of soul and contentment of spirit could be found in regular work and the ordinary happenings of day-to-day life as I lived it in this place.

And so life for us all settled into a rhythm of passing days and seasons; of moons waxing and waning; of dawns and dusks and the marking of the solstices to ensure protection for ourselves and for our loved ones.

I must admit I never had any time for party politics. None of our family was overly interested in the ebb and flow of political power and we rarely gave active support to political parties.

"Freedom may come, landlords may go, governments may rise and fall, but the lot of the poor peasant will remain the same." Father would shake his head and dismiss any further discussion.

It has often occurred to me that whenever politics, whether local or national, takes hold of the human mind, reasoned thought and plain facts are ignored or twisted to suit various "ideals". The bonds of families and friendships are broken or, worse still, abandoned or betrayed, and often good men will destroy their lives and the lives of others, and die or be sacrificed in the name of political idealism. You only have to look at history to see that this is true.

But then what do I know of the world of politics?

"What do women know of politics?" I once heard a wag say in the pub one night. "Politics is about the great affairs of men."

"Politics is the pursuit of trivial men," I answered him across the bar top. "And, when they succeed at it, they are thought highly of by other trivial men. Women have more important work to be doing in their lives."

I admit I had read it somewhere, but I was pleased that I remembered it, and I quoted it with great gusto, earning a loud cheer of approval from the twelve apostles.

In those times, women still did not have the right to vote and, not being too interested or involved in politics, at that time, I was actually of the opinion that the business of politics was indeed men's business.

In any case, politics, as I found out while running Bessie's bar, went to men's heads like strong whiskey and often with similar results. Through my observations, I came to the conclusion that too much politics played havoc with men's humour, their common sense and their God-given reasoning power. Too often did I witness friends and neighbours – sometimes brothers and blood relations – argue, abuse, insult and defame each other over some political triviality.

I witnessed the blood of otherwise meek and gentle men come to such a boiling point in the heat of political debate that they became a danger to themselves and to others, and I watched men who would not dirty their hands to do an honest day's work for family, love or money, swear on their mother's grave they were ready to "spill blood for the party and for Ireland!"

I often marvelled at how otherwise sensible and reasonable men were prepared to follow lesser men to the ends of the earth for some political ideal.

Election times were always times of high tension in the bar. These were times, in my opinion, when the mixture of strong drink and political discourse made for poor bedfellows. It got so bad coming up to election day, with tempers flaring, insults hurled and sometimes blows struck in the heat of argument, that I decided to put an outright ban on the discussion of politics in the bar after the hour of 9 p.m.

This, I have to admit, was not a house rule which was greatly enforced, as it seemed neither my regular patrons nor passing customerss had any inclination or interest in any topic other than the politics of the time.

All other topics and interests were suspended till the elections were over and life got back to normal.

In truth, the whole business greatly confounded me, and none of my experience of studying human nature offered a satisfactory explanation.

But, as I mentioned, politics was in the air like pollen after a summer wind. Now there were self-appointed politicians and experts at every faction fight, cattle fair or crossroads *céilí* on every street corner or bend of the road. But there were few real leaders of vision or statesmen who had the lot of ordinary men and women or the downtrodden at heart. In any case – according to Father – there had been only one true Irish politician and patriot worth listening to or following, and that man was Charles Stewart Parnell.

"He came to the land as would a Messiah, and they brought him down like wolves would their prey. It was the priests, the profiteers and the power-hungry who laid Parnell in an early grave." Father neither forgave nor could he forgot the sad end of the great Irishman. The very mention of Parnell's name in his company always drew comment. "Parnell was destroyed by underhand gutter politics, religious interference and self-interested factions, and we won't live to see his likes again. Willie Redmond is a good man and a fine politician, but he's no Parnell!"

Since Parnell's death, Captain William Redmond had held a seat at Westminster as a member of parliament for Clare.

How well I recall that bitterly cold January morning back in '85 when Father, Brian and I drove in the trap to Ennis to witness the great man, Parnell, come among us. His business that day was the turning of the sod with a silver spade for the commencement of construction work on the long-promised West Clare Railway Line. Michael could not have been more excited if the Pope himself was coming to visit the county.

As I gazed over the heads of the pressing throng milling excitedly all about this tall, dignified and handsome man in a top hat and morning coat, I though I saw the ghost of poor dead Alexander McNeil at Parnell's elbow as he declared the dawning of a new age for Ireland and for the Banner County. A great "Hurrah!" arose from a thousand throats, and hats and caps were hurled high in the air.

Michael pressed close and reached for Parnell's hand. He turned, smiled and returned the handshake warmly. Till the day he died, Father never forgot that moment.

"To have shaken the hand of the greatest living Irishman!" He repeated this many times on the journey home that evening and for years to come.

But in the years I speak of – those years of 1916 and '17 – both Parnell and Michael were long dead and in their graves. Once again, the hand of history was upon the land with talk of secret organisations and daring plots; of strike, dissent and rebellion; of revolution, of war and of freedom.

Freedom. Yes, that was the word that had fired men's hearts and imaginations ever since Pearse, Connolly, MacDonagh and the rest of them had been martyred in its name following the Rising in Easter of 1916.

How I wish Tommy Reilly were alive so he could relate, chapter and verse, the litany of terrible events that befell the land in those troubled years: those years of blood and death and suffering during the War of Independence that led to the signing of the Treaty in '21 and the terrible Civil War that followed. There was no day but would come the awful news of yet another tragedy: the desperate attacks and counter-attacks; the ambushes, bombings, murders and burnings, and the fierce reprisals which surely followed to bring bloodshed, suffering and the death of many innocent men, women and even children.

"What's the news today, Tommy?" we would ask Tommy Reilly when he had perused the newspapers.

"These days there's no news but bad news," was Tommy's usual answer, and you could but agree with him.

It was Tommy who broke the news of the death in France of Captain Willie Redmond, our Clare MP for twenty-six years, killed alongside so many other Claremen fighting the Germans at the front in June of 1917.

Parnell was dead. So, too, were Pearse and Connolly, and now Willie Redmond, in whom we had had so much hope. I prayed that day for his soul and was glad that Father had not lived to see this day and the turbulent days that followed.

From that day on, the talk was of little else but politics and the election that was soon to follow to fill the seat at parliament left vacant by Redmond's death. There were two candidates in the running, but the name on everybody's lips that year, and in the years that followed, was that of Éamon de Valera, one of the Easter Week Rising heroes. Unlike Pearse, Connolly, MacDonagh and the others, de Valera escaped the Sassenach firing squads because of the fact, and the twist of fate, of his American birth.

"Up the Republic!"

"Up the Rebels!"

"Up the IRA!"

"Up Sinn Féin!"

"Up Dev!"

We heard little else but these shouts and chants whenever and wherever groups of men gathered at hurling and football matches or at cattle fairs, house *céilís* or funerals. Party men of every political hue, canvassed door-to-door or speechified from platforms, timber boxes and barrels, tables or chairs. Or from pony traps, jaunting cars or from atop stone walls outside churches after Sunday mass, to call on the people to vote.

The people did indeed cast their vote, and the result was in no doubt: de Valera emerged the clear victor, though not to everybody's satisfaction. In the week that followed, there wasn't a single town or village square, hill or country crossroads in the entire county of Clare that was not ablaze with a bonfire to celebrate. Not that the country's troubles ended with Dev's election.

They were just beginning.

CHAPTER TWENTY-SEVEN

"MARIAH! MARIAH! GET inside the house and close the door. It's the Black and Tans!"

I can still hear Robin's urgent shout of warning from the roadway on that fresh spring evening in late April of 1920. I was out in the yard feeding a young calf being weaned from its mother. Brian was ill and confined to his bed that day. Robin had milked the cows, turned them out and driven them to grass in the lower field by the river.

On his shouted alarm, I looked to see a lorry approach from the direction of the village. I did not go indoors as Robin ordered but stood my ground to get a good look at our unwelcome visitors. The lorry turned at the crossroads and came to a noisy, spluttering halt under the chestnut tree just outside the farmyard entrance. From the canvas-covered back of the Crossley lorry jumped six or seven soldiers, dressed in oversize grey and black uniforms, to stand at their ease leaning on their rifles close to the vehicle. A few lit up cigarettes, and I could hear them laugh and talk among themselves. A tall man in a smart uniform – I assumed him to be an officer but I later learned he was a sergeant – stepped forward and hailed Robin.

"So these are the famous Black and Tans," I said to myself.

The Black and Tans! The latest army force of military occupation sent here by Lloyd George to help the RIC and put manners on us unruly Irish. Their sole purpose was to make, as Lloyd George himself said, "Ireland a hell for rebels!" The British prime minister must have been proud of his army, for ever since their arrival in Ireland the previous March, they had earned a reputation as being heartless, cruel and ruthless killers, spreading fear and mayhem among the ordinary country folk. It was said the English government, most of whose regular army was away fighting the Kaiser at the front in France and Belgium or in India, had opened the jails and mental asylums of England to fill the ranks of this latest conquering army.

One of their ranks is reported to have said later, "In England they gave me life in jail for murdering my wife. Here in Ireland – as a Black and Tan – they pay me five pounds a week for killing Irishmen and women."

As I looked at this rag-tag group of armed men, I could hardly stop myself from smiling. This was my first sighting of the feared Tans, and from where I stood, the six or seven young lads in this squad did not seem old enough to sport the moustaches they were attempting to sprout. Nor did they look desperate or fierce enough to have gained the fearful reputation they had earned for themselves since their arrival in the county a few months before.

The soldiers were hardly off the troop ship in Dublin Harbour when they were promptly named Black and Tans. They were so called, some said, because of their khaki tunics and black trousers and tam-o'-shanter berets or caps. Others swore they were named Black and Tans after a pack of mad hunting dogs in Limerick or Kerry. As they were to prove in the two years they were in Ireland, these Black and Tans had more in common with those mad-dog animals than they had with decent human men.

"Oi! You there, Paddy. We need some wahaa here." The

sergeant spoke in a clipped voice and in a strange accent, sharp and unmusical and harsh-sounding to my ears. Obviously Robin could not understand the soldier's words either and remained where he stood by the yard gate.

"Oi! Paddy! You deaf or whaa? I said to fetch us some wahaa! We need it for this blasted truck."

The sergeant pointed to the lorry, which was now belching and hissing white smoke from the front engine, as the driver raised the bonnet and stood back to survey the machine.

"Water! They only need water." I found the soldier's accent almost indecipherable. I breathed a sigh of relief and moved slowly towards the door and the safety of the house.

Robin made no reply but proceeded to fill a bucket with water from the water barrel by the house gable and carry it to the group of men standing by the lorry.

As the driver poured the water into the steaming engine, I saw the sergeant mutter something to one of the soldiers, a pasty-faced lad of no more than eighteen, who instantly put out his cigarette under his boot, cradled his rifle and walked up the yard towards me.

"'Ose in the 'ouse?" the soldier asked as he approached the door. He raised the butt of his rifle and with it pushed open the door. "'Iding any Paddy rebel bastards in 'ere, are we?" I remained silent.

"Are you fackin' deaf or whaa?" he snapped loudly and turned his rifle towards me. "'Oo else is in this 'ouse?"

"Nobody within but my brother." With the rifle tip not an inch from my breast, I felt a wave of fear wash over me. "He's in his bed. . . unwell."

"In 'is bed, eh?" The lad sneered and moved to within inches of my face. "Unwell. . . wot with?"

I looked him straight in the eye; I could smell liquor on his breath.

"Consumption," I said, quietly. "My brother is in his bed with consumption."

His face paled, a look of terror came into his eyes and he stepped back from the door.

"Fackin' Paddies," I heard him mutter as he turned on his heel. As he walked back towards his companions standing by the lorry, he kicked out in anger at a bucket of fresh milk cooling by the side of the house. The bucket clattered and rolled away on the stones as the contents spilled out on the grass and gravel.

"Shit!" he roared. In that moment, the other soldiers came to full alert and brought their rifles to their shoulders.

"Thompson!" the sergeant shouted. Everybody froze.

At that moment, our old faithful dog Charlie, who had been with Robin, rushed toward the soldier and, snapping at his heel, attempted to sink his teeth into a leather gaiter. The soldier kicked out at Charlie, who growled and rushed and made a second grab at the man's heel. In a wink of an eye, the Tan brought his rifle to his shoulder, aimed and pulled the trigger.

Kraack! The loud report from the rifle made me fairly jump out of my skin. I had never heard such a sound up close before, and it caused my ears to hum and buzz as the shot echoed around the yard. A second later it echoed back at us from the hills, accompanied by the screaming and loud cawing of a thousand rooks, crows and starlings, who had risen in panic from their nesting places in the trees about the house.

In shock, I looked down to see poor Charlie lying still on the ground, a dark stream of blood flowing from his head to form a pool in the gravel. At this awful sight, I called out "Charlie!" and made a move to rush to his side to pick him up in my arms.

"No, Mariah. Don't move!" Robin whispered to me in Irish and placed a firm hand of restraint on my shoulder. "These bastards are drunk. They'd as soon shoot you as the dog." His voice

228

signalled the grave danger that surrounded us all at that moment.

"Thompson, what are you doing, man? Make safe your weapon. All of you! Put up your weapons," the sergeant snapped at the men. "Shooting a miserable dog! Christ almighty, this is not what we are here to do."

"No," one of the smirking Tans sniggered in the background. "We're only 'ere to shoot Paddies, ain't we?"

At this his companions laughed and lowered their rifles.

For a long while nobody moved and nobody spoke.

At last, the sergeant gave a curt command, and with that the men slung their rifles over their shoulders and climbed up onto the back of the lorry. The driver slammed down the engine bonnet, climbed aboard, started the engine, and the lorry moved out on the road and headed away towards Kilfenora.

I was very shaken and greatly upset as Robin herded me inside the house before going to Brian's bedside to explain to him what all the commotion was about.

"Stay indoors, Mariah. I'll take care of poor Charlie." Robin went outside to take Charlie's body away and lay him in the barn.

"How could they do such a thing? To shoot a poor dog. The cruelty of it," Brian said.

I was still much disturbed that old Charlie had been killed in such a way, and the echo of that terrible gunshot still ran around inside my head. Robin and Brian, too, were deeply upset at the loss of our fine and faithful dog. At that time, Charlie had been with us for a decade or more, and we loved that old dog as one of our own and part of the family.

"These Tans are paid killers and assassins. Do you think they care a jot for man or beast? These men would shoot you dead as soon as look at you. May they rot in the fiery pits of hell!"

Robin spat into the fire and crossed himself. We spent an unhappy, uneasy night, and before sleep came, I prayed that I would never again lay my eyes on a cursed Black and Tan soldier. Early the following morning, before I arose, Robin had carried poor Charlie's remains from the barn and, as I had requested of him, buried the unfortunate animal close to the lightning tree in the upper meadow field. When he returned, he promised that as soon as possible, he would find a good sheepdog pup to replace our loss.

If the shooting of the odd dog were the only crime that might be levelled at the Tans as they patrolled the countryside, it would not be too cruel a story to tell. But the callous brutality and barbarity of their actions in every village and in every town, townland and parish left a wound that has not healed to this very day.

You can read the terrible litany of the bloody doings of those murderous Tans in the history books. As for me, I can recall from memory the crimes that touched us here in this place; or those we knew locally or in the three parishes during those troubled days of 1920 and '21.

In Miltown, three men were shot dead by a drunken Tan patrol while attending a bonfire celebration in the town square following the release of one of their rebel comrades from jail. As they drove through the village of Kiltartan, near Gort, they shot dead a young mother – Ellen Quinn was her name – whose only crime was that she was sitting on a wall outside her cottage while holding her baby in her arms.

The Tans later said they saw a weapon, and not a baby, cradled in the girl's arms. Nobody paid a price or was punished for this heinous crime.

A few weeks after the shooting of Charlie here at the house, they went on the rampage about the county – "putting down the general uprising" was their stated excuse. If that was the case, every man, woman and child who came in their sights was a rebel or suspect rebel and so deemed a legitimate target.

They shot and wounded Seán McMahon as he saved hay in his meadow. Around that time, they shot Albert O'Brien as he cycled along the road going about his daily business. They left him bleeding to death on the roadside as they drove away laughing at the sport they had just enjoyed. Albert was no more than an innocent lad and had never taken up a weapon nor conducted an unlawful deed in his life.

A poor hunchbacked boy was shot dead in east Clare as they ransacked his home in search for rebels who had long departed the area. They murdered that innocent lad out of sheer frustration, rage and badness.

Not a day passed without more and more stories of shootings and killings and the wanton destruction of property and all manner of violent assaults on home and hearth carried out by these unruly, drunken Tans.

Was it any wonder, Robin mused, that each and every day more and more men and women flocked to join the Volunteers to fight these barbarians and drive them forever from our lands?

CHAPTER TWENTY-EIGHT

"UNDERTAKING! THAT'S THE only business to be at if you want to make a shilling profit these days."

So Tommy Reilly used to say when talking about life and living in this country between the years of 1916 and '25. Tommy spoke these words in jest, but we knew there was a truth in them, too.

The undertaker was indeed a busy man in those years; the murderous Black and Tan soldiers saw to that. When they left, we saw to it that we ourselves supplied many customers to the busy undertaker. There was no day but we either attended a funeral or heard of a tragic death in the locality. To die of old age or natural causes was the exception, especially during those five cruel years of terror and killing between 1920 and the end of the Civil War in '25.

There were so many poor fellows that lost their lives on both sides. RIC constables were killed while patrolling country roads, on the streets of Ennis or in their barracks. Some were shot to death while off duty at home with their families. Rebel Volunteers were shot while attacking those barracks or unarmed in their beds by the Tans on reprisal raids. During these raids, totally innocent men, women and children who happened to get in their sights often fell to their bullets. The ambushes and killings went on apace, and all through that summer of 1920 the blood of the flower of the land was spilled for "the cause". We thought then that things could not be any worse, but what followed the ambush of Rineen showed that war is a well without bottom.

It was late on a fine September autumn evening, and Robin had been fishing upstream in the Fergus River. He arrived breathless at the door, and called out.

"Mariah! Brian! Come out and look at this!"

We followed him on the grassy pathway to the higher ground at the back of the house and stood in the softening ledge between twilight and all darkness.

"Will ye just look at that!" Robin said, pointing at the sky to the south-west, now aglow with dancing, flickering colours leaping upwards to the red and pink clouds.

I had often seen some colourful sunsets, but never anything quite like this sight.

"What is it?" I asked. The darkening sky was a slow churning of colour with great arrows of crimson and green rising and falling, rising and falling.

"It's a blaze, and a big one at that," Brian said, bringing me back to the present. "Somewhere between here and the sea. Might be a stack of wheat or a hayshed maybe? God forbid it's some poor soul's house."

"There's more than one hayshed or house afire from the looks of that western sky," Robin said as we headed indoors. "Maybe a ship ablaze and sinking off Spanish Point?"

Robin was no doubt thinking of the great passenger liner, the *Lusitania*, sunk off the Head of Kinsale by a German submarine with terrible loss of life three years earlier, in 1915.

233

"Whatever it is, it is not in the control of man," Brian added. He was right.

The following morning we heard the terrible and terrifying news. The glowing western sky we had witnessed at dusk the night before was the town of Ennistymon and the village of Lahinch all ablaze.

"Attacked, sacked and burned to the ground!" – so the post-man related to us – by the Black and Tans in retribution for an ambush carried out by the rebels on one of their patrols at Rineen.

His information was patchy, but in the days that followed we were able to piece together the events of that night from people who lived or had relations living in or near by the villages.

In any event, the next published issue of the *Clare Champion* had the whole story in all is gory details.

It happened that on the night of 20 September 1920 a body of armed rebels lay in ambush for an RIC patrol at Rineen, on the coast road near Miltown Malbay. When the fighting was over, six RIC men lay dead on the road by their lorry and two of the rebels were wounded.

Two nights later, the Tans reaped a terrible vengeance and went on a rampage of killing, plundering and burning. Farm-houses and small cottages were burned to the ground in Rineen and shops burned in Miltown and Lahinch.

But it was Ennistymon that had to suffer the brunt of their wrath and anger, for it was there – so they suspected – that the rebel ambushers were living or being given sanctuary by the townspeople.

As the sun set behind the Cliffs of Moher, the Tans came rolling into the town in their Crossley lorries and commenced their deadly work. They burned out the homes and shops of the Stacks, Davitts and the Madigans, leaving them homeless on the streets. They dragged Tom Connell from his house, for they

234

believed him to be one of the ambushers, and threw him back into his burning home in full view of his wife and children. They then managed to lay hands on Patrick Linnane, who had been at Rineen, and he suffered the same awful fate. They stormed and wrecked Tom Shalloo's pub, while Tom, a Volunteer commandant who the Tans suspected of being among the ambushers at Rineen, along with a comrade-in-arms, Cyril Hynes, managed by the skin of his teeth to flee the enemy through a skylight window. They both made good their escape across the rooftops and then up a back lane to the graveyard perched high on the hill behind the village, where they hid out among the headstones till the soldiers departed the town.

The Tans then set the Town Hall on fire, and Joe Salmon, a visitor to the town, was shot dead while he gave aid to an old woman they had clubbed to the ground with the butts of their rifles. It was indeed a brave or foolhardy man or woman who would have ventured out on to the streets as the Tans rampaged through the town on that night.

Leaving the town in flames behind them, they then turned their attentions on Lahinch by the sea, where they commenced to burn seven or eight houses and lay waste all about them.

Later on that same night, leaving a trail of blood, death and destruction behind them, they turned their wrath on simple farm cottages near the burning towns. They even destroyed the very crops in the fields and in the barns: wheat, oats, barley, potatoes and so forth.

Those poor people! Think of what they had to face when the sun arose the following morning, and the hardships they had to endure in the weeks and months that followed. How we pitied them and how maddened we were on learning the full facts. Whatever had gone before, this was an act of outright war. We realised that, from that day on, as far as the Black and Tans were concerned, there would be no quarter given or expected.

The burnings and killings that night had the effect of winning new recruits for the Volunteers, and Robin, without us knowing of his actions, had that very day gone to the village and joined the Volunteer brigade there. Brian, too, would have volunteered but for his failing health.

With all the troubles visited on the people all about, we now had our own troubles under our very roof.

Of all the diseases to plague the people, none was feared more than consumption, which claimed so many people all about. When consumption crossed over the threshold in those days, the angel of death usually followed close behind to lay his icy hand on one, or many, in that household.

That same black angel visited Uncle Patrick's house in 1919. In the passing of but a single year, he lost four strapping sons, a daughter and his wife Brigid to consumption. Six people from one household, laid out in their grave shrouds, leaving six empty chairs at the table. Six wakes and six coffins carried from one house between one Christmas Day and the next!

Even as they sickened and died one by one, Uncle Patrick called for Brian and me to come to their bedsides, but we had not the power in us to save a single one. Our hearts were sore and near to breaking, but what could we do against this scourge of God for which there was no cure?

It tore the very hearts from Uncle Patrick's family, and from our family as well, as we were close blood.

The boys were still a-growing – all in their twenties – and the young girl, Delia, coming on her prime with a mind to be married.

That terrible year of 1919 came to be known in the family as the year of the coffins. Only Uncle Patrick, along with his remaining youngest son Pat Joe, just turned seventeen, and Anna, the youngest, escaped the touch of the angel's hand and so was spared this terrible plague that stalked and ravaged the land.

Our hearts near broke to realise that, with all our powers of healing, we were powerless to save their lives. They say that the good Lord does not send us trials and sufferings that we cannot endure. But to watch each of six people from one family in turn fade and die was more than a human person should bear. When I think of that time, the keen blade of grief turns again in my deep heart.

Yes, there were healing powers and cures that we did possess and which we would put to good use many a time, but we possessed none to ward off consumption. Only God had that power, and He had deserted our family in the terrible year of the coffins. It was whispered by many in that year, that this disease was a curse visited on the family because of the cure we possessed. If we had believed then that this was the true cause, we would never again have lifted a finger to help or heal.

Before a single member of the family had taken ill, Pat Joe, being the youngest boy, had his mind set on leaving soon for the Americas.

A few days after the last of those six coffins was carried out of the house and was laid in the grave, Father Murphy, came to the house. He begged the lad not to go. He begged him to consider his leaving and not to leave the land. He begged him to stay and not abandon his grieving, heartbroken father and be a support to him and his young sister in their time of greatest suffering and their greatest need. Young Pat Joe had no choice but to stay and be the man of the house and to support those that God had spared. He knew it was the right and proper thing to do given the circumstances.

After Joe, the last of the brothers to die in that terrible year, was buried, they lived then each day in mortal fear for their own lives. A simple cough or a sneeze or a headache could be the signal that might mean the oncoming of that terrible sickness, and that another grave awaited one of them.

So, one frosty winter morning, soon after Joe's funeral, we all gathered at Uncle Patrick's house, as we would for a harvest *meitheal*. Our purpose there that day was to strip the house of anything that might carry the consumption plague, take it outside and burn it all in a fire: window curtains, bedclothes and pillow-covers, quilts and sheets, cushions and drapes, old clothes, papers, books. Everything! Even the timber from the parlour floor and the bedroom wallpaper was stripped from the walls and taken outside the house to be consumed in the purging flame.

It broke all our hearts to witness books, letters, pictures and picture frames being burned. Only the family Bible was saved from the flames. Job himself had not been visited by such suffering or tested so hard.

It was a pitiful and forlorn house we left that evening to return to our own home.

I remember Pat Joe as a youngster before that terrible time. He was a young rascal: always laughing and smiling. He would come to this house and play his tricks on us.

Brian and Robin and I enjoyed and looked forward to his visits. There were so few young children who lived close by, and to see the play of a child and hear a child's laughter was a rare and beautiful thing, like listening to the song of the lark or the first cuckoo of spring.

After the terrible year of the coffins, he rarely visited our house as his work kept him busy from dawn till dusk. I saw him grow to manhood, yet I don't remember ever again seeing him laugh or smile or make merry as he had as a lad. I never saw my Uncle Patrick outside the house ever again either. It was as if a shadow as black as coal dust had settled over their household and remained as a shadow on their lives from then on.

Old Uncle Patrick lived with his grief and pain for another twenty years, but young Pat Joe and Anna survived, and given the weight of troubles that had visited their poor home, they grew and prospered well enough.

I prayed nightly for Uncle Patrick and his family, but I also prayed for my own family. As time passed, a change had come over Brian. I could see it and so could Robin. The years of isolation and persecution – for that is what it was – had taken their toll. Where once there was a tall, straight-backed, youthful-looking figure, now before us stood a thin, slightly bowed, grey-haired man, aged beyond his years. Gone was the youthful spring to his step, the quick laughter and easy, positive way he faced his every trial or tribulation. Gone was a certain light from his eye, and where once he was outgoing and sociable, now he was often withdrawn and given to being alone with his thoughts, reading and – more and more – removing himself from social contact with all about him.

Sometimes, in the quiet of evening, I would catch his eye to see there some cold glint of loss – or perhaps it was a grief? A knowing of some deep unspoken truth, a haunted, lonesome look which now flickered and lingered there.

Robin – who shared the attic bedroom with Brian – whispered to me one morning that Brian's sleep was often bothered by dreams and he sometimes cried out and waved away some unseen spirit or ghost that troubled him nightly.

I once attempted to get him to talk to me about what it was that ailed his spirit; to unburden himself of whatever weight he now carried.

"Who heals the Healer?" Brian just shook his head and of his pain he would not speak more.

With a growing, gnawing pain in my gut and an ache in my heart, I saw the passing weeks bring about a physical change to my beloved brother. I watched as he pushed his food from him when he sat down to eat. I took notice of his sickly pallor and his increasing bouts of breathlessness. Most of all, I was gripped by the icy fingers of fear when, in the dead of night as I lay in my bed, I could hear Brian's body-wracking cough pierce the silence of the night. I knew Robin was as pained and bothered as I to see Brian suffer so.

As Brian's sickness progressed, I felt both frustrated and powerless in the knowledge that not one of our cures or charms, healing potions or incantations could fight this most feared intruder. Other than commenting on the "severe cold that was going around", Robin and I tried to make light of his weakening condition. Neither did we talk of it or speak its name out loud, fearing that to do so would make it real. We knew, however, that it was now just a matter of time.

As the days turned into months, I watched the disease take hold of Brian, and both Robin and I watched over him and nursed him as best we could.

When all seemed black and hopeless, I would go and sit beneath the lightning tree to share my deepest fears and say the words I could not say to a living soul.

"Dear God," I prayed, as fervently as I ever prayed before, "don't let it be this. Don't let it be like this!"

CHAPTER TWENTY-NINE

W E LAID BRIAN – then in the sixty-third year of his life – in our family grave by the south-facing churchyard wall on a sultry, overcast day in August of 1922. Robin and I stood dry-eyed as we watched our beloved brother being lowered down into the black earth to join his ancestors in their eternal rest. Whatever tears I had left to cry had been shed in the long days and the bleak, lonesome nights that had led to this day.

I will not speak now of Brian's brave struggle with the consumption during those days. But I tell you truly, there were times when I would have gladly taken on his burden rather than have to stand so helplessly by and watch the life-force being sucked out of his failing body and watch the spirit light dim in his eyes.

His suffering ended when he slipped away from us on the evening of August twelfth. I well remember that day and date, as the great Irish hero Arthur Griffith died in Dublin on that very day. Twelve days later – on the twenty-second – General Michael Collins, who had visited Ennis the day after Brian was buried, was ambushed and shot to death by the republicans at an ambush at Béal na Bláth in County Cork.

Robin made the comment later that he was glad that Brian had passed before news of Collins' death reached us. Brian greatly admired the man and saw him to be "a true Irish hero and as great a patriot and leader as was Parnell!" He would have been sorely grieved at the news of Collins' brutal and senseless killing in this awful Civil War that now raged through the land.

Brian was well waked with keening and whiskey, stories and song, tears and laughter, tobacco and snuff, and Jack Fogerty, Frank Neylon, Tom Collins and Robin shouldered his coffin every step of the road from house to church and from church to graveyard.

When Father Murphy spoke from the altar of Brian's life and the great loss to his friends and neighbours, he made no mention of Brian's "troubles" with the church all those years before. It mattered not, as now all Brian's troubles were behind him.

A hushed silence fell over the crowded graveyard, the mourners pressing ever closer as the four men lowered his coffin gently down into the cold grave. Still there was a silence as the men commenced to shovel in the black earth mixed with the bleached bones of those who had gone before him on his cold bed of rest. Robin stood all the while at my side, and as I felt his trembling hand squeeze hard on my shoulder, I shivered in the full heat of that August day.

As the final shovel of earth fell soft on the grave, a single skylark began to sing his piping song high above our heads, and for a long while we stood nigh the grave, hardly daring to breathe, as this free spirit sang a final song of farewell to our brother Brian.

They said later it was one of the biggest funerals ever seen in the three parishes. Brian was well liked and respected by all who knew him, and his fame as a healer caused those he had cured to travel from great distances to be with us in our grief and be with him on his final journey. There were many who commented how many more mourners there would have been in attendance that day had the railway tracks on both sides of Corofin not been blown up by the republicans.

When at last we moved away from the graveside, Robin – along with many neighbours and the gravediggers – repaired to a pub in the village to wash the dust of the grave from his hands and sup a well-earned mug of porter. I walked home alone. The afternoon was warm and humid, but the atmosphere within the house had the chill of winter about it and seemed to me as lonesome as the grave. I immediately set about making myself a hot brandy punch and decided that, rather than let my grief overcome me, I would set myself to writing a long letter to our brother Frank in Australia to break to him the sad news of our loss.

I soon had to abandon my writing, for even as I penned the opening lines to say that his beloved brother Brian now lay in his grave, my tears fell to mingle with the ink, and I sat for a long time, staring through a gauze of white mist at the wet, smudged paper on the table before me. In my mind's eye, I tried to see my distant brother's features and imagine what he would look like if he were to walk in the door that instant.

Try as I might, Frank's face would not come to me. I could only dimly see that youthful tear-streaked face reach down to kiss me goodbye before getting aboard the pony and trap with his young wife Margaret to begin the long sea-journey that would take them to Australia and a better life.

That was more than fifty years before, and Frank and Margaret now had family of their own. In the early years we heard from him often, but since Mary Ellen's death he seemed to lose the will and urge to write, leaving that duty to his daughters Margaret or Theresa, who usually wrote at Christmas and Easter with all their news. In those last months of Brian's illness, I have to admit that I too had neither the energy nor the inclination to write to Frank and his family of our bleak news from home and of the Troubles that still beset our land.

"If you can't write good news," I can hear Mother say still, "then write no news at all!"

When at last I finally composed myself, I sat down at the kitchen table to complete this long-overdue missive, and in the writing of it, some of the lonesomeness, heartbreak and dreary gloom that so pressed on my spirit lifted somewhat as I related the events over the previous days, weeks and months that had led to this sad day.

Brian, I believe, knew from the outset of his illness two years earlier that there could only be one outcome, and so he prepared as best he could for that inevitability. The previous September, Robin and I had managed to persuade him to take two weeks at Lisdoonvarna to take the healing spa waters.

"It will make a new man of you," Robin said.

As he mounted the trap that was to transport him the twelve miles to the Spa Hotel – a comfortable enough hostelry where he was to stay – he said with a weak smile, "Maybe I'll get myself a wife there!"

There was a long tradition in the spa town of matchmaking during the month of September, and many a bachelor or spinster came home with the promise of a wife or a husband.

Mishearing his words, I answered, "Of course you will get your life there. You'll outlive us all."

"You hear me wrong, Mariah. I said I might get myself a *wife* while I was there." He gave me a look that broke my heart. "I doubt if there will be as much 'life' granted me as will get me to this time next year."

I was embarrassed then that I had misheard his comment, and it lingered on to nag at me till his return some weeks later. As he stepped down from the trap and we greeted his return, he turned to me and said, "Well, Mariah, I don't know about getting a *life* at the Spa, but I can tell you I didn't get a wife either."

As autumn slipped into early winter, it did seem as if there was an improvement in Brian's general health, but when the chill and wet and damp of January came, he weakened. Though we prayed that it might be different, we all knew in our hearts that it was but a matter of time till he left us. I stayed close by his sickbed and nursed him night and day especially during his final months. Robin, too, had it hard, for now he had to do the work of two men as he ploughed and sowed, cut turf in the bog and worked every hour God gave in the meadows and gardens to put food on our table. I don't know how he would have managed without the help and generosity of our good neighbours, especially at bringing home the harvest, when there was always a *meitheal* in attendance to share the labour.

Brian called me to his bedside one day in early summer. He was now greatly weakened, and his coughing – that still cut into my very soul – continued to rack his frail body.

"Mariah," he said, his voice weak and feeble-sounding, "I want you to help me do something I've been meaning to do this long time. I want you to write down all my cures. I want you to copy down, exactly as I tell you, the listings of ingredients and recipes for all my potions and pastes and healing bottles. You and Robin will have them, and you will make good use of them when there is a call for them. I don't want my cures to go to the grave with me as some of Michael's went with him to his grave."

We had often spoken of what old knowledge was lost when Michael died; for other than what he passed on orally, he never wrote down a single one of his hundreds of cures.

So it was I sat by Brian's bedside for most of those warm June afternoons with my paper, pen and ink, and wrote down, page after page, the many cures he had in his possession, as he dictated them to me. When he had finally exhausted his memory, I gathered the pages, tied them with a ribbon and placed them within the pages of the family Bible for safekeeping.

All this I related to Frank in my long letter to him and finished with the hope that he would say a prayer for our dead brother and for those of us that survived him to live out our days as God pleased.

That evening, as the sun slanted towards its setting in the west, I walked out the fields to my usual spot by the lightning tree, and for a long time I sat quietly by its withered bark. How peaceful it was to sit here by my old hiding place. How calm and serene it was to be close to this withered bark that had borne the weight of my troubles and tears down all the years.

Birds wheeled and soared high in the air, and the light all about was soft and peach coloured. I looked toward the graveyard not a hundred paces from where I sat under the lightning tree and listened as a gentle breeze stirred the nearby plum trees with a murmuring voice.

"Don't be sad, Mariah," the voice seemed to whisper. "I'm at peace. I'm at peace."

Suddenly, I felt a great, black cloud, the heavy weight of grief, lift from my shoulders, and for a brief, fleeting moment, I fancied I caught a glimpse of Brian's face – youthful and smiling and happy, without care or pain – in a shaft of dancing evening light.

My heart now lightened, I arose and walked the short distance back to the house. The setting sun had dipped below Clifden hill and the afterglow cast long shadows all about me. As I passed the orchard, I stopped for a moment to breathe in the perfume of the dappled twilight all about me. I turned towards the graveyard to bid a sweet goodnight to my sleeping brother.

A lone swift flew and swooped with heartbeat speed close to my head to disappear high into the twilight glimmer. From a nearby laden apple tree, a single apple fell unseen, but I heard it touch the earth as soft as the kiss of a petal's fall on a fresh grave.

CHAPTER THIRTY

A ND SO THE years passed and people continued to come to our door to ask that I – or Robin – attend to their various ills, and we never refused a single soul the comfort of the gift of our cures.

Some came with other motives on their minds.

"Who will heal our ills and maladies when you're gone, Mariah?" Anastasia Carty – a bitter old woman reputed to have a cure for warts – said to me one day, with more than a hint of sarcasm in her voice.

The same woman had turned her face from our family when Brian was going through his purgatory following his excommunication. Now, although I had not laid eyes on her for several years, here she was, sitting in my kitchen and acting as if I owed her some debt of loyalty.

"Would you ever think of passing on your secret cures? If you do, I would be glad to take them for you. I'm sure you know that I, too, have a gift of healing. You won't forget me, will you?"

I could hardly believe my ears. Here was this woman, as brazen as could be, asking me to hand over to her my – and my

247

forefathers' – store of healing lore as if it was an old worn jacket or a piece of cheap jewellery.

I looked her straight in the eye.

"Well, Statia," said I, "what knowledge I have to give cannot be passed or handed on as would a simple story, song or rhyme. It has to be understood, and it has to be earned. I also intend to take my cures, along with my memories, with me into the grave when I finally decide to go. In any case, I intend to outlive you and everybody else in the three parishes!"

That put a halt to her gallop, let me tell you! It was then I began to give serious thought to what exactly I should do with the sheaf of pages containing the knowledge that Anastasia Carty – and God knows who else – was so keen to get her hands on.

In the years after Brian's death, I had begun to write down – just as I had done for Brian in his final days – all the cures and herbal pastes and potion recipes I had in my head. I was amazed to see that my scribblings over the years added up to a thick parcel of single, yellowed, handwritten pages and old school copybooks.

I was not getting any younger and I knew I had to make a decision as to what to do with this collection. So a few years ago, I decided to give the entire bundle of knowledge to Pat Joe, my neighbour and blood relative. Pat Joe, the only male survivor of cousin Michael's family. I well remember him as a small lad running about my feet on this very floor, and he was now a grown man with wife and children of his own whose own fame as a powerful healer of animals had spread far beyond the three parishes. So it was to him – and only him – that I wanted to make a gift of those fading pages.

He visited one evening and we talked long into the night – with glasses of hot brandy punch in our hands. I told him of my wish that he, my only living relative in this country, take into his keep those cures that had been given me in my time.

I could see he was both glad and honoured – so he said – to be offered this gift, but his fear that it would draw the wrath of the clergy on him should he make use of this knowledge left him no option but to refuse my offer.

"As you know, Mariah, my family has the cure for animals, and the clergy never give us bother on that score for they say that animals have no souls. If I was to take on your knowledge, we might draw the Church down on us and have to suffer some of the troubles your own family had to endure."

I was sad that he should refuse my offer, though I had to admit to myself I could well understand his reasoning. Leaving me that night, he did, however, take with him a selection of old recipes for all kinds of stews, puddings, custards and cakes that I had written into a notebook back in 1927.

"I know Sadie will make use of these."

I knew Sadie, his wife, to be a fine cook, and when she visited me a few weeks later with one of her fresh-baked porter cakes, she told me how glad she was to receive those old recipes.

Later that night, I determined on a course of action. Rather than let my old cures fall into hands that did not deserve to receive them after I had passed on, I decided I would place the entire collection of pages – lying safe in my sea-chest – beyond human eye or hand.

My plan was a simple one. I would place both my and Brian's pages in an old leather satchel and bury them in a secret place. I knew exactly where I would find such a place.

As the sun set that same evening, I took a small shovel from the barn and went to the lightning tree. Ensuring that there was no person in sight to witness my activities, I scooped out a deep hole at the centre of its rotted body and in it carefully placed my satchel full of secrets, and covered it with a thick layer of earth from around the base of the tree.

With the moon rising in the eastern sky, I turned my back and walked away from the lighting tree. The world had turned and changed in its turning. I had played my part and now it was almost over.

In a strange way, I felt as if a great weight had been lifted from my shoulders. I felt as light-headed, free and at peace with myself and with the world as I had in many a day.

Robin died in the spring of 1950. He had been ailing for many years and passed away one night in his sleep. As he wished it, he was laid out in his coffin and buried in his black coat, red waistcoat and with his silver watch and chain. I miss both my brothers: Brian for his good humours, lively conversation and his energy; Robin for his wise old head and listening ear and his gentle, quiet, thoughtful ways.

It has been a hard and lonesome time for me since his passing, for now apart from Bruno, my old dog, I am alone in a house full of ghosts. If it wasn't for my good neighbours and friends, I think I would have soon followed him to the grave. But I remain. I live on, and though I feel the long shadows daily growing, I am not afraid to peer into the heart of the darkness.

Since Brian died in '22, the years since have flown by on swift's wings. I wish he had lived to see Ireland free, though his heart would have been broken – as mine was – to witness the Civil War and the hatred, suffering and death that followed independence and the signing of the Treaty.

When the next Great War broke out in '39, I turned my face from the ways of the world and the madness of men. 'The Emergency' they called it here, those that governed us pretending it had nothing to do with us, that it was not our fight and none of our doing. But there were many from here and from all over Ireland who saw and feared the Fascist evil that was loosed on the world, and took up arms against it.

How quickly did all those years fly by!

Though now that I think on it, I have seen such marvels in my lifetime. Marvels that would have been seen as magic, or miracles, by those that went before me. I have seen the coming of the train and the great western railways. I travelled on it one Garland Sunday to Lahinch to take the air and see the great Atlantical Ocean. We truly thought there could be no greater invention or advance of man's ingenuity. I have seen the coming of the motorcar and the aeroplane and have travelled on one but not the other.

I have seen the coming of the telephone. Biddy Joyce, the postmistress, had such a speaking machine installed in her post office back in the '40s, but I have not had the opportunity – nor the inclination – to speak or listen into such a contraption.

I have never seen those pictures that move like ghosts across white screens that are to be seen in the towns and cities all over the country.

Neither have I ever heard the sounds that swim in on unseen waves of air to the radio and, at the turn of a switch – so they tell me – voices and music can be heard as if they are with you in the room.

So many wondrous things in one lifetime.

How marvellous! How extraordinary! How miraculous!

CHAPTER THIRTY-ONE

I HAD A visit yesterday from a man in a suit. He caught me snoozing in my chair. I do that a lot these days. It was late afternoon, and I had supped from a glass of brandy punch and had nodded off in the comfort of my armchair. I heard a sharp rap on the door followed by a cough, and I awoke to see a figure standing in the shadows of the open doorway. Right away, I came fully awake. In my experience, any time an official-looking stranger in a smart suit ever called to my door, it usually meant trouble or news I did not wish to receive.

"Who have we here?" I asked.

"My name is Mr Canny. . . Tom Canny," was his answer. "I'm an engineer from the offices of the County Council."

"Come in," I said. "For a second there I took you to be the undertaker."

He stepped forward into the room, came toward me and offered me a hand in greeting. I saw before me a tall bespectacled gentleman in a heavy black overcoat and carrying a small brown briefcase. After introducing himself and conversing about the weather and the poor crops this summer, he opened his brown case and removed some papers from it.

"Miss Mariah," says he, all official-like, adjusting his spectacles on his nose, "you'll be seeing some activity all about here over the next few weeks. A gang of our Council workmen with machines – that sort of thing – will be at work on the roads and surrounds out at your crossroads. Considering you live in such close proximity to this necessary work, I just wanted to inform you of these plans. It's the Council's hope that you won't be too inconvenienced or disturbed."

"And why should I be disturbed?" I politely asked him.

"The plan is the clearance of that site out on the roadside there to prepare for further improvements: widening and tarring, that sort of thing. Improvements long overdue. That humpback bridge on the road below, for example – that will be removed. As will that bad bend on the road by the graveyard. Oh yes, and that old tree out at the crossroads? That's in the way and will also have to be removed. All part of the Council's plan for general road improvements." "Improvements!" He used that word a lot in his speech to me.

"You're cutting down that grand old tree?" He could see the look of shock register on my face. "How in heaven's name can the cutting down of that noble tree be regarded as a road 'improvement'? What harm is it doing to anybody where it stands?"

He had no answers, except to repeat that the tree – and the old stone-cut bridge and the road bend – had to be removed in the interests of "improvement" and "progress".

"This is 1953," says he, as if reading from a prepared speech. "Ireland – and the county – is moving with the times, and very soon we expect a great increase of business, which will lead to an increase of traffic on these roads, especially motorised vehicles transporting all manner of goods from place to place. There are major plans afoot to improve all roads in every corner of the county, especially following the advance of the Rural

253

Electrification Scheme and the coming of electrical power to the Burren. Imagine it. Light and heat and power in every house at the flick of a switch! That's what I call progress. You will be getting in the power, I take it?" asks he, a big smile on his face.

"Indeed, I most certainly will not!" My bile was up now and I let him know it. "I and all who came before me survived right well with the power of the open fire, the power of the oil lamp and power of the penny candle. And when we didn't have any of those, we survived on the inner power and light of our great faith and our imaginations. There will be no new-fangled electrical power running about or through this house – not while I live here."

At that, the smile faded, and I could see his face take on a hard, imperious look.

"Well, be that as it may. But it's my duty to inform you today that work on road improvement – road widening and tarring and the removal of the old humpback bridge and that tree out there will commence at eight o'clock sharp on Monday morning next. I bid a good day to you, ma'am."

And turning on his heel, he was gone from my floor like a scalded cat.

For the rest of the morning I sat and though of naught else but the words spoken by this unwanted messenger. Progress and improvement indeed!

It was true that the world was changing. The papers were full of it, also the letters from our friends and relatives at the other side of the world, and I heard it from the lips of politicians asking us for our votes.

Times are changing and people are on the move and changing with them, so they tell me. There is no day passes now but I see or hear the sound of an aeroplane high in the sky overhead and the sound of a motorcar or two pass by out there on the road.

I have a notion in my head that all this coarse noise is driving the singing birds from the skies and shy animals to their dens. Motorcars are taking over. The day of the horse and cart, the side car and the trap are over. Even the old horse-drawn funeral coach is being replaced by a long, black motorised hearse vehicle. Where's the style, the grace – or the dignity! – in that, I ask you? I for one have no wish to be transported to my final resting place in one of those machines. If a proper funeral coach, drawn by two plumed black horses, can't be had, let four good men shoulder me from church to graveside. That is all I ask.

So I think of that old chestnut tree standing out there, and I can hardly bear to think of it being cut down. I cannot imagine it no longer being there when I look out my gable window in winter to view its leafless branches; or in spring and summer when I walk out to the crossroads to linger awhile, as I have done all my life, beneath its leafy shade.

As with my lightning tree, over the years, this old chestnut tree has practically become part of my life, as friendly and familiar as a family friend. Nothing now remains of the lightning tree but a wizened old stump – a bit like myself – but that old chestnut out there at the crossroads is still alive and strong and in the full of its health.

For as far back as I can remember, the chestnut tree has stood at this place, spreading its great boughs over the meeting of the roads. What a life it has had. What events it has witnessed! As youngsters we would play and cavort about its base and clamber high to hide or just to sit amid its branches. Father often said that the tree was already fully grown when he was a boy, and there is nobody alive today who can remember a time when it was not there. I cannot bear to imagine it gone. It sorely grieves me to learn that very soon it will no longer stand as a sentry and guardian and shelter for us all. And now its days are numbered, as are my own. I am sad at the thought of its going.

I will not be the only one who will miss that tree.

It was here beneath these spreading boughs that old men would gather after Sunday mass to talk politics and about the ebb and flow of their lives and labours on the land. It was here, on Sunday afternoons, countless carefree lads and lassies from the three parishes gathered to play the game of pitch-and-toss, to talk and argue about football and hurling and to tell old stories and tall tales. It was here on spring and summer evenings some would spark and court and play the games of innocent youth beneath its flowery shade.

It was here, too, that on dark nights of the Troubles, many brave men gathered to whisper of their schemes and dreams of rebellion and of freedom.

So, too, beneath this tree were promises made and pledges broken, bonds of friendship forged, happy greetings and sad farewells enacted.

It was from beneath this tree that Mother and I waved our final goodbyes to my brother Frank as he set off with his newly wed wife, Margaret, in the back of the cart pulled by Paudie and driven by my father to take him to the boat coach in Ennis to commence his long journey to Australia. I was but five or six then, and I watched as our heartbroken mother flung herself on the tree and howled with grief at the sight of her first-born heading off down the road, and she never to lay eyes on him again. It was our last sight of him and his last view of his birthplace and the woman who bore him into this world.

In one of his letters to her, he recalled how even in far Australia he kept alive that memory of looking back through the veil of his own tears and seeing Mother and me standing under that old chestnut, waving goodbye forever. I have no memory of it, but his letters said that he still had a small branch of the tree that I had given to him as he departed, and he had kept it with him, all those years later in his new home in Melbourne, Australia.

It was here, more than eighty years ago, on a bitter January evening with troubled rain clouds tumbling in from the west, I came on a young woman, barely out of her teens and ragged and thin as a skeleton, huddled and trembling beneath the tree and cradling a small infant in her arms.

I could see that she was in some distress from the look in her haunted eyes, and the cries of her little babe pierced me like a knife. I was about ten years of age and well used to meeting poor travelling people, often hungry and destitute, on the roads, but I could see that this wretched woman and her baby were soon to cross over to join the pale people whose spirits walked these roads.

I came close to the couple and stood for a moment. She said not a word but looked at me with eyes that still haunt me to this day. I knew right away what I must do. I quickly ran inside the house and filled a mug of buttermilk and ran to her and offered it to her. With a bony, trembling hand reached from inside her tattered shawl, she took the milk and began to feed her baby. For a moment the crying was stilled and she spoke in gentle tones to her infant.

A cold rain began to fall and a wind unsettled the branches above us. An icy chill ran down my spine, for I could see a pale glow all around her, and I could see the mug shake in her shivering hands. I knew that unless she received some food, warmth and shelter, neither she nor her baby would survive this bitter night. Young as I was, I could not walk away from this pitiful sight.

"Come with me," I said to her. "You can stay in the barn for the night. It's warm and dry there, and I'll bring food and drink for you and your baby."

Without a word, she slowly arose, clutching her baby to her breast, and the desperate couple slowly followed me into the farmyard. I led her to the barn and showed her inside.

"You're an angel sent from God to us this night." She reached her hand towards me, and I reached to take it in mine. In that moment I felt my strength leave my body and rush out through my fingers to her fingers and into her body. She smiled as her cheeks lost some of their deathly pallor and a light flashed for a moment in her sunken, sad eyes.

"I must get you food and drink," I said at last and headed for the barn door. "Rest yourself here and I will be back by-and-by."

I quickly went inside the house to tell Mother and Father about our visitors and prepare food. In no time at all, Mary Ellen and I returned to the barn with a lantern, a bowl of chicken broth, a wedge of brown bread smeared with home-made butter, and a mug of porter and milk.

"This will bring back some strength to the poor woman's famished blood," Mary Ellen said. "There is great nourishment in milk and porter."

We watched in silence as she ate and drank as much as she was able of her simple meal.

Outside, the heavy rain fell on the barn roof.

Before I bid the poor wretch a goodnight and left the barn, the woman stood and pressed an object wrapped in a ragged piece of cloth into my hand. In the light of the lantern, I unwrapped the object and could see that it was a small, silver-tipped hammer.

"God give you grace and protection for all your life for your kindness to us this night. This is the only thing I have to give you as a parting gift. It was passed down to me from my grandfather. It has the power. Use it only for good and keep it near you always. The *leanbh* and myself have a long journey ahead of us. Remember us both and say a prayer for our souls, as I will for yours."

I arose as grey dawn broke and rushed out to see how they both fared through the long night. The sight I beheld then is with me yet. The poor woman and her helpless babe lay together in the hay and straw, white and stiff and cold. Together they had died sometime during the cold night.

Father went immediately to the neighbours for assistance, and while Mother dressed both the woman and her infant, I was sent to fetch a priest. Before the day was out, we had given them both as decent a burial as we could in an unmarked grave in a corner of the graveyard. I realised then that I had not learned the name of either mother or child.

"They will be known to their God," Mary Ellen said, a tear wet in her eye.

I could only pray that at last they had both reached a place of lasting peace and found the warmth and sanctuary this world could not give to two innocent souls.

Not a decade later, I stood again under that same tree as I bid my last goodbyes to my one true love, Alexander McNeil, before the cruel lake waters took him from me. We had spent the afternoon walking in the hazel groves on the hillside and, as the hour was late, it was time for him to return to his rooms at the Butlers big house. I walked with him to the crossroads and stood for a moment beneath the great tree.

We kissed and embraced, and I shyly withdrew from his arms and stood with my back to the cool tree trunk. I still see myself there, standing beneath the gently waving boughs, my hands pressed against the tree trunk, and watching him walk away and seeing him turn and smile and wave and me never knowing that it was a final goodbye and I would never see his face no more.

It was here, too, in this very place a few years later that I first heard Grace Furey, an old travelling woman, sing her lonesome song of love that flooded my eyes with tears of loss.

I was shelling peas in our kitchen garden one autumn evening when I heard the sound of singing floating in the clear air. The sky to the west was peach coloured, the darkening clouds to the east tinted salmon pink.

I stopped what I was doing to listen to her voice, and as I did I was filled with a great sadness. I walked out of the garden into the yard and out to the gate to come closer to the singer and the song.

From the gateway I saw the stooped figure of Grace – who I knew well from her many visits to the locality – wrapped in her black shawl, sheltering beneath the tree. Over an open fire she had built inside a small circle of stones, she stirred a small pot while singing her song of love and loss that was to fill my eyes with stinging tears and break my heart in two.

She finished her song, sung in the voice of a woman of all ages and in the tones and tongue of her people, and I roused myself from my trance and moved closer and greeted her.

"You're welcome back from your travels, Grace. What is the song that you sing?" I asked her.

"It is known among the travelling people as 'The Lament for Donal Óg – The Grief of a Girl's Heart'," she replied. "I learnt it from my mother, who got it from her mother." There was a far-away look in her eyes. "It is the greatest and saddest song of heart-break any woman who knows of men and of lost love can sing, God knows, but I have earned the singing of it."

Grace threw her grey-haired head back, and again her broken but beautiful voice rose up from within her soul to repeat a verse from the song that pierced deep into my heart.

Again my heart grew heavy inside my breast and tears welled to fill my eyes, for she was singing of my heart's core, of my grief, of my loss and of my sorrow. I knew she was singing the song of my life, and even though I felt as if I could not bear to hear her truth, my heart cried out to me to listen.

Her song stays with me and will to my dying day.

You have taken the east from me;
You have taken the west from me.
You have taken what is before me
And what is behind me.

You have taken the moon,
You have taken the sun from me
And my fear is great that
You have taken God from me.

And now comes this man in a suit from the town to tell me that this tree – which means no more to him and his fellow Council officials than some soulless, dead thing – is standing in the way of "progress". And to think the deed will be carried out by men who know well the history of this tree and who themselves sheltered under its leafy cover on many a happy day of their lives.

Shame on them, I say!

There is nothing I can do about this. If I were younger, I would climb high into the branches and remain there till they abandoned this crude and unnecessary course of action. But I will not stir abroad on that day.

I have heard this judgement, but I will not witness the execution; for that is what it is. I will not witness the death of the last of my living old friends.

But I will wake it as I would a dead relative. I will raise a glass to its passing and praise it for being staunch and faithful and true and for always being there: for me and the men and women of the three parishes.

If this old tree could speak, it would tell my story. If this tree could speak, it would tell us a truer, more honest history of this place than you will ever read in books.

CHAPTER THIRTY-TWO

"An rud a líonas an tsúil líonann sé an croí."
"What fills the eye, fills the heart."

S O WENT THE old saying, as I recall it now. But it was a tear that
filled my eye and an ache that filled my heart when I stepped
out my door a few days ago to view the desolate scene before
me out at the crossroads. The old chestnut tree, more than twice
as old as my five and ninety years, had disappeared.

In its place and space was now an acre of emptiness.

One day last week, four workmen arrived promptly at eight in
morning with horse and cart, hatchet and saw, and commenced
their road-clearance work as instructed by their foreman. I stayed
indoors well out of sight as the men chopped, hacked and sawed
their way through all those years of life and growth till, following
a mighty ripping, tearing and groaning of wood and earth, I
heard the great tree fall as would an old warrior in battle. While
the men filled the cart with the sawed logs, branches and boughs
and set a fire at the base of the tree stump, one of the workers,
Petey Murphy, came and knocked at my door. Petey knew my

feelings as expressed to his boss, Mr Canny the Council engineer, about the destruction and removal of the tree, and I could see that he was hesitant and shy to speak to me.

"Mariah, before we clear up out here, I'll fill your woodshed with some of this timber. It will give you a good supply of fire-wood for the coming winter."

I just thanked him for his kind offer and made no other comment.

"Sorry about that old tree, Mariah," Petey said as he departed. "But orders are orders, and we have our job to do."

When I finally emerged to view the scene the following day, I stood and gazed for a long while on a landscape I hardly recog-nised. For a moment, it was as if I had stepped out from some house other than my own, and I felt again the familiar stab of loss twist in my heart. The empty space where the tree had stood now seemed to me disturbed, unsure, unsettled – as I did myself at that moment.

Judging by the troubled squawking from the bushes and hedges all about me, the birds too shared my upset at the sudden disappearance of our old friend.

"Progress!" In my head I heard Mr Canny say the word. This was a word that appeared often in the *Champion* and other news-papers. It seemed to me that these days the word always appeared in the same sentences as the words "rural electrification", "aero-plane travel", "moving pictures", "telephones", or "radio". The country, indeed the world, was changing in the name of progress, yet I could not help but wonder how many other great trees would have to fall in its name.

With the aid of my walking stick, I walked then to visit the light-ning tree and was happy at least that what remained of this old tree, now aged, decayed and ravaged by the years as it was, was still standing.

"We're still here," I said, laying my hands as in greeting on the gnarled, twisted husk. "After all the years and all the storms you and I have weathered, we're still on our feet."

I peered into its bowled, hollow centre, where I had so often, as a child, hidden and curled up in safety, and my heart skipped a beat. There, sprouting from the damp, black earth and mulch at the centre of the lightning tree, was a fresh, strong, young ash sapling.

Life springing from where, for so many years, there was only death and decay!

My eyes misted over, but my heart sang out at this glorious sight. In my mind's eye, I saw – in the fullness of time – this young sapling grow and rise and spread, high into the clear air to claim its place on this earth.

I knew, too, that here, while my bones turn to dust in my grave, will stand again a great tree to guard over the treasure I placed deep within its bosom.

CHAPTER THIRTY-THREE

SPRING ARRIVED LAST night like a flight of angels. I heard its beating wings as it swept across the land, trailing behind a flight of wild geese on their way to their summer feeding grounds somewhere in the far north. The sound of those great swishing wings fell brokenly on my ears in the grey hour before dawn, and I knew and recognised it as I would the voice of an old friend singing a familiar song.

I can hardly count the years since I first heard that sound, and yet, as I listened deep in the warmth of my bed, I was filled with such a longing and restlessness, just as I was as a youngster all those years ago.

"Wild geese!" The old people would say with wonder in their voices and yearning in their hearts, and they would cock an ear to the skies. Listen to them sing their song of their leaving."

And we would be silent then and listen, our hearts filled with some unknown longing; our imaginations flying to be with them up yonder in the free sky – to be part of that beautiful flock slicing and beating the clear air with great feathered wings scenting of bog and wood, lake and marshland.

"The music of wings: it can make a priest forget his prayers and a thief in the night forget his purpose."

So I once heard an old man say about the song of the wild goose or swan as they ploughed a swathe through the cloud-waves of the northern skies. There were some humans who did succumb to the wild-swan siren-song and who did follow and take on the plumage of wild goose or swan and were never again seen in their human forms.

They say the wild swans of Inchiquin – and I counted fifty-two one time, one for every week of the year – are but those who once had human form and were changed to swans by some evil druid or witch. It is they who return to live out the swan lives on the lake only to be near their homes and their people.

It happened once that a young chieftain of the O'Quin Clan – Conor, son of Donal, was his name – was hunting deer with his comrades in the foothills and by the shores of the lake not too far from his castle. You can still see the ruined walls on the northern shore. Conor broke away from his comrades as he tracked a wounded stag in the woodlands running down to the shore by Clifden Hill, and as he did, he saw three beautiful snow-white swans drifting on the still lake waters. As he watched, they swam ashore, and there on the land cast off their snowy plumage, turning into three beautiful young women. In amazement, the young lord ran forward, and as he did, the swan-women – save one – donned their white feathered robes and flew away across the lake, leaving their deserted sister alone and weeping on the shore.

O'Quin moved swiftly, and, seizing the young woman, he right away took her back to his castle keep. There he comforted her, cared for her and, before too long, fell in love with her.

Eventually, so the story goes, the handsome young lord won the love of the lovely swan-maiden. After a year and a day in his keep, she agreed to marry him, but only on three conditions: that

266

their marriage be kept a secret; that he should never indulge in gambling or games of chance of any kind; and that no member of the O'Brien Clan should ever be invited to spend a night under their roof.

So enthralled was he by her beauty and by the great love he felt in his heart for her, that Conor, without question or hesitation, heartily agreed to each of her conditions. She went on to warn the young lord that if ever he should break even one of his promises, she would disappear from his life forever.

And so the young chieftain and his swan-maiden were soon wed and lived happily and peacefully for seven years and had two children in their stronghold castle by the lake.

Then one fateful day Conor went to the races of Coad, where the man elected chieftain had to measure up to the height of the huge standing stone at the corner of the race course and where the clans met once a year to show and to race and test their finest horses. It was at this event that the Lord O'Quin met with Taigh O'Brien, an enemy chieftain who sometimes waged war with the O'Quin Clan, and invited him to his castle keep by the lake.

Throughout the night, they continued to eat and drink freely and make merry into the early hours. They commenced to gamble until eventually Conor, abandoned on this fateful night by Lady Luck, lost all his lands and property to the rogue O'Brien. In this dark time, in the deepest night, with all lost to his wily enemy, he suddenly remembered the promise made to his swanbride seven years before. Coming to his senses, the poor, distraught man ran to seek out his only remaining possessions, his wife and children. High and low he searched the castle and finally came to the tallest tower where, at last, he found his wife.

He was not prepared for the sight he now beheld.

His beautiful wife was no longer in her human form. She was now in her swan-clothes with a little cygnet under each wing. Without speaking a single word to her husband and with a forlorn look, the swan spread her great white wings and, with her cygnets, flew from the high castle tower over the misty lake towards the rising sun and disappeared forever from his sight.

Though he mounted his fastest horse and searched the lakeshore, hills and woodlands all around, he found not a trace of his beloved family. He never laid eyes on his swan-woman wife or his two children again in this world.

Poor Conor was to live out the remainder of his short life as a lonely and miserable man, a dependant of that scoundrel Taigh O'Brien, who allowed him to dwell as a vassal in De Clare's Court or O'Quin's Ruin – as it is often named – where the Fergus River flows into the lake named after his noble clan.

That's as my mother told the story to us young ones. And to this day I can never see a single swan and her two cygnets on that lake without wondering.

Late last evening, when I heard the air full with the beat of wings, I longed to be away with them; to be adorned in the full snow-white plumage of their royal family and setting out on their great journey towards the fading light and the Northern Star.

"Come away," they seemed to sing out, and the music of their wings in flight resounded in the deepest heart and soul. "Come away and leave the sad old earth behind you."

In that moment, my spirit arose from within my breast and wished itself free to follow wherever the winds might take us. But I was what I was! I was but an earthbound human, heavy of heart and unable to depart this weary body to fly up to be with them.

Yet I imagined myself free of my tired old human bones and one of their kind, my wings beating out time to that old music, while down below the people would look skyward in wonder.

"Listen," they would whisper, their aching hearts and spirits stirring within them. "Listen. There they go. Wild Geese on their way home to the Northern Star."

CHAPTER THIRTY-FOUR

I THINK A lot about my past life these days – how I journeyed down my nine decades to this moment. Some days the memories come to me jumbled and confusing, like the spilling out of the box of old, musty clothes, faded, raggy patches and other odds and ends I have under my bed. On those days, I don't attempt to sort them into any order. I just sit and watch and let them flow by, as would a river winding its way through my mind.

That's the trouble with old age. It is not for the faint-hearted. And worst of all, you really have to work hard at getting your memories to behave long enough to tell you the story of your own life.

I think a lot about Death, too, these days. But I don't fear it. Why should I? I have been in Death's company so many times in my long life; I know the darkness of his shadow, the cold of his fingers and the ice of his breath. I know his many faces, I know his humours, his suddenness, his violence. But I know too his compassion and the relief he sometimes brings. When Death comes for me – as one day soon he surely will – I will welcome him as I would an old acquaintance.

On my next birthday, if I live that long, I will have seen six and ninety summers. People say I will make the century. But old age never comes alone. So they say, and I now know that to be true. My old bones creak and complain, and the veil of mist that has descended on my eyes has me wearing a pair of eyeglasses that Mary Ellen once bought from Thread-the-Needle the hawker.

I used to relish the winter months. Now the blood grows thin and cold in my veins, and in the quiet of the sleepless hours before dawn, I feel my lifeforce being tugged from my body, like a withered piece of seaweed from the strand by an ebbing tide.

I have now outlived all my old friends and all my family: my father and mother, my brothers Frank, Brian and Robin. Now they visit me in dreams, and they call to me to come and join them beyond the veil that separates us from the world they now inhabit. In these dreams, I am invariably lost and searching for a way back home. When I awake, I am filled with a great aloneness and a feeling of abandonment. So I prepare for the hour and moment of my leaving, which cannot now be too far distant.

I remember our kind old teacher Mr Moloney teaching us "The Old Woman of Beare".

"The oldest poem in Ireland," so he would tell us. "And one some of you will come to understand in the fullness of time."

I still recall much of that poem.

The Old Woman of Beare am I
Who once was beautiful.
Now all I know is how to die.
I'll do it well.

Look at my skin
Stretched tight on the bone.
Where kings have pressed their lips,
The pain, the pain.

The young sun
Gives its youth to everyone
Touching everything with gold.
In me, the cold.

Unbidden, those lines come into my head a lot these days, and I suspect, like all old women everywhere, I have indeed become that Old Woman of Beare.

I heard somebody once say that we should ask only children and birds how cherries and strawberries taste. It being such a lovely autumn evening, I walked out in the fields last evening, searching for wild garlic and other herbs, and I came on a small cluster of wild strawberries tucked away between briar and stone. I plucked and ate them there and then. On that first taste – in that moment – I was again young and tasting this wild fruit for the first time.

I abandoned my hunt for garlic to go directly to a small grove of plum and crab apple trees that grow some way across the fields behind the house.

My heart leapt to see the plum tree laden with ripe purple fruit, and I plucked a single juicy plum from the tree and bit into it. Its bittersweet juice filled my senses, and still it tasted as delicious as it did when I was a child.

"So," I said to myself, savouring the moment, "the good Lord has left me with some of my faculties." I remembered, too, that it is said that *in extremis* our sense of smell and taste are the last things to abandon us. I filled my basket with the ripest of fruit and slowly made my way home.

CHAPTER THIRTY-FIVE

YESTERDAY MORNING I saw my old friend the heron, wearing his rain face, back in his usual spot by the river bend, and rain from the west will as surely follow his visit as night follows day. I heard the tinkers' wagons – with iron pots, tin cans, pony tackling and harness all a-jingle, goats bleating and the laughter of children – pass by on the road to take up their winter quarters. One of the tinker children, a red-haired scamp of ten or so, came to my door to beg for bread and milk, and he told me he and his clan would lodge tonight by the castle and lake by Drummore Woods.

Later in the evening I watched the swallows and swifts fill the branches of every tree about the house in preparation for their leave-taking.

This morning the trees are bare and the skies are quiet. Sometime before I awoke, the swallows silently departed to their winter nesting grounds somewhere to the distant south.

My heart is heavy to see them leave, and I thank them for the music they made for me all through the high summer. I will surely miss that.

Mostly I am sad today for I feel I will not be here to welcome them when they return in spring.

I cannot tell you why or how I know this, but I know it. Like the cold that now creeps into my marrow, I feel it keenly in my blood and bones that I am close to the end of my journey through this world.

I do not fear the journey's end. Fear can be excused in the young, but never in the old.

I came awake from a light dozing sleep to the sensation that my body floated somewhere between sky and ground. In that moment, it seemed to me as if I had ceased to breathe, and all about me was silent as the grave. In that moment, it seemed, too, as if the whole world – Time itself – had ceased its breathing. But the moment slipped from my grasp, and once again I find myself sitting in my old rocking chair by a dying fire.

From my window I see a dark cloud move across the face of the winter moon, and I see a star winking bright in the east. It's going to be a cold night.

I hear a soft rapping on my windowpane. It may be a gentle night wind with its mournful message of the coming season. It may be a small night bird seeking a safe nesting place. Or perhaps a ghost moth attracted by the light? It may be any one those night visitors – I cannot say – yet I sit and listen to its soft thrum, and my heart hears its rhythm, and my heart knows.

I give thanks I have lived this day, and for all my days past and gone and the days that God in His mercy may yet grant me.

I am weary now and I must pray before I take my rest.

GLOSSARY

Alanna Child; pet name

a ghrá My love

cailín óg Young girl

cuaird Visit; round of visits

Leaba Dhiarmada agus Ghráinne (Diarmuid and Grainne's bed)
   Passage grave

leanbh Child

meas To have *meas* on: to think highly of.

meitheal A traditional gathering of neighbours to help with farm
   work such as threshing, hay-making or saving turf

mór Big

Nollaig na mBan 6 January. Known as Women's Christmas or
   Little Christmas

Oíche na Gaoithe Móire Night of the Big Wind

piseog, pl. *piseoga* Old saying or superstition

poitín Home-distilled (illegal) whiskey; poteen

púca, pl. *púcaí* Spirit; hobgoblin

riasc Marsh; bogland

RIC Royal Irish Constabulary

Sassenach Englishman

sí gaoithe Fairy wind

tigín A small house, hut

turlough A field in limestone areas which holds water and
   becomes a small lake in winter.

uilleann Elbow

Acknowledgements

During the writing of this book, a number of good, true and dear friends were unstinting in their continued help, advice, inspiration, encouragement, friendship, support, patience and refuge which saw me through to the end.

I therefore wish to acknowledge and sincerely thank the following people: Geraldine Bird (Clare), Phil Cousineau (San Francisco), Pat Costello (Shannon), Garret Daly (Dublin), Toni Dearsley (New Zealand), Maribeth Gus (Idaho, USA), Leo & Claire Hallisey (Connemara), Mick Hanly (Kilkenny), Deirdre Herbert (Galway), John Keane (Kilfenora), Cormac McConnell (Shannon), Mike Mulcaire (Ennis), Pat Musick (Colorado), Dave Reid (Gibraltar), Gaye Shortland (Cork), Alice Lawless (Dublin) and Eddie Stack (Galway).

Special thanks to my sister Mary, my brothers Gerard and Michael and their families.

Also to Steve MacDonogh at Brandon, who saw some worth in the original manuscript.

PJ Curtis

THE BESTSELLING NOVELS OF ALICE TAYLOR

The Woman of the House

"What shines through in *The Woman of the House* is Alice Taylor's love of the Irish countryside and village life of over 40 years ago, its changing seasons and colours, its rhythm and pace." *Irish Independent*

ISBN 9780863222498

Across the River

"Alice Taylor is an outstanding storyteller. Like a true seanchaí, she uses detail to signal twists in the plot or trouble ahead. It is tightly plotted fiction, an old-fashioned page-turner." *The Irish Times*

ISBN 9780863222856

House of Memories

"*House of Memories* shows her in her prime as a novelist." *Irish Independent*

"It is Alice Taylor's strength to make the natural everyday world come alive in clear fresh prose. In this book, as in her memoirs, she does so beautifully."
The Irish Book Review

ISBN 9780863223525

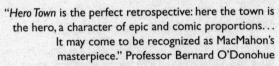

BRYAN MACMAHON
Hero Town

"*Hero Town* is the perfect retrospective: here the town is the hero, a character of epic and comic proportions... It may come to be recognized as MacMahon's masterpiece." Professor Bernard O'Donohue

"For the course of a calendar year, Peter Mulrooney, the musing pedagogue, saunters through the streets and the people, looking at things and leaving them so. They talk to him; he listens, and in his ears we hear the authentic voice of local Ireland, all its tics and phrases and catchcalls. Like Joyce, this wonderful, excellently structured book comes alive when you read it aloud." Frank Delaney, *Sunday Independent*

ISBN 9780863223426

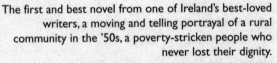

JOHN B. KEANE
The Bodhran Makers

The first and best novel from one of Ireland's best-loved writers, a moving and telling portrayal of a rural community in the '50s, a poverty-stricken people who never lost their dignity.

"Furious, raging, passionate and very, very funny."
Boston Globe

"This powerful and poignant novel provides John B. Keane with a passport to the highest levels of Irish literature." *Irish Press*

"Sly, funny, heart-rending... Keane writes lyrically; recommended."
Library Journal

ISBN 9780863223006

TONY KEARNS AND BARRY TAYLOR
A Touchstone for the Tradition – The Willie Clancy Summer School

Text and photographs providing a unique portrait of traditional Irish music in action.

"Succeeds admirably...There's beauty on almost every page." *Irish Examiner*

ISBN 9780863223082

HELEN BRENNAN
The Story of Irish Dance

"This is a lovely book, excellently researched and written with authority, yet managing to be entertaining and very readable." *Books Ireland*

ISBN 9780863223280

FRANK CONNOLLY (ED)
The Christy Moore Songbook

Over a hundred songs, with music, illustrated with photos

"Christy Moore is the most successful solo artist in Ireland." *In Dublin*

ISBN 9780863220630

WILLIAM WALL
No Paradiso

"In addition to the author's alert, muscular style, his painlessly communicated appreciation of obscure learning, his vaguely didactic pleasure in accurately providing a sense of place, many of these stories are distinguished by a welcome engagement with form... In their various negotiations with such tensions, the stories of *No Paradiso* engage, challenge and reward the committed reader." *The Irish Times*

ISBN 9780863223556

CHET RAYMO
Valentine

"Such nebulous accounts [as we have] have been just waiting for someone to make a work of historical fiction out of them. American novelist and physicist Raymo has duly obliged with his recently published *Valentine: A Love Story*." *The Scotsman*

"[A] vivid and lively account of how Valentine's life may have unfolded... Raymo has produced an imaginative and enjoyable read, sprinkled with plenty of food for philosophical thought." *Sunday Tribune*

ISBN 9780863223273

KATE MCCAFFERTY
Testimony of an Irish Slave Girl

"McCafferty's haunting novel chronicles an overlooked chapter in theannals of human slavery ...A meticulously researched piece of historicalfiction that will keep readers both horrified and mesmerized." *Booklist*

"Thousands of Irish men, women and children were sold into slavery towork in the sugar-cane fields of Barbados in the 17thcentury ...McCafferty has researched her theme well and, through Cot,shows us the terrible indignities and suffering endured." *Irish Independent*

ISBN 9780863223389

SEAN O'CALLAGHAN
To Hell or Barbados
The ethnic cleansing of Ireland

"An illuminating insight into a neglected episode in Irish history... its main achievement is to situate the story of colonialism in Ireland in the much larger context of world-wide European imperialism." *Irish World*

ISBN 9780863222870

DAVID FOSTER
The Land Where Stories End

"Australia's most original and important living novelist." *Independent Monthly*

"A post-modern fable set in the dark ages of Ireland. . . [A] beautifully written humorous myth that is entirely original. The simplicity of language is perfectly complementary to the wry, occasionally laugh-out-loud humour and the captivating tale." *Irish World*

"I was taken by surprise and carried easily along by the amazing story and by the punchy clarity of the writing. . . This book is imaginative and fantastic. . . It is truly amazing." *Books Ireland*

ISBN 9780863223112

MANCHÁN MAGAN

Angels and Rabies: A Journey Through the Americas

"Each chapter is gripping because truly insane things happen around the author: war breaks out in Ecuador; a famous Hollywood actress falls into his arms... It is a warm, well written and entertaining book." *Village*

"Frightening, funny and lovable." *The Sunday Times*

"[Magan's] writing is unashamedly sensual and he has an engagingly confessional narrative voice; his adventures are as poignant as they are hair-raising." *Sunday Telegraph*

ISBN 9780863223495

MANCHÁN MAGAN

Manchán's Travels: A Journey Through India

"Magan's writing is as unique as his TV style; endearing and honest, his personality shining through. He succeeds in bringing the Indian landscape, the country, to life, but his real talent lies in the people." *Irish Independent*

"As off-beat as it is entertaining, taking a look at the often surreal nature of life in modern India." *Traveller*

"Magan has a keen eye for the hypocrisies of elite urban India and artfully evokes the 'fevered serenity' of the Himalayas." *Times Literary Supplement*

ISBN 9780863223686

TOM HANAHOE

America Rules: US Foreign Policy, Globalization and Corporate USA

The disturbing, definitive account of globalization and the new American imperialism. Rather than serving as a global protector, the United States has shown contempt for the ideas of freedom, democracy and human rights.

ISBN 9780863223099

LARRY KIRWAN

Green Suede Shoes

The sparkling autobiography of the lead singer and songwriter of New York rock band, Black 47.

"Lively and always readable. He has wrought a refined tale of a raw existence, filled with colorful characters and vivid accounts." *Publishers Weekly*

ISBN 9780863223433

DESMOND ELLIS

Bockety

"The various adventures of a boy, living in less complicated times are recalled with humour and authenticity... The imagery is evocative and witty and Ellis' book is an easy read, avoiding sentimentality as it lilts through amusingly recounted, people-focused stories." *The Dubliner*

"Genuinely funny. It is enlightening to learn that, despite the censorious and tight-arsed approach of the Catholic Church and its lapdog politicians, working class people were quite subversive in their attitude to life back then. Straight-laced they certainly were not. *Verbal Magazine*

ISBN 9780863223648

MÍCHEÁL Ó DUBHSHLÁINE
A Dark Day on the Blaskets

"A wonderful piece of drama-documentary...
entertaining and captivating. It's an evocative story, a
portrait of a young woman and her times, and an
engrossing description of a beautiful place at a turning
point in its history." *Ireland Magazine*

"A fascinating insight into Blasket Island life, life on the mainland, and life
in Dublin in the early part of the last century." *Kerryman*

ISBN 9780863223372

GEORGE THOMSON
Island Home

"Imbued with Thomson's deep respect for the rich oral
culture and his aspiration that the best of the past might
be preserved in the future. It is when the deprived and
the dispossessed take their future into their own hands,
he concludes, that civilisation can be raised to a higher
level." *Sunday Tribune*

ISBN 9780863221613

JOE GOOD
Enchanted by Dreams
The Journal of a Revolutionary

A fascinating first-hand account of the 1916 Rising and
its aftermath by a Londoner who was a member of the
Irish Volunteers who joined the garrison in the GPO.

ISBN 9780863222252

DRAGO JANČAR
Joyce's Pupil

"Jančar writes powerful, complex stories with an unostentatious assurance, and has a gravity which makes the tricks of more self-consciously modern writers look cheap." *Times Literary Supplement*

"[A] stunning collection of short stories... Jančar writes ambitious, enjoyable and page turning fictions, which belie the precision of their execution." *Time Out*

"[E]legant, elliptical stories." *Financial Times*

"Powerful and arresting narratives." *Sunday Telegraph*

ISBN 9780863223402

AGATA SCHWARTZ AND LUISE VON FLOTOW
The Third Shore: women's fiction from east central Europe.

"A treasure trove of quirky, funny, touching and insightful work by 25 women writers from 18 countries in the former communist bloc. Flipped open to any page, it offers a window into unique worlds – some political, all intensely imaginative and often unexpectedly funny." *Sunday Business Post*

"These stories are exciting, intriguing and never predictable. For all their startling narrative tricks and puzzles these stories will appeal for their wide range and honesty." *Books Ireland*

ISBN 9780863223624

NENAD VELIČKOVIĆ
Lodgers

"[A] beautifully constructed account of the ridiculous nature of the Balkans conflict, and war in general, which even in moments of pure gallows humour retains a heartwarming affection for the individuals trying to survive in such horrific circumstances." *Metro*

ISBN 9780863223488